I0618456

The Moonstorm Series

Volume One
Land of the Frozen Sun

Volume Two
Book of Dreams

Volume Three
Destiny's Children

Volume Four
Time Weaver

Volume Five
Death is the Door

Volume Six
Aranae in Red

Special Thanks:

Peter Gawtry
Stephanie Gawtry
Ren Johnson
Chris Mayer
Pat Sullivan
Jack Svenningsen
Ricki Terry
Tracy van der Leeuw
Christopher West

A. P. Malloy

The Moonstorm Series

Ardilla Blanca

ISBN 13: 978-0-578-82397-3

Cover design and artwork: Mari Fridley Larsen
marilarsen.com

Learn more about the series
and order promotional copies:
moonstormseries.com

The author welcomes correspondence:
apmalloy1@gmail.com

CONTENTS

CHAPTER ONE	Survivor	1
CHAPTER TWO	Accrete	14
CHAPTER THREE	Meeting	32
CHAPTER FOUR	Promise	53
CHAPTER FIVE	Captain	73
CHAPTER SIX	Feud	98
CHAPTER SEVEN	Ghost	120
CHAPTER EIGHT	Blood	153
CHAPTER NINE	Skull	169
CHAPTER TEN	Sister	191
CHAPTER ELEVEN	Vow	219
CHAPTER TWELVE	Parting	241

CHAPTER ONE
Survivor

JEREMIAH THE STORYTELLER will open his book. It will be the next day, and most of the chores will be done. All that will remain is the anticipation. But guests will arrive when they arrive, and no one will be able to say for sure when that will be. Wishing will not make it happen any sooner, though some people will try.

"Could be tomorrow, could be a week from now." That's what the adults will say, which will be entirely unsatisfactory to the children.

"Page four hundred seventy-six," the boy named Bo Lin will say. He will sit, as always, right up front.

Jeremiah will nod and smile, turning pages and clearing his throat. The rain will fall gently outside the mining compound—gently for now, as a family feud is brewing in the heavens. Three of the five moons are slated to appear in the coming hour, and another will be close behind. Woe to those without shelter!

"Can we just skip to the good parts?" the girl named Natalia will ask.

"No skipping!" several children will call out, some older than Natalia, some younger.

Jeremiah's audience will have evolved since the story's beginning. Some listeners will have deemed the tale "boring," others, "confusing." Those will have gone off to help—or simply watch—final preparations for the festival. The entire colony will participate in one way or another, for their guests' arrival is an event they will have waited for all of Jeremiah's thirty-seven years of life. And the storyteller himself will have a role: occupy the youngest and keep them from getting under foot. The story will have largely done that, in spite of attrition, some of which will be unavoidable. Folks will have different tastes, after all. But for every loss, there will be two more audience members gained, and now some adults will join the listening, those with infants held close.

"Yes," one such parent will agree. "No skipping."

"I just read what's in front of me," Jeremiah will say, and he will turn to page four seventy-six.

"Please tell me it's about kezel," Bo Lin will say.

"Blah," Natalia will stick out her tongue. "Let's get to those Moondwellers. They're up to something."

"Actually," Jeremiah will say, "this chapter starts in Albion—with Viktor, the Old Magister."

"Excellent," a nursing mother will murmur.

"Scion are important," a father to her left will agree, bouncing a baby on his lap. "Many lessons to be learned." But Bo Lin and other children will make a fuss.

"That old bugger is gross," Natalia will say.

"He's mean," Bo Lin will add.

"Kezel! Bombas! Moondwellers! Rock and Crag!" It will seem every child in attendance has an opinion about what part of the story deserves to be told next. But Jeremiah will merely hold one finger to his lips and say,

"Shhh..."

And at last, they will settle, allowing him to take a deep breath and begin.

+ + + + + +

He may be missing an antenna, but that doesn't prevent Viktor from sensing the approach of tey Ramota with the one he has remaining. Pain travels from its quivering tip and takes up lodging behind his left eye. It tells the old scion that soon after completion of the Circle, which he hears in the west like a rumor of trouble, land to the north of Albion will tremble and wrench. Toxic smoke will billow from newly formed chasms, and anyone near the landfall will be crushed or cast over the edge.

Normally, tey Ramota would follow the floods, churning the soil and allowing the water to reach deep below the surface and nourish the lova pods hibernating there. But for many moons, the Circle has been an empty promise, bringing no water. Without it, there is much quaking and spewing, but no lova rises to be harvested. The spongy plants that had greened the floodplain known as the Bacca stay buried deep, and the scion who depend on them grow anxious, their numbers dwindling.

Water this time, does Old Magister think? asks Viktor's companion, one of the last soldiers still loyal to him—though that has earned him a demotion to drone. Once ranking in the hundreds, he is now an "it," numbered accordingly, Eight Thousand and Two.

Viktor buzzes in a harsh tone.

It will focus on counting the lova. Flood or no flood, he wishes to be out of this hole as quickly as possible.

Eight Thousand Two chitters unhappily, and he runs black forelimbs over his antennae, trying to preen away the discomfort growing there. As with Viktor and all scion, the approaching tey Ramota aches in his head like unrequited longing. His eyes grow dim as he casts quick glances at the large, bristly soldiers who stand guard, a pair of Queen's chosen, blocking sunlight from the hole's only exit. Even they, robust and scintillating, feel the mounting tension behind their eyes.

Yes, the drone thinks. *Count quickly!* He keeps his thoughts tightly focused for Viktor's mind only. But the guards are distracted by their desire to join the Circle and pay little attention to their duty or the conversation. And so, the drone adds, *But Old Magister is wise. He already knows how much lova there is: not enough. Not nearly.*

Queen wants a number. It can complain to her.

The drone bows and dutifully joins his master in the job before them. They work from one end of the hole to the other, cataloging each of the flat, thick leaves piled in neat rows. Using nothing but memory, they check each leaf for turgidity and rot, noting variations in color. Viktor moves with a distinct limp in his rear four legs.

Old Magister is insulted working here, thinks his companion. *He should be honored at the Circle.*

It must be still! It makes him lose count.

But this treatment enrages! It offends! Proud soldiers turned into drones through no fault of their own. The queen Adira lost trying to solve the mystery of the drought. Viktor, Greatest Magister of all, left queenless and bereft of Command, counting lova in a hole!

Viktor whistles softly. Eight Thousand Two is not wrong. Adira had been very brave. But she had also been prideful and foolish. She had ignored his advice and dared to violate the Prohibition, approaching Ozag's Hold in an attempt to beseech the Undying for aid against the drought. She had not returned. Viktor, clinging to the last of his Command, had gone in search. But he and his soldiers had been spurned by Ozag, injured and driven away from the Hold, and he had returned to Albion defeated and discolored. His name had been revealed, and when a new queen arose, his successor had been chosen.

Ex-Magister, he corrects. *Old Magister.*

Not to his loyal soldiers. Albion would have floods if he *were closing the Circle. Not like this New one...*

New Magister is not his concern, thinks Viktor. *He is more interested in the mutant vumierre.*

And the glowing thing, yes? His companion rubs his forelimbs together, raspy and slow. *Princess felt it was important. What does he think it was?*

Viktor has been wondering the same thing since his last team of soldiers had captured the mutant and its strange artifact. Indeed, he has thought of little else. He had assumed it to be of vumierre design, but the more time he had spent with the singular object, the more he had come to doubt that. It had no smell, for one, and the way it gobbled up sunlight was unique in his experience—and disconcerting. But if not a creation of the vumierre, then whom? Ozag herself?

New Magister presented the mutant to Queen as if he had captured it, the drone recalls bitterly. *Getting honor for their work!* He continues counting the lova, but his pace is so slowed by his complaining that he scarcely works faster than his limping companion.

It won't matter, thinks Viktor, *if Princess keeps her promise.* He moves closer to the drone, his thought faint like a whisper. *She swore when he gave her the location of the hidden artifact that she would find a way to free him—and his few remaining loyalists.* Viktor stops to rest his legs. *Is it still in contact with the others?*

Often! They are as unhappy as he.

Patience. Their fortunes have turned; they will turn again. The next time it is in the towers, he will need it to share a message with the others. It will tell them...

Viktor's thoughts trail away. A faint sound, neither the Circle, nor tey Ramota, tickles the sensitive membranes on either side of his cloudy, black eyes.

Does he hear that? his companion wonders.

He does.

It is familiar, yes?

It is familiar, no.

The sound grows, and it does so rapidly, soon becoming louder than the Circle itself. Even if moons were due, their thunderous voice would be different, not this sustained rumble, growing to a roar.

Viktor limps to the exit, unsure if the guards will let him pass, but they have already left their post to investigate. Eight Thousand Two is faster, reaching the sunlit opening and scurrying outside. Following as quickly as he can, the old scion hears and then feels a tremendous impact and a concussive explosion that drives him to the dusty ground. Outside the hole, his companion whistles in shrill panic.

Viktor's senses are dashed away like sand before a breaker, and he reels from the sudden awareness of thousands of scion minds reacting in terror and blinding pain. Then, there is nothing. Their thoughts are simply extinguished. He stumbles out of the hole, greeted by a low-rolling cloud of smoke and dust expanding outward from a Circle that is devastated in fire. He ducks his head and turns away from the cloud, chittering anxiously as he waits for it to pass. When it does, taking with it a terrible smell of burned flesh, the sun shines down unhindered on a holocaust.

The giant hexagonal bowl, filled with flame.

The eastern bridge broken, cast into the lake.

Beasts of all types escaping on foot and wing.

Nearby, Eight Thousand Two continues his terrified whistling. He casts frantic gazes from the carnage to Viktor and back, his antennae waving madly and his eyes crazed with glittering light.

She is dead, he thinks. *Queen is dead.*

The drone begins scurrying aimlessly, describing misshapen ovals in the dust and repeating news Viktor can sense for himself. Queen Benica, along with every other scion in the Circle—including New Magister—is dead and gone, their remains spiraling upward in a tower of black smoke bent by southern winds.

It will keep its head! thinks Viktor.

But his companion has come unhinged and is beyond reach, stumbling blindly into rocks and clicking maniacally. After several moments of this, his sapphire skin changes to match the parched ground on which he totters like a disconnected marionette. Shortly after, he disappears entirely, with only tiny dust clouds to show his meandering, eastward path.

It will come back! thinks Viktor, but his effort is wasted. Queen is dead; all those enthralled have been cut free of her guiding force. Though once a soldier, Eight Thousand Two had been reduced to a drone, and drones are more Queen-dependent than any other member of the hive. The miserable creature, along with others like him, will stumble along blindly until they are overcome by the elements. Without a Queen to lead them, many will wander into the Great Saline, to be found later washed up into the rank grasses of the river delta.

Assuming anyone else survived, thinks Viktor, and his antenna quivers. Limping toward the Circle, he seeks to learn the answer.

+ + +

By the time Viktor reaches his destination, guttering flames and dark, oily smoke are all that remain of the mighty conflagration. The Circle itself has been ruined, its terraces and columns melted, their faces smooth and shiny like volcanic rock, the water at the bottom of the bowl vaporized. The scent of roasted flesh rises on the wind, but stronger yet is the foul aroma of whatever caused the fire, some synthetic accelerant, undoubtedly a vumierre design. For the first time, Viktor is glad for his failing sense of smell. Had time and trauma not dulled his perceptions, the scent would have overwhelmed him. As it is, he can barely breathe.

The first survivors he discovers are a dozen bristled handlers, returning from the east, their every skill applied to driving an alp, its tentacles thrashing, back to the moorings nearby. With the beast secured, they approach Viktor, but their eyes are on the Circle.

What has happened? they think. *The Circle...*

Yes. The Circle...what of New Magister?

Yes. And what of Queen?

It is a dream, yes?

It is a dream, no, thinks Viktor, and he watches as all twelve handlers begin to tremble and buzz.

No Queen, they think. *They are lost...*

Yes. Lost. Cut loose...

Yes. No purpose, no Command...adrift.

And even as they think this, they turn slack-limbed and begin to disperse, each in a different direction, as if trying to remember an errand or heeding a distant summons. But Viktor will have none of this.

They will halt! he thinks. *He reclaims the Magistery! He has Command. They will come back!*

He could just as well have asked the charred skeletons at the bottom of the Circle to rise up and bring him fresh lova. The handlers disregard both his order and the ululating alp and totter off haphazardly, antennae drooping. Viktor runs forelimbs over his eyes, chittering to himself as he cleans away the smoky film.

Fools and weaklings, he thinks. *Never mind! It's the towers for him.*

But the eastern road has been blasted from the shore, and his limping journey to its southern counterpart is slow and painful. He encounters occasional drones and awlers, excluded from the Circle because of duties or punishment. Some pass by without remark, vapid shells on a mission to nowhere. Others stand frozen, their eyes fixed on empty space. When he finally reaches the southern road, Viktor must stop to rest. The towers, lit by the sun, glare down at him, and he feels sure he is the target of some collective blame, an accusation and a dare.

This is his doing, he imagines the towers thinking. *He failed to keep Queen Adira at home and earned the wrath of Ozag by daring to approach Her Hold. He will come inside and see what his impotence has wrought—if he has the courage.*

No courage, he thinks. *But stubborn pride.*

And so, gathering his energy, Viktor turns up the road and resumes his stuttering journey toward the towers and whatever truth lies within.

+ + +

He is a soldier by birth, and later a magister, so Viktor has always found the Queen's tower disorienting. His expertise is in pursuit and capture, combat and killing. An entire tower dedicated to cultivating life by the thousands is so foreign an endeavor as to be vaguely menacing. The effect is doubled now by the absence of tenders or other scion. Usually bustling and full of sound, the tower is now dead silent and appears to have been entirely abandoned.

Tenders, he thinks. *Drones. They will come out.*

But none do.

He is Viktor, he amplifies his thought, casting it high and far. *He is Magister once again. They must come out and take their orders! He Commands it.*

And yet, as he navigates the angled corridor and comes to the central chamber, resplendent amber and filled with wriggling life, no other adult scion show themselves. They may have scattered at the explosion or may be walking muddled hexagons on nearby levels, able to sense him but oblivious to duty.

They will come to him! he thinks, pushing his mind to its limit. *There is work to be done!*

Some of the languorous prisoners floating in their stacked cells turn to face him, but they are incapable of responding. The amber fluid in which they stew seems to fill every cell equally and completely, but a closer examination reveals small pockets of air in those on the lower levels. He is no expert on the process, but when the larvae in those cells have consumed all the fluid, he knows they will chew their way to freedom and become breathers of air—if they are mature enough. If not, they will simply run out of food and die, never leaving their single-occupant home. Only tenders know for sure when a larva is ready, monitoring fluid levels, re-filling some cells, withholding from others. Viktor guesses the larvae nearest him approach the time of emancipation. Their squirming in tight quarters speaks of desire to see a larger world.

Dead within a moon unless he finds some tenders, he thinks. And as he wonders what he should do next, a thought enters his mind, strong but incredulous.

Viktor! it thinks. *It is Viktor, yes?*

It is Viktor, yes, he thinks. *Who is that?*

Across the chamber, a soldier comes into view, fit and bristling. He hurries forward.

He is Twenty-Seven, the soldier thinks, clicking steadily. *He remembers, yes?*

He remembers, no. Viktor bends his antenna to this newcomer, who reciprocates in kind. He is a fine specimen, worthy of his high number, strong and bright, with eyes whose facets catch and reflect amber light like a memory of Viktor's youth.

He was part of his first cadre as Magister, thinks Twenty-Seven. *Viktor said he had good potential.*

He says that about all the soldiers he chooses for a cadre. Or he used to. But he was correct about this one. He has a strong mind, not undone by Queen's passing. Why was he not at the Circle?

He and his team were sent to find the...the... Twenty-Seven pauses, struggling to create the proper thought. *Viktor witnessed the brown vumierre, yes?*

He witnessed, yes.

How it fell from the sky, tied to a broad sheet that seemed to slow its descent?

Yes.

Some claimed to have seen it be...spit out of a large flying object that passed to the west. Since then, Queen Benica has been sending teams to search for this object. His was the latest, but they were no more successful than the others. The object has passed from Albion, into the realm of the Cyclonian queen, he believes, and they were late in returning for the Circle.

Twenty-Seven's buzzing is rich and resonant.

As they approached the Royal River, they saw that sharksha in one of the confinement pits had been freed. Two teams of handlers and a dozen soldiers were killed. He sent his company ahead to alert New Magister while he stayed behind to track the prisoners.

Twenty-Seven's eyes grow dim.

He sent his soldiers to their deaths, yes?

He did, yes, Viktor confirms. *But he is blameless. He could not have known. And the sharksha?*

Fled to the north, a dozen or more. He dared not pursue them so outnumbered.

And since then?

He has been searching for other survivors.

And?

Few—all addled, walking circles or stiff and unresponsive. Who has Command? Who has Power?

But Viktor does not answer right away. He considers Twenty-Seven's news of the sharksha escape. How it could have happened he can't guess, but it is of no consequence. They are long gone now. All that matters is the present, which is difficult enough on its own.

Viktor, Twenty-Seven repeats, *does he have Command? Is he Magister again?* The supplicant tone is unfit for his robust appearance, as if a scared pupa looking for reassurance is trapped inside.

He has Command, Viktor thinks, but he knows at once the soldier is unconvinced. *He will prove,* he thinks, trying to assume a bold manner, as much to assure himself as anyone. *He will hear his plan, and he will see.*

\+ + +

Twenty-Seven attends carefully as Viktor shares his thoughts, but he is unable to shelter the doubt he feels. When done, he dims his eyes and bows his antennae, turning to make his way to the southern exit and the first stage of Viktor's plan. Watching his fit, zig-zagging stride and iridescent skin, Viktor wonders how long his reputation will hold the virile soldier enthralled.

Enthralled, he thinks bitterly. *Too strong a word. One misstep and he will be as lost as the others—or try to take Command himself.*

So worrying, he makes his way out of the courtyard and then down, to lower levels only royals and magisters visit, storage rooms with the last remains of vintage lova. He hasn't been inside for many moons but takes no time to reminisce. Instead, he focuses all his energy on extruding white filament from his midsection and wrapping as much lova in a bundle as he can carry. His body has not been taxed in this way for a long time, and his store of webbing barely suffices. Once complete, he places the parcel on his back, where it adheres in a wobbly, uncertain fashion as he limps out of the storage room and toward the tower's western exit.

The journey to the sharksha pit takes twice as long as it should, and Viktor must stop to rest along the way, often pausing to listen and look, hoping for Twenty-Seven's return. But the soldier is nowhere to be seen. As he shuffles across the bridge and the exhausted Royal, he returns to the mystery of the sharksha. Arriving at the pit provides few answers. The scene is just as Twenty-Seven described it. The babelrack, disconsolate and lowing hungrily, stands guard over an empty enclosure. At the entrance, numerous handlers lie torn to blue shreds. More dead scion lie outside the pit, near the unmistakable signs of the sharksha trail. Their heavy, clawed feet mark a northerly course across the stricken land, disappearing over the horizon, along with the river.

Back to the land of snow, he guesses. *And a good riddance to them. May he never see them again.*

A regular, massive stride comes from the east, hammering steadily closer. Soon, a giant, tentacled head comes into view, joined a moment later by the enormous body of an alp, ridden by Twenty-Seven and a team of handlers. In spite of his aching legs and the weight of the lova, Viktor's spirits rise.

Commendable! he thinks, and he passes his burden up to the scion perched aboard the alp. Climbing to his own place takes longer than his pride cares for, but he is eventually secure in the lead position, which Twenty-Seven relinquishes without question.

Viktor has Command, the soldier thinks to the others. *Viktor is Magister now.* The handlers buzz and click to one another, as if debating the truth in this claim. To their eyes, the hearty soldier whose mind cowed them and led them to this end seems a better option.

Twenty-Seven whistles sharply.

They will repeat!

Viktor has Command, yes, the handlers think as one. *Where does Magister wish to go?*

They will release the babelrack first, thinks Viktor. *It will starve otherwise. Then they will seek the royal stores and bundle all the lova they can carry. When they have loaded the alp, they will drive it west to the Cyclonian hive. There, he will barter with their queen for tenders to care for the larvae now left in Albion's towers.*

The handlers chitter amongst themselves but do not disagree. They dismount their alp and hasten to obey, cutting the babelrack free to lumber north in search of food. When they have moved back toward the towers and have passed beyond thought range, Twenty-Seven rubs his forelimbs together.

On the way here, he thinks, *he smelled something. There was a queen nearby, not long ago. Just transforming, and not fully grown.*

Then the princess survived, yes? thinks Viktor.

So it seems, yes. But she is gone now, along with her pluripotents. Why? Why not stay and tend the larvae? And where did she go?

That is not his business. They have little time, and none for the answering of pointless questions.

And yet, as they wait for the handlers to return, Viktor considers this mystery. A single, immature queen with no tenders to rule would be unable to care for so many larvae by herself. Perhaps she has already gone to pursue the very same plan he has devised. Or perhaps the inexplicable devastation has undone her mind and she is wandering senseless like the others. There is no way to tell, and searching for her is a waste of time and energy. She could be anywhere!

When the handlers return, shuffling beneath the weight of bound lova, Viktor whistles.

Off! he commands. *All haste! To Cyclonia!* And the alp strides away as soon as it is loaded, guided by the handlers who have returned to their positions clinging to its bony plates. They whistle and chitter, and the beast slowly gains speed until its thundering passage is all they can hear.

Chapter Two
Accrete

THE SUGARFOOT KEZEL reach the first of the living stalagmites, towering lavender fans and twining, yellow forks, just as Submission has regained most of his senses. The fog of repeated scion bites is slow to dissipate, but the edge of his reason sharpens with every northern step. When at last he gazes at the boundary of his home, his eyes are bright, and his nose is active.

The clan is five thousand snowy strides west of where Lightning and Thunder discovered the Thing, having left the banks of the River Tongue that had wound to their right. That had been Bridger's idea; she had judged crossing that ill-fated land an inauspicious homecoming, and Submission had agreed. Feather, however, a Bristle by birth, had parted ways with them at that point, eager to follow the Tongue north into her own range.

Once she is gone, Submission turns to Bridger.

You've been a good leader, he thinks.

She bows, her tail lowering to the snow.

I didn't want the job. I'm glad you feel better.

Better, not great. I'm still going to need help.

Then, if you don't mind another suggestion, I say scout before going in—I know folks are impatient, but who can say how things have changed?

This is another point on which they agree, and Submission, after assigning the task to Measure and Bone, gathers the clan together, rowdy wabis and all.

We wait until the scouts return, he thinks. *Settle in; it might be a while.*

More than a few grumble at this delay, anxious to

quit the open plains and its unceasing wind. Still, they do as they are told, hunkering down in the crusty snow or seeking shelter among the tussocks of grass, their long, yellow blades bending to the north.

What about them? one of the bibijas wonders, a white-spiked male by the name of Crunch. His question is echoed by others, and they look to the west, where scion both bronze and blue surround a figure of winged gold, the onetime Princess Shimmer, now Queen. Submission imagines them buzzing and clicking amongst themselves. What thoughts they might be sharing are a mystery, as they remain far out of range, rarely venturing near the kezel by whom they are generally despised.

What about 'em? he thinks.

Are we really letting them in the accrete? an ibiwa replies sharply. She is the broken-snouted ah-lah named Stone, and her tail, some of its spikes worn away, lashes side to side. *After what they did?* Other adults bare their teeth, shaking their heads at the thought as if troubled by pestilent yits. But Bridger waves a clawed hand.

Enough! she thinks. *We've been over this. Don't make Bruiser's job any harder than it already is. They keep their word, they get to tag along.* She curls her lip, exposing large, white teeth. *If we're lucky, they'll break their promise and we can tear 'em all to little bits.*

Submission nods.

We can only hope. But Lightning thinks they're OK. Until that changes, keep your peace. My honor is at stake, and right now that's about all I have.

This sentiment is greeted with ambivalence, but none dare challenge. They idle impatiently, waiting for the scouts to return, and Bridger scowls.

Where is Lightning, by the way?

With the blue one, thinks Submission. *They're saying goodbye to the bomba.* His eyes grow narrow, and he wrinkles his snout. *There's something I never imagined myself thinking.*

+ + +

Ansel perches in the crooked arms of an enormous cobalt accrete, three hundred strides to the east. He cranes his neck and peers down with bright, green eyes, his crimson head cocking right to left. Lightning bows low before glancing up to address him.

Will you come down to say a proper goodbye? she wonders. *Please? You deserve a thank you, at least.*

Ansel squawks loudly, and he spreads his wings, rainbows arcing from his broad back.

I have no plans to say goodbye to you, kezel, he thinks. *Properly or otherwise.* He spears an unsuspecting yit as it strives against the wind, gulping it down. *I will share Oracio's last message, as I swore I would, then I will leave this despicable place.*

Where will you go? asks Joy.

Not the maison! The tone of Ansel's thoughts is pure acid. *You have ruined that place for us. White worms infest all the lower levels now, and the memory of my brother's death echoes still.* He hisses and turns away from them. *I will fly to the Eye Tower, our temporary home. I will meet with the claw that promised to wait for me there, and together we will follow the brood.*

But Ilda can't fly, thinks Joy.

Ansel flexes his talons, scratching them across the scaled surface of the accrete.

Many old bombas set out for the Eye Tower on foot, he thinks, *fleeing the worms you released. I expect to find a trail of their corpses in the snow.*

Lightning grimaces. The thought of Ari, dead because of her curiosity, drags her heart to a low place where injuries and doubt overshadow hope. Images of Oracio and Ilda struggling across the plateau plague her imagination. She knows she must offer some thought, some recompense, but her mind is empty.

I wish we could help, she thinks.

I wish the same thing, kezel. But can you travel back in time? Can you undo what you have done?

Lightning casts her gaze downward, tail drooping.

You should hurry home, thinks Joy.

Ansel cackles, but the sound is not a happy one.

I do not need your advice! Oracio told me to forgive you, but I am not the bomba for that task. Listen to his last message, then leave me. I must rest before I fly.

Lightning finds the strength to look up. Ansel's beak flashes side to side like a blade.

Kezel, he thinks, *my nester believes you are the steward of a power greater than you understand. I can only imagine he refers to the blue one. He begs you guard it with your life in the hope that he may see it again.*

Her, Lightning corrects, but it is simple habit; her mind is distant as she reflects on Oracio's words.

He will see me, thinks Joy.

Maybe, Ansel replies. *Maybe not. But if so, bring no trouble with you this time.*

+ + +

Measure and the Brigadier Bone return not long after Lightning and Joy have made their way back to where the kezel gather near the edge of the accrete. As the bibija scouts stride toward them through the wind-swept snow, Lightning turns to look at Ansel one final time. Even at this distance his brilliant plumage stands out against the cobalt, but he soon moves deeper into the shadows, disappearing from view.

He hates us, she thinks. *But he still helped us.*

Bombas have good hearts, thinks Joy.

The scouts share dark, sheltered thoughts as they approach. They address only the other bibijas, as well as Trapper and Old Buttons. But it is to Submission and Bridger they primarily direct their report. Lightning maintains a respectful distance at the edge of thought and catches only the first part of what they share.

It's not hostile, thinks Bone. *As far as we went.*

Not hostile, adds Measure, *but not pretty.*

What they think next, or how the others respond, Lightning can't determine, and she knows better than to get caught eavesdropping. While ibiwas stand watch and oversee energetic wabis, zealous to explore the accrete, Cliff limps up next to her, his gray eyes moving from her to Joy to the ongoing conference.

There's gonna be a lot of angry kezel when they see how bad it really is.

Are you worried they won't keep their promise?

I don't need to worry. I didn't burn the accrete.

Lightning's growl is low but sustained.

Neither did we.

No, Cliff agrees, *but if they're mad enough, they might forget that part.*

Joy clicks a faltering rhythm, but Lightning dismisses the lame kezel with a snarl.

Promise breakers are the first to doubt.

I've kept my promise!

Then you should know they'll keep theirs. But as she thinks this, the council at last adjourns, and Lightning feels a doubt she can only hope remains sheltered.

Submission waves her to approach.

Wants us to visit your princess, she supposes.

Not princess any more, thinks Joy. *Queen.*

+ + +

Shimmer awaits them in her basket. Five of its six sides are a lattice of woven hexagons, but the front panel is open for easy access. When resting on the ground, it makes a perfect throne for audiences like this. Her gold skin mirrors them as they approach. In total, four dozen refugee scion gather unhappily in the cold. Most are as blue as Joy and have equally black antennae and eyes, but though fully grown, they are each no larger than she. Some bear woven parcels on their back, fully loaded. The six bronze among the scion are larger and winged like their queen. They huddle close to her basket, ready to bear it aloft at her command.

When Lightning delivers her message from the kezel leaders, Shimmer is not happy.

Queen desires no more delays and discussions! Al-

ready she has come far out of her way. The heroic derka, whose body lies resting in Albion, was most clear: her answers lie to the north and east of here, at Far Colossus and Ozag's Hold, not in this terrible place.

Maybe, thinks Lightning. *But the clan is going in, and we're going with. You're welcome to stay here or come along until we figure out what to do with you.*

Shimmer's buzzing is harsh and loud.

Hideous sharksha do not intend to keep faith.

They will keep faith, Joy replies. *Lightning says.*

This revolting beast? Does it say when? Queen's lova will not last forever. Nor will her awl.

Soon, thinks Lightning. *And we can get you awl.*

Shimmer whistles a discordant melody.

Can the beast clarify "soon"?

Once Gapi-kan has passed.

What is this? It will speak plainly!

Gapi-kan is Grandfather Red, thinks Joy, and she tilts her head skyward. *The moon.*

The other scion, who have been attending every thought, buzz amongst themselves, unhappy with this response. Shimmer's antennae quiver.

Albion's destroyer may die of old age before Queen can get her revenge. Her eyes sparkle. *The beast should remember its debt. It owes her its life!*

Oh, the beast remembers, thinks Lightning. *Which is why she hasn't let the others tear you to pieces.*

Queen fears them not! She fears only delay, the postponement of retribution!

Her followers click and chitter their consensus. But Shimmer is a creature of hots and colds. As quickly as her fury rises, it abates, and she turns away.

The beasts will conduct their crude business in the shadows if they must, she thinks, as if discussing a trifle. *But scion will not join them. They will shelter beneath the ground; better to suffer digging than a foray into the hideous world of sharksha.* She waves her forelimb at Joy. *The Oddity will return when the Red has passed.*

The dismissal is obvious. Joy clicks a slow tempo,

looking back only once as she and Lightning make their way toward the accrete.

+ + +

The clan uses what had once been a major route from the plains to the foothills. Well-maintained in the past, the way now lies under many moons of snow, shaped by the wind and littered with tracks, none of them kezel. Submission and Bridger lead, walking abreast. In this fashion they plow an opening for those who follow. With Cliff on her left, carrying her pack and limping gamely, and with Joy on her right, Lightning takes a place near the end of the line. She casts gazes to the canopy in vain hope of glimpsing Ansel.

As they move from the skirts of the accrete into its depths, there is at first no anger, in spite of Cliff's worry. The point at which they have entered is healthy, full of sounds and smells they have long dreamed of. They step lightly through the snow, their breathing easier than it's been in moons. Wabis born in scion captivity, for whom the accrete is a wonder, scramble after yits with more will than skill, blithely stumbling over hidden stones and occasionally paying for their inexperience with plunges into icy streams. Their enjoyment can't be dampened, and it proves contagious, spreading to adults who haven't the heart to discipline even the most rambunctious. Seeing the accrete through the eyes of their young, they hurl balls of snow and chase each other's tails.

But when they have at last crossed the Spine and arrive at the first blackened fan, its scales melted, and the many hundreds of ashen stumps that march along behind it, terrible memories rise to the surface, and their mood darkens. Stone's thoughts are the easiest to read—and most foul—but as the band proceeds farther into the sunlit desolation, her mind is joined by others. What merit Lightning had earned from the rescue seems to evaporate before her eyes.

I'm moving up, she thinks, and Joy is quick to follow as she jogs forward to where Submission marches with Bridger at his side and Thunder close behind. Cliff glances at the curling lips and wrinkling snouts up and down the line, and he hastens to join her.

Good idea he thinks.

Thunder glances at them as they approach, but he keeps his thoughts to himself, much as he ever has since his rescue from Albion. He slows his pace to match that of Cliff, and the two jabis plod in silence. Lightning moves ahead to take Thunder's place at their api-kan's tail, holding her thoughts.

It's a good thing your little gold friend didn't come with us, Submission thinks after a time. *I wouldn't have been able to guarantee her safety.*

She's not my friend, thinks Lightning.

She is nobody's friend, Joy adds.

Submission turns and scowls at her.

The less folks sense out of you, the safer you'll be. He shakes his head. *I promised to protect you, but you make my job harder every time you open your mind—or your mouth. Lay low and stay quiet.*

Joy hugs close to Lightning, and in moments her skin changes to black. The only thing visible is the sparkle in her eyes and the sling over her shoulder.

That's not what I meant! You can't go randomly disappearing and expect folks to trust you.

Joy starts to buzz a forlorn tune, then thinks better of it and returns to her original blue.

I'm sorry, Lightning's api-kan.

But Submission only grumbles, and Lightning falls back to walk beside Thunder and Cliff, her mood pensive. When they reach the caves, Bridger goes in first, along with Bone. They return wearing morose expressions, and even the wabis can sense trouble.

They're filthy, thinks Bone. He sticks out his tongue. *Gonna take a long time to get 'em clean.*

Then I guess we better get started, thinks Submission, and he sniffs at the entrance.

There are...bodies, thinks Bridger, and her tone is

strained by suppressed emotion. *And skeletons.*

Submission's ears droop.

Then no wabis inside. Establish a perimeter, and everyone else get ready to work.

We should send out some hunters, thinks Bone. *Check things out and see what they can catch.*

Fine, thinks Submission. *But if they come across a Redtooth, they're not to start anything. Mark our turf and move along.* He turns to Lightning.

Stay close, Little Spark.

+ + +

At Submission's request, Lightning relinquishes her last remaining crystal. He snaps it into neat halves, passing one to Bridger. They split into two teams and make their way into the caves, accompanied by looming shadows and the shuffling of reluctant feet. Bridger leads her woli Stone, Measure, and Pounce. Submission goes with his two jabis, as well as Crunch and Cliff.

The space is much as Lightning remembers: rank with the smell of burned accrete, coated in dust, and littered with bones and the feces of small animals seeking shelter. On occasion, she catches the sound of scurrying feet, and more than once the glimmer of eyes recedes into the darkness before them. The sudden appearance of light-bearing kezel sends purple rixli scattering, often not quickly enough to avoid being squashed.

At the first branch, the teams split.

Keep an eye open for crystals, thinks Submission. *Or anything else useful.*

But Lightning knows they will find nothing.

Submission leads his team to the feast cave as Joy's rasping hands break the heavy silence. The crystal reaches neither the cave's ceiling nor its farthest walls, and they navigate the rough floor in a lonely bubble of light. A place Lightning once considered among her favorites fills her with dread and melancholy. The shuffle of their feet echoes like the whisper of conspiracy, and when

when Cliff sneezes from the dust, Crunch jumps and curses as if someone pulled his tail. A pile of deliberately placed rocks becomes visible in the shadows: Gami-kan's burial mound. Lightning glances quickly at her api as he approaches the cairn. His mood is difficult to read.

You built this?

Yes, sir. I know it's not traditional, but I had to do something, and we didn't have time to carry her to the High Step. I hope it's OK.

Submission releases a low, rumbling sigh.

Did you see...Do you know how it happened?

Lightning furrows her brow, but the question is directed to Cliff, not her.

The fumes from their burning, thinks Cliff. He wrinkles his nose. *It didn't blow away like normal smoke; it sank to the low spots and filled up the caves. Took forever for it to clear out.*

Submission squats by the cairn. Crunch places another stone and bows his head.

I don't think they suffered, Cliff offers timidly. *When I smelled the fumes, all they did is make me sleepy. I suppose they just drifted off...*

They?

As Submission thinks this, there comes from a distant cave the mournful howling of a kezel in grief. Not long after, it is joined by another, equally dismayed, but angry as well, coming from a cave on the opposite side of the complex. As the individual howling grows to a chorus, Submission's ears pin flat against the noise.

We should maybe go, thinks Thunder.

Yes, thinks Submission, his eyes on Joy. *You're not safe here.*

+ + +

The jabis follow Submission out of the feast cave through one of its secondary exits. A brief climb and another narrow tunnel leads them at last to the clean air and sunlit snow of a wide rock shelf overlooking the cave's main entrance. Below them, wabis chase one another and wrestle in the snow. Gully and Snapper oversee their play, scanning the skies carefully and often raising their noses to the wind. The low-riding sun shines unhindered; accrete that had once filtered its light now stand barely higher than the snow itself.

I'm sorry, thinks Lightning, though she is uncertain to whom. *I didn't know this would happen.*

Joy whistles softly but cuts herself short. Thunder and Cliff look away awkwardly.

Would it have made a difference if you had? Submission fixes Lightning with a discerning gaze.

Yes, she thinks without hesitation. *At the time.*

And now?

But Lightning lets this go unanswered.

Why didn't you tell me?

I...tried.

That story about your friend Ivy? You call that trying? Is there even a Bristle by that name? Thunder and Cliff hunch their shoulders, fearing an avalanche, but Lightning remains steady.

I should have trusted you, she thinks.

Yes! You should have. It was your first and worst mistake, and kezel may have died because of it.

From deep within the caves, muffled by stone and snow, the aggrieved howling continues. The wabis stop what they are doing, grimacing at the sound. Gully and Snapper herd them away to a small dell, looking up at Submission as they do, their expressions sour and their thoughts sheltered—a fact for which Lightning is grateful.

Cliff sidles up next to her.

Might be a good time to tell him about the awl.

Lightning nods absently.

What awl? asks Thunder.

Last time we were here, Lightning speared an awl. I helped, Cliff adds. *It's cached somewhere—or it was.*

Submission reads this thought.

Good, he thinks. *You two*—he points at Cliff and Thunder—*go dig it up and bring it to the wabis. No eating!*

It won't be enough to make folks forget what's happened, but we need to start somewhere.

Lightning shares directions to the cache and opens Cliff's pack, removing her rope to make more room. Then Cliff and Thunder climb down from the shelf and are soon out of sight. Submission glares at his woli, but what he thinks he keeps to himself, and neither she nor Joy have the courage to ask.

+ + +

When they finally reach the described location, Thunder and Cliff must move a great deal of snow and dirt—and some rocks—to get to the awl. But their effort is rewarded. Lightning's cache is carefully placed, and the awl they find is well-preserved, fully intact and redolent. Neither dare disobey Submission's order, though the food calls to them like a fancy. They bear it to the wabis unmolested and are thanked by being mobbed. Dropping the meat, they scramble away, casting wistful gazes as the awl is torn up and devoured.

They are returning to the rock shelf when the adults from inside the caves proceed solemnly out into the light. Their howling is done, but they are more menacing in silence than sound. Thunder and Cliff step away prudently, keeping their eyes averted and their tails low. The adults glance at the feasting wabis, then up to the rock shelf where Lightning stands with Joy in her apikan's shadow. The Brigadier Bone steps forward.

No amount of awl makes up for this, Bruiser.

It's not intended to, thinks Submission. *And if you can find a kezel here who hasn't lost someone, let me know, please. We have a responsibility, Bone. We need to find a way through this—and remember our oath.*

This call to duty is enough for the preeminent Brigadier, who clashes his teeth and sweeps his tail side to side but in the end turns away, grumbling. Others among the adults are not so easily deterred, two in particular: Stone and Fang, whose fancies Flake and Fall are among those lost in the toxified caves while trying to protect their wabis. Stone especially is beyond reason, for alongside Flake, her two wabis had also perished, Knit and Knot, as if they had died while taking a nap.

You say, "Without Lightning, we'd all still be scion prisoners." She snarls. *I say without her, we wouldn't have been prisoners in the first place. Come down here! Let me show my gratitude. You too, blueface.*

Joy clicks in spite of herself.

Yes, thinks Fang. *Come down. Your kindness deserves a reward. Or maybe we should come up.*

The two ibiwas, with Stone leading the way, step to the narrow path leading up to the shelf.

Don't be stupid, thinks Submission, and he growls with teeth bared. But Stone and Fang are wounded by grief, and their pain cries for a target. They start up the path, their eyes narrow and their lips curled. Before they have made it halfway, however, a mind comes calling from the west, followed closely by a barking voice. Both bear the same clear message:

Intruder alert! Redteeth on the range!

In moments, Blue comes into view, his steely, peppered spikes impossible to miss. He kicks up a spray of snow as he runs toward them, dodging the stumps of burned accrete. The other adults, even the angriest among them, turn away from Lightning. Stone and Fang leap down from the path. When Blue arrives, he is panting heavily, and a bloody scratch mars his flank.

Where's Bruiser? he demands. *Where's Bridger?*

Up here, thinks Submission. *Bridger's still inside.*

Better get the wabis there, too. Blue presses his flank against a mound of drifted snow. His eyes close, and he sighs. *I ran into a hunting party.*

Sensing this, Bridger exits the cave.

You weren't supposed to start anything.

Blue winces at her tone.

They didn't need any "starting" from me. They took care of that on their own.

Reluctant wabis are ushered into the caves. Bridger scowls at the remaining adults.

Are we listening to a story? Having a feast? Stone and Fang! Get to work! Partner up and take positions! She looks up at Submission. *Suppose we'd better go welcome our guests? They,* she indicates Lightning and Joy, *should probably stay where they are.*

Submission nods, motioning to Thunder and Cliff.

You two. On the shelf. Watch over them.

We don't need watching over, thinks Lightning, but when Cliff and Thunder join them on the shelf, she can't deny she is grateful for their presence.

+ + +

Submission and Bridger move west, away from the cave's main entrance, but they haven't gone far before four well-fed bibija Redteeth appear. They amble through the foothills as if on a pleasant tour of scenic vistas, not encroaching on contested territory devastated by fire. As with all Redteeth, they wear no clothes, though their eyes are thickly lined with black bomba essence. Their leader, his spikes brindled and his right eye missing, pauses to rase a leg and mark a charred stump of accrete.

You can have that one, Spike, thinks Bridger. *We weren't using it. I'm afraid the others are claimed.*

Bridger! thinks the Redtooth leader. *Is it you? And Submission? I didn't recognize you, Bruiser. Lose your vests? Or is this the new Sugarfoot style? Finally seen the light? Gotten over all that Moondweller rot?*

His companions clash their jaws and pin their ears, the entire party approaching until it is within a dozen strides. They stop to read the wind.

A whole pack of 'em, thinks one.

Suppose they're naked too? asks another.

What did you do to the accrete? asks Spike. *Your range smells as bad as it looks.*

It smelled fine until you showed up, thinks Submission. *You're a long way from home, Spike.*

Not as long as you might think. You maybe haven't

heard, but Redteeth are east of the wedge now. We'll care for it better than you did.

And I don't know if you've heard, Bridger wrinkles her snout, *but you're an idiot. I knew there was a reason I said no when you asked me to be your fancy.*

Spike snarls and takes another step forward. But one of his companions stops him, pointing to the rock shelf where Lightning and the others observe the encounter in silence. Spike's one good eye narrows to a mere slit. His growl is low but impossible to miss.

There's one who's not naked, he thinks, and he curses. *Black-vested and running with a blue freak.*

His companions scratch at the snowy ground.

Redteeth know all about this one, boss. Trespasser, she is. Murderer!

Redteeth know nothing, thinks Submission. *The only one of 'em with any sense was Ancian.*

That's another dead Redtooth we can blame on the dirty jabi, thinks Spike. *How many more are there?*

I'll give you a number, Bridger replies. *Four. That's how many breaths you have to show us your tails, or this conversation is going to get a lot less civil.*

The Redteeth flare their spikes and move closer, but Bridger immediately rises to two legs, joined by Submission, and in moments, Bone and Pounce step out from their positions inside the cave's main entrance. Measure and Crunch appear further to the east, flanking the Redteeth, their tails thrashing.

With a curse, Spike sweeps a huge, clawed hand through the snow, casting it skyward in a glittering spray that falls about Submission and Bridger.

Keep your precious murderer, he thinks. *And her little blue friend—for now. But don't get comfortable. You're not staying long...*

And the one-eyed kezel turns about, his companions quick on his heels.

\+ + +

Lightning's cached awl soothes wabi hunger, but it does little to dull the angry edge shared by Stone and others. For the moment, however, much of that anger is redirected at the transgressing Redteeth. And there is the business of burial to attend.

I'm not done with you, thinks Stone to Lightning, but her ami-kan Bridger ushers her away.

Come, she thinks. *Flake wouldn't want this.*

One by one, bodies are borne from the cave and up to the burial place on the High Step, the process sad and slow and accompanied by an awful silence. There goes Flake, and poor little Knit and Knot. And there, too, are Drift, and Shadow, and the gigika Prowl...

I'm going to be sick, thinks Lightning, and she turns away, slumping beside Joy. They wait on the shelf, expecting at any moment a storm to break the silence. And indeed, one does at last, a howling chorus of misery from the High Step, the worst sound Lightning has ever heard. She grits her teeth and pins her ears, but there is no escape from the mourning, no refuge.

Joy clutches her spikes.

It's not your fault, she thinks, which is true, of course, but it won't bring back the dead.

+ + +

Not long after the last body is laid to rest, hunters finally return with a trio of cremlins, two sour dow, and a full-grown sneer, three strides long. The adults gather for a somber meal, debating plans for the future. They do not share with the jabis. Cranny, Pockets, Edge, and Splay venture out on their own to seek a meal, but Lightning, Thunder, Cliff, and Joy remain atop the rock shelf, observing the proceedings with empty stomachs and closed minds. Finally, Lightning can take no more.

You need to ask him, she thinks to Thunder. *Just the leftover bones or skin.*

You ask, he counters. *You're his favorite.*

Says who? Lightning scowls. *C'mon! Ask him.*

Don't do it, Cliff worries. *It'll just make him mad.*

No, don't do it, Joy agrees, but Lightning's stomach growls almost as loudly as she does.

They won't leave any, she thinks. *Just watch!*

Thunder shakes his head and looks away.

Well that's just fine, thinks Lightning. *We'll fatten up on the smell of it.* She glares at her oti-mu. *What's wrong with you? Ever since we got out of that place, you've been stuck in your own head. Don't tell me you're not hungry! I know better...*

I'm just not looking for trouble, Thunder replies.

That's a good plan, thinks Cliff.

Now it is Lightning's turn to shake her head.

You had your chance, Cliff. It never occurred to you to bury a few chunks of that awl along the way?

I was just following orders. "No eating," Bruiser said. I wasn't trying to get bit.

Brilliant.

Lightning turns to the east, where a hint of movement catches her eye several hundred strides away. Soon after, a lone ibiwa emerges from the shadows of undamaged accrete, his tan spikes gleaming as he steps into the sunlit snow and charred spikes of black.

Digger's back, she thinks.

Bliss, too, Cliff points to the north, where a lanky, brown ibiwa leaps carefully from rock to snowy rock, following the downhill course of Sour Creek. The two scouts join the other adults, who welcome their return with the last of the cremlin.

This should be interesting, thinks Lightning, and Joy clicks slowly, though what it means is unclear.

\+ + +

You got off easier than I did, Blue complains to the other scouts, noting his lacerated flank.

Barely, Digger grimaces. *Redteeth have been all over the Spine, from the Bloodwater to the Tongue. Their stink is pretty much everywhere, even where that dirty lit-*

tle thief— He catches himself, bowing before Submission. *I'm sorry, Bruiser. I mean Lightning. The place she found the blue one. Redteeth all over that.*

And you? thinks Submission to Bliss. Rock's fancy stretches her long legs as if buying time.

The good news is the burning doesn't go on forever, she thinks. *Accrete are healthy north of the Sour.*

And the bad news? asks Bridger.

Redteeth are having a grand time hunting our talihew and dow, that's the bad news. The accrete is too quiet; even the virbles are on guard. Outside of the one that went with Lightning, there isn't a bomba in smelling distance—or a babelrack—and hasn't been for moons.

Same to the west, Blue agrees. *It's like they were afraid we were coming back, so they overhunted everything they could get their teeth on.* He licks his injury. *Only way we're making new vests is with Bristle help.*

Then you'd better have something to trade, thinks a mind, coming from the east.

The adults turn to see the ibiwa Melt, escorting Feather across the River Sweet and up the hill. With them is another Bristle, a bibija female with a striped coat of glistening spikes, an impressive, bushy tail, and a fine vest of sleek talihew. It is she who has sent the thought.

Look who I found, thinks Melt.

Feather! Back already? asks Bridger. *Life on the Bristle range too boring after your Sugarfoot adventures?*

I wish, thinks Feather. *Sorry to interrupt, Bruiser, but you're going to want to hear this.*

*Hmm...*thinks Submission, considering her tone. *Somehow I doubt that.* But he has eyes only for the striped Bristle, her hunting vest svelte and tanned to a dark brown. Even the least attentive of the kezel sense their chief's discomfort, his awkwardness at having been caught naked and bedraggled.

Hello Brook, he thinks.

Hello Bruiser, replies the bushy-tailed Bristle. *It's very good to see you again.*

Chapter Three
Meeting

SHIMMER WATCHES CAREFULLY. The moment all the kezel have disappeared into the accrete, she calls to two of her soldiers. They barely qualify for the title, having only recently been transformed from lowly drones by her new Queenly arts. They had been numbered in the thousands and are very slow to adjust. Their fangs remain underdeveloped, their frames gracile. Nevertheless, they are the best she has. They dim their eyes and bow.

They will follow the sharksha with greatest stealth, she thinks to them. *In particular the Oddity, whom they are to never let out of their sight. If it seeks to flee, or it looks as though it plans to leave this wretched domain without first consulting with Queen, one of them will return to alert her. The other will remain and follow.*

Yes. One will return.

Yes. And the other will follow.

Yes. It is clear.

Yes. Perfectly.

Shimmer pauses, considering something.

Utmost secrecy, she orders, *but...if they can approach close enough to the Oddity, they may be able to sense its thoughts—and those of the hideous sharksha with whom it conspires.*

Yes. Utmost secrecy. Downwind.

Yes. But close if possible.

Yes. Close enough to sense but not be sensed.

Yes. Sense the conspirators.

But...

Yes. But...

The soldiers chitter and click, and their hesitance is easy to read. Sharksha are known to them only as dumb, violent brutes, incapable of thought. What could there be to sense?

They are wrong, Shimmer scolds. *The beasts are indeed disgusting but able to think in ways unguessed. They will go now and not return until they have news!*

Bowing and buzzing, the soldiers change from blue to white, their zig-zag trails following the path of the kezel into the accrete, shadowy and forbidding. As they go, Shimmer regards the golden burnish of her skin, noting with a detached resignation how it has gradually spread to cover her entire body.

She is beautiful, thinks her prime pluripotent, who herself has begun to turn silver, preparing to fill the vacated role of princess. *She will be the loveliest queen ever. She is sure of it.*

Queen of refugees, thinks Shimmer, her tone scathing. *Queen of a wasted land. She does not desire this ascendance, lovely or otherwise.*

Her prime threshes her wings to keep warm and her antennae lay flat.

Does Queen wish the next ones to be summoned?

Which are the two highest numbers?

Seven Thousand Eighty-Seven, Queen, and Thirteen Thousand Sixteen.

Thirteen thousand! How is she to convert such a low rank? How will it prevail in the mission ahead? Shimmer's clicking is slow and morose. *Of no consequence. What choice does she have? Bring them to her.*

Her prime takes to the air, while the remaining pluripotents huddle close, trying to shield their queen from the wind.

The holes will be complete soon, thinks one. *Then Queen can take rest from the elements.*

Rest! Shimmer's eyes glitter. *She cannot see the time when that will happen. What other queen has been so unfairly taxed so early in her reign?*

No other, her attendants are quick to assure, and

they think with one mind.

Shimmer buzzes a mirthless tune.

Has there ever been a reign begun with such calamity or so many impossible choices?

None have faced a harder road, her pluripotents concede. *Unless perhaps Ozag Herself, when the Undying led scion from vumierre slavery.*

Ozag! They will not mention that name in her presence. Ozag the Forgetter! Ozag the Punisher!

The bronze creatures dim their eyes.

Hers is indeed a singular burden, they think. *None have suffered worse. Yet, she will prevail!*

Perhaps, thinks Shimmer. *If only she weren't so tired. She is not meant to convert drones and handlers to soldiers on such meager stores.*

She preens her antennae, whistling softly.

And yet, thinks a pluripotent, *they approach.*

Her prime flits toward them, trailed on the ground by a pair of scion whose eyes grow dim when they reach her, their antennae tilting forward to touch the snow.

Queen commands? they think.

She commands they ready for conversion. They will have fangs and learn to fight!

The scion chitter to one another, in spite of themselves, unprepared for such a revelation.

Queen is wise, one of them thinks.

Yes, thinks the other. *The wisest.*

But he is just a handler, adds the first.

Yes, and he just a drone. Simple and slow.

Yes, thinks the handler. *The slowest. And stupid.*

Yes, agrees the drone. *Not worthy of fangs.*

No. The stupidest. Not worthy at all.

This is sadly apparent, thinks Shimmer. *But she has no options. They are the best at her disposal and they will perform their roles as commanded.*

Yes. They will, thinks the handler.

Yes, thinks the drone. *Gladly.*

But they continue chittering nervously as Shimmer spreads her wings and bends her antennae forward.

Pheromones and brain waves mean nothing to the pair, but they feel their effects all the same. Their limbs relax, and their heads tilt as if hearing a pleasant sound. The subtle smell wafting from beneath Shimmer's golden wings buoys their spirits while at the same time making them very sleepy. They sway in waking dreams of sturdy, bristled limbs and marching drills.

They will have fangs, they sense, and though skeptical at first, they soon lose all doubt, and when they sense, *They will become soldiers,* it seems the most reasonable thing in the world.

Yes, thinks the handler. *Fangs.*

Yes, thinks the drone. *We will bite and fight.*

And like that, the spell is cast and the job done. Shimmer settles her wings and releases a deep breath.

They will seek the darkest hole, she thinks. *Only total darkness and torpor will complete the change. When ready, they will return and receive their orders.*

The pair turn and zig-zag away slowly, already half asleep, although no different to the eye than when they had arrived. If the conversion works, it will do so only with the help of time and sleep.

Sleep, Shimmer thinks, weary like she has never been. The thought of flying—or even walking—to her hole makes all three of her hearts quail.

She has overdone, thinks her prime, and the pluripotents hurry to retrieve her basket, assisting her inside before lifting her from the ground.

No choice, she thinks, her thoughts soft and blurry. *The road to Far Colossus is sure to be filled with danger. Who can say what form the obstacles will take? Her very life may be threatened. And she would not approach Ozag's Hold weak and unprepared. Someone must be made to pay! Thousands of larvae...thousands...*

But even before her pluripotents have carried her in to a neat, hexagonal hole, delved by buzzing drones, Shimmer is fast asleep.

+++ +++

What's happening down there? thinks Lightning. *I can't sense anything!* She strains to catch the thoughts being exchanged by the adults, but neither Thunder nor Cliff are any help. The former gazes to the south, his mouth moving soundlessly, as if chewing memories. Cliff lies curled up, his eyes closed tight. Joy fidgets restlessly, one hand inside her sling, caressing what is carried inside. She reads Lightning's frustration.

Submission said stay here, she reminds.

He didn't mean forever, thinks Lightning, though she has no evidence for that. *He wouldn't want us pooping by the caves, would he? I gotta go!*

This gets Thunder's attention.

Liar, he thinks. *You want to spy.*

Can't I do both?

Not without me. C'mon...but stay downwind and be quiet. Leave Cliff. He'll just get us caught.

With Joy walking silently behind, the siblings climb down from the rock shelf and choose a path that seems plausible for the stated quest of relieving themselves—but also passes close to the gathered adults, allowing them to hide behind a toothy barricade of stone.

They peer over this, their minds open.

\+ + +

I'm sorry we can't offer you better hospitality, thinks Submission. *As you can see...* He waves generally at the desolation around them as if it explains everything.

And I'm sorry, thinks Brook, *that we can't welcome you home with better news. The whole Bristle range was glad to hear you'd returned, that's for sure, but I'm afraid we haven't had time to celebrate—or rest.*

Or mourn properly, thinks Feather.

Well, prompts Bridger, *if there's bad news, better get to it. We have a lot to think about.*

The Bristles take places around the circle. Feather is already re-vested, and the Sugarfoot kezel squirm at their own nakedness in such close proximity. Brook takes a seat beside Submission, whose discomfort is apparent. He never makes eye contact, and when she leans close and their spikes touch, he twitches and shimmies to his right. Lightning is not the only one to notice, though she is the one, outside of Brook perhaps, most keenly interested in his response.

Well? he thinks, and his tone is gruff. *Get it out.*

Where do you want me to start? thinks Brook, a moment later answering her own question. *I'm chief now; I suppose you haven't heard.*

They have not.

What happened? asks Old Buttons, but her tone reflects the mood of the clan. None are eager to learn what they feel sure will be unhappy news. Brook's response spares no feelings.

My api-kan is dead, she thinks. *That's what. Last Wabi-la moon. He was surveying the Skull. It had been abandoned for a generation, you know, but the clan is growing, and he had thoughts of moving some families back in. Folks aren't as superstitious as they used to be, and the Skull doesn't scare 'em like it did. Anyway, he stumbled onto a Redtooth party. Spying on us, I guess, or conspiring with the rotter Whitetails. Not that it matters.* She bares her teeth. *They were quick about it; no one heard a thing. We didn't find his body until after the next sleep. They tried to hide the signs, but their tracks and their dirty smell were impossible to miss.*

For a time, no one comments on this, and they shelter their thoughts. But around the ring, a low growl moves from kezel to kezel. Trapper clashes his jaws,

Squall! he thinks. *As fine a Bristle as ever was.*

Handsome and brave, agrees Old Buttons. *He was like my oti-mu. Poor Squall...poor Brook!*

Poor all of us, thinks Brook. *Because they won't stop with murder. They aim to take the Skull. Your return complicates their plans, but I doubt it will keep them from making the attempt. They re-built the northern crossing, you know. Our scouts report a lot of activity.*

When, do you think? asks Bridger. *How long?*

You mean will they attack before the Red or after? Until you showed up, we thought after, for sure. Why risk getting caught aboveground when Gapi-kan shows up?

But now, guesses Submission, *they figure the more time we have to prepare, the more help we can be.*

I'm pretty sure that's the way of it, thinks Brook. *From their point of view, the faster they move, the sooner they take hold of the Skull. Once they're embedded, that'll be that. But if they wait 'til after the Gapi-kan, you have a chance to get organized—and maybe put your throwers to use. Then their little plan might not go so well.*

*Hmm...*thinks the Brigadier Bone. *About that...*

Yes, thinks Submission. *About that. I'm sorry, Brook, but there are no throwers. I don't know who took 'em, but they're long gone. Cutters, too.*

Brook's eyes close, and her ears droop.

Gone? she thinks. *Are you saying the Redteeth might have them? All of them?*

It's possible—all but one.

One that doesn't work, adds Bone.

The mood of the two Bristles is spoken through the deflated hope visible in their eyes and postures.

Then the Skull is just the start, thinks Feather. *They'll come for the home caves next. Yours too.*

Somber, lengthy silence and sheltered thoughts greet this unhappy prediction. Finally, Bridger looks up.

How long before Gapi-kan gets here?

Three sleeps, thinks Submission.

My counters tell me two, thinks Brook.

And how many stationed at the Skull?

Eight.

That's not enough, thinks Bone.

It's all we could spare. If Whitetails are making a move on our eastern range, someone needs to stay home.

More growling around the circle.

Dirty Whitetails, think some. *Cowardly Redteeth,* think others. *Thieves and murderers,* they all agree.

Yes to all of that, thinks Bridger. *But we're not going to win a fight with name-calling. What's the plan?*

I can't say, thinks Brook. *I had hoped...* And here, she looks at Submission, seeking his eyes. He resists at first, but he can't maintain this for long with everyone's attention on him. Wrinkling his snout, he finally matches her gaze as if it causes him pain.

Of course, we'll help, he thinks. *But I don't know what the plan is either. If they have our throwers...*

He flounders and looks away.

One step at a time, thinks Bone. *That's what Ancian always used to say. We can't make any kind of a plan until we have more information.*

And Submission nods, sighing heavily.

She also said a tired mind makes a lot of mistakes, and I'm about to fall asleep on my feet.

You're not wrong, thinks Trapper.

And you're not alone, adds Old Buttons.

Bridger takes this cue to assume the leadership, and she organizes a team to reset the southern crossing, their goal to scout the length of the wedge, determining Redtooth location and numbers—and if they are armed. As the conference adjourns and kezel move to their respective duties, only Submission and the two Bristles remain. With a quick glance from Brook, Feather steps away, making a show of conferring with her dear friend Bliss. Submission squirms and fidgets.

I know this isn't the time, thinks Brook.

No, thinks Submission. *It isn't.*

But I've missed you.

Hmm...yeah...well...yeah.

I'm sorry. I know you just got back from an awful ordeal. Feather told me everything. Poor Rock and Crag. She leans forward as if to touch noses, but Submission draws away, rising to two legs.

We're not giving up on them. They're out there somewhere. He pretends to read the wind.

Bruiser...

But Submission continues as if he was alone.

They might make a play on the Sugarfoot caves, he thinks. *We're going to need all the throwing rocks and rol-*

ling boulders we can find. If we can hold them off the high ground long enough, Gapi-kan will drive their dirty tails back across the wedge.

Submission...

I'll get the ah-lahs and jabis working on that right now. But we need sleep. We're pretty banged up. Maybe rotating crews, some working, some sleeping.

Bruiser...

But Submission has reached the limit of his pride. He lowers his head and steps away, moving back toward the caves, his tail dragging.

You're welcome to come inside, he thinks. *Until the scouts return.* But he does not look back to see if his invitation is accepted.

+ + +

Lightning and her fellow conspirators have little time to discuss what they have learned, for not long after they have hurried back to the shelf, they are ordered to gather rocks and boulders for the defense of their home.

They wake Cliff from his nap.

Where are the other jabis? he grumbles.

Hunting, foraging, shirking, thinks Blue. *But don't worry about them, Three-legs, just get to work.*

And work they do, overseen by Trapper and Old Buttons, for the gigikas consider themselves experts on which rocks make the best missiles. They search for ones with the ideal heft, the most comfortable fit in the hand. These are stockpiled in strategic locations best suited to rain destruction on enemies foolish enough to climb the hill. Stones large enough to maim or kill are rolled into place by the ibiwas Digger, Bliss, and Blue. One good push will send them over the edge, and then watch out! to anyone in their path. The Bristles put their backs into this effort as well, but even with their help, there is a great deal of huffing and puffing, and curses flow freely.

Cliff spends much of his rock gathering time complaining to anyone willing to give him their attention (not many) about his hunger and fatigue, but Thunder keeps his mind sheltered and dives into the work as if trying to prove a point. Lightning and Joy work together, occasionally exchanging thoughts but more often lost in their own heads, each pondering different dilemmas. Bridger has chosen their most vocal detractors for the scouting duty, so as they work, they are able to do so in peace.

Who's this Brook? Lightning wonders.

Ami-kan's friend from back in the history days, Thunder replies. *That's what I heard, anyway.*

Why does she make Submission so uncomfortable?

I don't know. Why are you asking me?

Lightning scowls as she watches the two Bristles persuade a chunky boulder into position. Their loyalty is unquestioned by the others; that should be enough for her. And yet, in Brook's presence her api-kan is reduced to a simpleton, and this sits uneasily with her. In fact, since the conference, he has remained out of sight, doing what, she can't say.

Probably hiding, thinks Cliff, intruding on her thoughts. *It's what you do when...you know...*

No. What?

You know...when someone...you know.

No, she snaps. *I don't.* Though in fact, she does, now that Cliff has expressed it in that awkward way. She stuffs a last stone in her pack and wrinkles her snout.

Let's put these up on the shelf, she thinks to Joy. *I've seen enough down here.*

\+ + +

Joy tucks two more rocks in her sling, careful of the artifact riding inside, though it seems impervious to their rough edges. As they make their way up to the shelf, she caresses its smooth face and ponders the mystery of its properties. She had told Lightning not to worry, that the device did nothing, but that had not been entirely true. Nothing malicious, is what she had meant, nothing troublesome or untoward. But it most definitely did something. That had been clear from the first.

Though she had needed no further proof of its ability to magnify and clarify the thoughts of others, their recent foray into spying had cemented the fact. The adults had been on the edge of thought sense, almost out of range, and had at times taken care to shelter their ideas—and yet she had sensed them, clear as if they were right beside her. Lightning and Thunder had as well, though she doubts they know just how much help they had been given by the device, via her own mind.

Upon unloading their bounty, piling the rocks in a neat pyramid, they pause for a moment, weary and hungry. Their fingers are achy and bruised, their feet and backs cramping. Just as they debate making another trip, Submission finally exits the caves.

Time for introductions, he thinks, and he calls down the hill to Brook. *You wanted to see,* he thinks to the Bristle chief. *Here's your chance.*

+ + +

Moments later, Lightning and Joy find themselves sitting amid the ruined accrete, joined by Submission, Bridger, and their visitors from the east. Feather is no longer amazed by Joy, but Brook paces side to side, her eyes locked on the blue creature, her nose twitching.

I know you told me, she thinks, *and I thought I would be OK with it, but...*

You're not alone, thinks Bridger as she grooms her tail. *Shakes up the world, doesn't it?*

I don't see why it's such a big deal, thinks Lightning, for she is tired of seeing Joy treated like a freak on display. *Turns out lots of creatures think.* But she stops herself from further comment. Submission's curled lip is all the warning she needs.

About that, thinks Brook. *Feather says bombas are on that list. Babelracks too.*

It's true, thinks Submission. *If we can believe this one here,* and he inclines his head to Joy.

You can believe it, she thinks. *And the scion, too.*

Who? asks Brook.

The blue ones who caused all this mess, thinks Feather. *Like the ones we left on the edge of the range.*

Brook blinks rapidly and runs claws through the spikes cresting on the back of her neck.

How many more, do you think? Which others?

Who can say? thinks Submission. *For all we know, they can all do it.*

Not virbles or sneer, thinks Joy. *Not yits or cremlins.* But her thoughts are timid, and she glances to Submission, afraid to be out of order.

This... Brook's thought trails off. She settles to her haunches; the weight of this new reality is too much to bear standing. *This changes things, doesn't it? I mean... doesn't it? And this one can sense them?*

Her name is Joy, thinks Lightning by old habit, grimacing when the bibijas glare at her.

Apparently, thinks Bridger, *not only can it—she—sense them, but when she's nearby, we sense them too.*

But not otherwise?

No.

But...but how?

We don't know.

Brook considers this. The others wait in silence, reflecting on their own sheltered thoughts.

Well, she thinks finally. *I'm going to have a hard time at the next babelrack feast. And bombas? Are you saying we should...what? Treat them like equals?*

Submission runs his claws through the snow.

They saved Lightning's life—twice, the way I understand the story. I don't know about equals, but...

At the moment, thinks Bridger, *we need as many allies as we can get. I say until we know more, bombas are off limits. Babelracks too.*

Brook and Feather look glum. Their ears droop.

Then I guess it's a good thing most of them have cleared out or been killed, thinks Feather.

But you'll never gain your weight back, frets Brook.

What about awl? Or talihew? Can they think too?

Not that I know, thinks Joy. *Can't say for sure.*

Feather mentioned something else, thinks Brook. *Something about a promise to those...those blue things gathered on the fringe. Those scion.*

Submission answers by explaining the situation with Shimmer and the vows made to secure her assistance. Brook doesn't waste time suggesting the promise be broken; she knows her hosts too well for that. Still, practical considerations nag.

What does it mean? she thinks. *You're not going to run off on some fool's errand while Redteeth are threatening our ranges, are you?*

Of course not. Submission growls. *We'll deal with the scion when the Redteeth have been shown back to their side of the wedge.*

Will they help us? Brook wonders. *If they know we can't give them what they want until this threat has been eliminated, maybe they'll lend a hand.*

Maybe, thinks Joy, but her tone is doubtful.

It's worth asking, thinks Bridger.

Agreed, thinks Submission. *That's why I'm going to go with Lightning and...and...*

Joy, thinks Lightning, and she resists the urge to scowl. *Her name is Joy.*

Yes. We'll go together and talk with these scion. But nothing can happen until we've gotten some rest. Will you stay? he asks Brook, in a tone that suggests he hopes she will not. The Bristle chief shakes her head.

We've done what we came to do. I need to get back and marshal defenses. You'll come to the Skull?

As many and as soon as possible.

\+ + +

Miraculously, Splay and the other jabis return bearing a large awl, and they are at once forgiven for missing the rock party. Using Lightning's cutter, Submission renders the awl, laying it out in ceremony. When he carefully extracts the glands at the base of the awl's brain and hands them to Bridger for safekeeping, no one questions it. Then he helps Old Buttons rise to two legs, and all but the wabis follow her example.

We stand in honor of the Moondwellers, the bow-legged gigika thinks. *Stand as they did—as they do—and use the weapons they left behind to prepare the kill. But we need no help...*

She stops. Her grizzled snout wrinkles, and her lip trembles as if preparing to snarl. She can't go on.

...we need no help hunting, continues Trapper. *And we never cook the meat.*

Never cook the meat, the others echo, but their thoughts are subdued like a mumble, their focus split.

Meat! think several of the wabis, who have yet to learn the order of a feast. In any case, the affair is more informal than in moons past, when piles of food, not tight rations, were the rule. Snapper is doted on, so pregnant she can barely stand, and the victorious jabi quartet get their hunter's share. After them it's the gigis, bibis, and ibis, in that order, chewing more thoughtfully than is usual. Lurking around the perimeter, Lightning, Thunder, and Cliff must wait and worry, sensing the adults' conversation but not participating.

Moondwellers, thinks Bridger. *Do you think that's what they really were?*

Submission licks clean the awl head.

No way to tell, I guess. No one's ever seen one.

Ancian described 'em just like that, thinks Crunch. *I knew it as soon as I saw 'em.*

Others grumble general agreement. But Snapper, rubbing her distended belly, takes a less positive view.

She also made it seem like they were a great help in time of need. Didn't notice those three sticking around to lend a hand. And only one of 'em dressed!

Yes, thinks Serenity. *What was that about?*

Several kezel turn spiky heads to peer at Joy as if she might have an answer, but she cowers under their gaze and keeps her thoughts tightly sheltered.

When I asked them, thinks Bridger, *they didn't have much to say about it. Said they might be related to our Moondwellers, but that they'd never been to any of our moons. They had more questions than I did.*

Where do you suppose they are now? thinks the Brigadier Bone. *And are there more of them?*

But no one has an answer.

Ancian always said they'd come back, thinks Bridger. *But this isn't how I imagined it.*

What do you think a Redtooth would say if a Moondweller walked onto their range? wonders Crunch.

Let's hope they're smart enough not to find out, thinks Submission. *If not, we've seen the last of 'em.*

+ + +

With their meal done, the adults chew their thoughts for a time. Recognizing at last the sorry lot of those who still wait their turn, they step away from the scraps and gather on the hill outside the caves' rear entrance. Sitting back to back, Lightning and Joy lick and gnaw at their sole share of the feast: shreds of skin to which cling precious bits of stringy meat and a thin veneer of grease. As the adults discuss what was learned by the scouts on the other side of the wedge, Joy surprises Lightning with a question, so tightly focused and subtle she knows it is intended to be secret.

Promise don't be mad?

That depends. Mad about what?

I might have lied.

OK. About what?

Promise?

Lightning gnaws the awl skin, extracting every last calorie before spitting it into the snow.

I promise not to get mad, but that doesn't mean I'll be happy. The longer you stretch it out, the worse it gets.

Joy buzzes, quiet and low, conscious of the jabis bragging to Thunder and Cliff not far away.

That thing I found, she thinks.

Yes?

It does do something.

Like what? Please give me some good news.

It helps my thinking, is Joy's simple response. *It makes things clear.*

Clear. What do you mean? No. Hold on.

And she leads Joy away from the caves, where they can be free from prying minds. Here, Joy explains her experience with the artifact, how, since its awakening, it has enhanced her ability to sense, increasing her range and comprehension. She also adds the belief that it improves her ability to help dissimilar thinkers understand one another.

Well, that sounds useful, at least, thinks Lightning. *Better than it could have been.*

There might be more.

Like?

Joy pauses and considers. The wind, sailing unchecked through the ruined accrete, pipes a conflicted tune as she thinks, and the low-riding sun burns dimly in her eyes. How to express what has been happening in the last few sleeps? How to make it sensible?

It's about my dreams, she thinks.

What about them?

Joy finishes the last of her awl and casts the inedible skin into the snow.

It talks to me, is all she can think. *It...has a name.* She wonders if this sounds preposterous, but Lightning's ears perk up, and she turns to face her.

Petros, she thinks.

Joy whistles keen surprise, hunching her shoulders when Bliss and Blue pass by.

You dreamed it too! she thinks when it's safe.

Yes. The last sleep before we got to the accrete. I had no idea what it was. But someone kept saying: "I...' What was the word? "I...illuminate." Yes, that's it. "Illuminate the Way. My name is Petros."

Yes!

What in holy pockets does that mean?

I do not know.

How do you know the dream came from that thing?

I know.

How?

I...I just do, thinks Joy. *And it kept repeating...*

Yes?

This part's really important.

OK.

Joy's antenna dip low, and her thought is so subdued that Lightning can barely sense it.

It must remain secret.

Hmm... So why are you telling me?

Joy answers the question with one of her own.

What does "allies" mean?

Allies? Um...well, an ally is like a friend, I guess. A helper, someone you can trust to watch your tail.

Ah, that makes sense. Joy's eyes brighten. *Because it needs allies,* she thinks. *And it trusts you.*

Well, that makes me feel better, I guess.

The others will ask, thinks Joy. *They mustn't be told.* The tone of her thought is intense in a way Lightning hasn't sensed before.

OK, she thinks. *And I'm not mad. But if this thing... Just tell me what you sense, yes? If I'm only dreaming part of the story, I want to know the rest.*

You will.

+ + +

After the watch is set, the clan tries to rest their worried heads. Lightning and Joy make the rock shelf their bed, no grass or fur to soften their repose.

You can sleep inside, you know, thinks Submission. *Don't believe that nonsense about a curse—and don't worry about the others. They're still mad, but they're past doing anything stupid.*

But Lightning declines.

Thank you, Api-kan, but no, it's not that. We're just...we'd like to be outside is all.

And Submission lets it go at that. But in spite of his claim, he is reluctant to leave them alone, so he curls up below, blocking the path from the caves to the shelf and asleep almost the moment he lies down.

Will they ever forgive? wonders Joy as she preens Lightning's spikes. *You did rescue them.*

Let's hope I don't live to regret that decision.

You don't mean that.

No.

Lightning rises and stretches. Her injuries have begun to heal, but recent exertion has taken a toll; she is as tired as she can remember being.

And that's saying a lot, she thinks. She curls up in a ball, her tail wrapped around Joy, who in turn hugs the artifact and stares at the sun. *Get some sleep while you can. Who knows what the waking time will bring?*

\+ + +

But Joy doesn't sleep at first, though Lightning's regular breathing turns quickly to snores. She sits taking in the jabi kezel's scent and caressing the artifact, trying to drive away hungry thoughts of awl and lova by contemplating the device's origin. She has asked it this question before, but she tries again.

So, what are you?

She doesn't expect a response, so when one appears in her mind, she can barely restrain a surprised whistle. There is no mistaking the thought's origin.

I am Book Thirteen Eighty-Two, the artifact thinks.

Joy sits up; her antennae straighten.

Not just a dream, she thinks. Nothing about the artifact has changed. It swallows light and refuses to reflect her image as it always has, its surface implacable yet pleasing to the touch. She wonders if it does indeed have a name, as she dreamed. But only when she turns this curiosity into an actual question does she receive an answer, clear as a trilling rixli.

My last Readers called me Petros, it thinks.

Well! thinks Joy. *Nice to meet you.*

She waits for it to offer something further, but the device falls mute. She raps it lightly with her knuckles.

Hey, don't stop now, she begs. *So, what are you?*

I am an Illuminator. I illuminate.

You what?

I light the Way.

The way to what?

Read and you will learn.

Read? What is that?

You're doing it right now. You're a Reader.

Oh, thinks Joy, startled once again, but in a different way. It is as if someone has rolled a stone away from the entrance to a musty cave and revealed a small, glimmering treasure. *That's what I am?*

Among other things.

What does it mean?

That you have an important job.

Which is?

To Read me. To share what you learn. And, as I have been hinting in your dreams, to keep me secret from all but another Reader—or trusted allies.

Other readers? Joy's grip on the artifact tightens. *There are other...me's?*

Several, once upon a time. But now only one. And that may have changed.

Where?

At the moment, unknown.

Joy considers this. A Reader. It certainly doesn't sound very important. In fact, she remains unclear on what the word means. For all she knows, it's another way of saying dung collector or servant to fools. Still, it's the first time anyone has provided her with a concrete term, an identity and purpose, whatever it might be.

I told my ami-kan, she thinks. *Like the dream said.* The artifact greets this with no response until her patience grows thin. *Did you sense me?* she thinks.

Yes.

It's OK she knows?

Only time will tell.

Is she a Reader?

No.

But we share dreams, thinks Joy. *Why?*

Because your minds are connected. Hers is open and compassionate, and yours is strong.

Oh. Joy had known some of this already; it was evident in every step Lightning took, every plan she made and thought she shared—and it was a sentiment reciprocated beyond measure. But the last idea? She had never thought of her mind as particularly strong. What would make the artifact think such a thing? For that matter, what would make it think anything at all? What in the world is it?

I am an Illuminator, it repeats when she asks the question again. *I light the Way.*

Yes, you said that, she clicks tersely, but then she pauses to reflect. What would a strong-minded person ask next? *Where are you from?* is what she decides.

Olon Prime, originally, the Castellar system in the Kebadov arm of spiral galaxy Ess Jee Too.

What...where is that?

Very far from here.

Farther than the Moondwellers? Thinking to show how much she has learned about the world, she adds, *Where's your flying vessel?*

Much farther. And I have no vessel.

How'd you get here?

I was left by my creators, long ago.

Why?

To engage and cultivate Readers. It is my sole reason for existence. I am, after all, a Book.

That's a funny name.

The artifact neither agrees nor disagrees.

Where are your creators?

I do not know. Very far from here, I suspect.

Will they come back?

Unlikely.

Are there more of you?

Many.

Close? Here? On Aranae?

No. Very far away.

Joy rubs fingers along her antennae, trying to smooth the edge from her mood. All these questions and partial answers are both tiring and addictive. She feels the artifact is doling out just enough information to motivate yet another question, and she has so many.

She takes a deep breath and continues the asking.

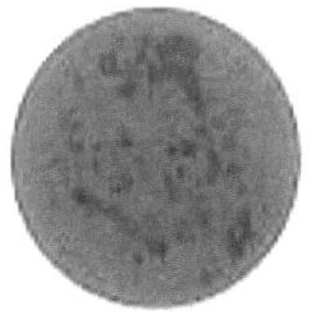

Chapter Four
Promise

LIGHTNING WAKES REFRESHED, body and spirit, surprised at how much better she feels, in spite of having slept in the open sun. Some hurdle has been cleared during her sleep, she is sure, some threshold crossed, but what it might be, and to what end, she can't say.

A new start, she thinks. *That's what it feels like. Beginning again, with new eyes.*

She rises carefully, peeling herself from around Joy, who—quite out of character—remains sound asleep, the artifact hugged close and her eyes dim. Seeing the object calls to mind dreams which do not remain in detail and whose impressions are no more unusual than they have ever been in Joy's presence. To the contrary, whatever the dreams may have been, they have the lingering quality of a good meal, like a feast for her brain, though she can't recall what she ate.

She stretches, testing her injuries and reading the wind as she looks down from the rock shelf. Submission is gone from his post. In his place are Thunder, Cliff, and the jabi Edge. Though they do not intend to share their thoughts with her, she senses them clearly.

Bruiser was pretty sure about it, thinks Thunder. *He's going to the Skull.*

Not by himself, I bet, thinks Cliff.

Not with me, thinks Edge. *I'm done traveling.*

I guess you'll go if he says go, thinks Thunder, to which his companions have no reply.

I miss Shadow and Drift, thinks Edge after a time, referring to the jabis lost in the scion encounter.

Cliff nods, though Lightning guesses he is simply being agreeable. His experience with his peers has been largely unpleasant, and she doubts he misses any of them. Thunder's response is absent at best. and for a fleeting moment, Lightning senses he is not thinking of jabis at all, but the ibiwa Hail, in thoughts that are fleeting and sheltered. She turns away from the discussion, her gaze falling again on the object Joy holds in a tight embrace. Its power is apparent to her; without it nearby, she would have been unable to sense the conversation taking place below—or secret thoughts.

So. You do something after all, she thinks. *Just like Joy said. What are you? Where do you come from?*

The artifact offers nothing in reply, but she feels no worry about its nature or motivation—if it has one. Her early feelings about it, rooted in disastrous encounters with the foreign and unnatural, have changed, though she isn't sure why that should be. There is nothing in its form or lack of smell to endear it to a kezel, but there it is, nonetheless. For reasons that are beyond her, she trusts the object and is glad for it.

Remembering Joy's insistence on secrecy, she adjusts her sling, hiding the object from view. But a moment after she has done so, Joy—still sound asleep—pulls the sling away, exposing the artifact to the sun and buzzing softly. Her eyes remain dim, her breathing deep.

Fine, thinks Lightning. *Have it your way,* And she climbs down from the shelf, navigating the stony path to where her oti-mu and his companions remain in discussion. Thunder is the first to notice her.

It's about time, he thinks. *I thought you were going to sleep forever.*

Nobody's business if I did, Lightning replies, but she offers the thought in kind tone.

You're in a better mood, thinks Cliff. *What's up?*

Food, I hope. What's news on the hunt?

Submission's sending us out as soon as he gets back, thinks Edge. *We get to keep what we catch, so the news is good.* His tone suggests folks are well aware of his hunting prowess. Lightning is not, and she hasn't forgotten his role in her exile, moons ago. Despite this, she sees no reason to cast shadows on the endeavor.

Want to come along? thinks Cliff. *We could use another nose.* But Thunder growls.

Our noses are fine, thanks. Anyway, he turns to Lightning, *Bruiser wants to talk to you when he gets back. He's got other plans for you.*

Like?

Like ask him yourself. Thunder nods in the direction of the caves, where Submission and Bridger come walking out into the sun, deep in thoughts so well sheltered Lightning can sense only their tone, anxious and stern. When they part company, Submission continues on toward them, offering no greeting as the jabis relax their ears and drop their tails, keeping their gazes averted until addressed.

Are you ready? he asks the ah-tahs.

As sharp as they're going to be without a proper stone, thinks Thunder, flexing his claws. Edge bares his fangs as his answer, and Cliff minds his posture, coaxing his defective leg to an angle befitting readiness.

Hm. Good enough, thinks Submission. *Keep it simple and keep it close. Within howling distance!*

West? thinks Thunder. *North?*

Neither, is Submission's firm reply. *South or east, but stay off Bristle turf. We need them in a good mood.*

If we bring back something to share, wonders Edge, *can we sit at the head of the feast?*

There won't be a feast. Haven't you heard? There's a feud to be won! Stop puffing up your spikes and go.

And so the three hunters depart, arguing almost at once about the plan. When they are out of thought range, Submission turns to address Lightning. She is careful to remain deferential. A storm is brewing inside her api-kan; she dreads its arrival, though she knows she is neither its cause nor its target.

Won't matter if I get caught in its path, she thinks.

What's that?

Nothing. I'm sorry. I was...nothing.

Good. Then get your...your...Joy, and get ready. We're going hunting.

The three of us?

I hope it meets with your approval.

Of course! But...

Don't worry. I saved some awl. Enough so that neither of you will have an excuse for a bad hunt. I expect to bring back something to share.

Yes sir.

While we're out, I'll tell you the plan.

The plan?

Strategy! The feud! Or are you not interested?

No sir. I mean yes sir.

And she turns quickly and climbs to the rock shelf where Joy sits, recently wakened and staring at the sun. She buzzes quietly and gets to her feet when she hears the jabi kezel approach.

We are going hunting, she thinks.

We are.

Submission saved some awl.

He did.

Joy places the artifact carefully in her sling, which she drapes over her shoulder.

Let's learn the plan, she thinks.

Lightning removes then hastily reties her mask.

My thoughts exactly.

+ + +

When they climb down from the shelf, Submission is waiting for them with some filleted awl and Lightning's cutter and thrower riding in their belt around his thigh. Most of the awl he stashes in Lightning's pack for a later, unspecified use, but he allows a small portion for each of them. They devour their breakfast with many thanks to which he does not respond. Turning without a thought, he strides to the south, clearly expecting they will follow.

They do.

Their path follows the meandering Sweet, first to the west, passing by the High Step, then south. Submission seems content to weave his way through the ruined accrete while he organizes his thoughts, none of which he shares. This is fine with Lightning, who has, since her api-kan's awakening on the plains, been satisfied with nothing more than to be in his presence—whether angry or buoyant, troubled or at peace. That what she had so longed for in her younger moons should now happen in a time of such duress does complicate the experience, but it doesn't change the essence. She trails after her him, comparing their prints in the snow and glad for his scent on the southern wind. Joy follows close and silent, toying with her hair.

The caves have fallen out of sight behind them and the first undamaged accrete rise into view when Submission finally opens his mind.

Assuming I ever get a new mask, he thinks, *how am I supposed to proof it against rixli if bombas are off limits? It won't take long before the dirty eye biters smell kezel have returned to the caves.*

That is a question Lightning had not considered. Had her mask not been several times too small—and had all the bomba essence not been washed off long ago—she would have donated it in a heartbeat. As it is, she has nothing to offer. Her reed of essence hadn't evaded Oracio's scrutiny and had been discarded at his insistence, tossed into the nacht.

Maybe bombas could help, thinks Joy.

Help how? By jumping into my mouth with no complaints? Volunteering their skin?

Joy rubs her hands together, raspy and quick.

They know about rixli, she thinks simply. *Maybe they could help.* How, she does not specify.

Maybe, thinks Lightning. *When we see them, we can ask.* She intends this to sound hopeful, but the thought of how far away their friends are, and of the many obstacles between them, sobers them both.

One problem at a time, I guess, thinks Submission.

Let's talk plans. You heard about Stone?

No. I don't think so. What about her?

You know she was sent scouting along the wedge?

Sure. With amoti Pounce and the rest.

Did you know Pounce saw her with a Redtooth?

No.

Well, he did. He was too far away to tell what they were thinking, and Stone made a big show of chasing the Redtooth off when she realized Pounce was watching. Said she came on him by surprise and was trying to lure him into giving away Redtooth secrets. Said she threatened to tear him up when he wouldn't co-operate.

But?

But Pounce isn't so sure. It sounds likely enough, and the conversation clearly ended on the verge of a fight.

But...

No buts. That's all. Stone stumbled on a Redtooth, they exchanged words, she chased him off.

So, what part doesn't Pounce like?

The timing. The part where Stone only got aggressive when she knew she was being watched.

They walk on for a time as Lightning considers this. What does it mean?

You tell me, thinks Submission, reading her unexpressed question. *Assume the worst.*

Um. It's hard to say.

Because it hurts to imagine, but say it anyway.

Lightning scowls.

The worst is that Stone is somehow working with the Redteeth and can't be trusted.

And?

And the Redteeth know what she knows.

Which is?

How many of us there are. What condition we're in. Our commitment to help defend the Skull. And the fact that we only have one broken thrower.

Submission opens his mouth as if planning to bite an imaginary enemy, and his ears lay flat.

Nasty to think about, but it could be. No point ask-

ing; she'll deny it if it's true, be offended if it's not.

So, what do we do?

Again: assume the worst—and use your imagination. If you were the Redtooth chief, and you knew what Stone knows, what would you do?

That depends. Do I have the Sugarfoot throwers?

Assume yes.

Do I have anyone who can use them?

Again...

Lightning allows her mind to roam across the wedge, drawing on what she had learned of Redtooth life over the moons of Gami-kan's training.

But I thought they hated anything that has to do with the Moondwellers. Thought they would never use a thrower any more than wear a vest.

Are you willing to bet your life on that?

Lightning swipes her tail side to side.

No sir. And I know they'd love to have our caves. Probably only stayed away 'cuz they thought there was a curse or something. But now we're back, and they see the place is livable. I was always told there's no way the home caves could be taken if there was even one healthy defender at each entrance. Too steep from the north, and too exposed from the south—even more so, now there's no accrete. But if they have our throwers...

Then "no way," Submission concludes, *suddenly becomes possible. So, what do you do if you're them?*

If I have throwers, attack the Sugarfoot caves.

And if you don't?

Then go for the Skull. It's easier, yes?

Much. Needs twice as many to hold off an assault.

Which the Bristles don't have.

Not while they're occupied with Whitetails.

A righteous curse comes to Lighting's mind at the mention of this name.

Then if I'm going for the Sugarfoot caves, she thinks, *I wait 'til after the Red. There's no point in rushing and getting caught out in the storm.*

But...

But if it's the Skull I'm after, I go as soon as I have enough fighters to take the place. I have to risk the storm, because if I wait too long, Sugarfoot reinforcements will get there first and I'll have no chance.

You've got the sense of it. Submission nods. *And there's this, too: if we have a traitor in our camp, we can't let her know we know, we can't let her out of our sight, and we can't let her in on our plans. Understood?*

Yes sir. But what are our plans?

We'll know that soon enough. For now, focus on other things; it's hunting time.

They have come to a place where healthy accrete bring a return to the range's normal sights and sounds. Yits squeak and flutter their way through shafts of sunlight, cremlins hoot nonsense while leaping from one fan to the next, and the sound of virble chatter everywhere reminds Lightning of her river voyage. She hopes her api has other game in mind.

Dow, he thinks a moment later. *That's the target. Not far from where the Spine curves west there's a pool, hidden from the path. Your ami-kan and I used to...* He releases a great sigh. *Anyway, we'll need to ford the Sweet to get there. Once we do, be quiet and be ready. If Redteeth haven't ruined it—and if we're careful—we might be able to surprise a couple before they can get to the water.*

He comes to a sudden stop, turning to face Joy.

Unless you're going to tell me dow are thinkers too? Good friends of yours?

The light fades in Joy's eyes.

No. Dow don't think.

Submission curls his lip.

First good news I've had in a while. He turns and resumes his trek, more slowly now, and with deliberate, stealthy intent. Lightning and Joy follow, sharing a brief glance but daring to exchange no thoughts.

+ + +

The pool is indeed secluded, a placid sheet of blue,

striped in forking shadows. Its surface is broken on occasion by the fall of scales shaken loose by the wind, but the wind itself can't reach the sheltered water, tucked inside a circle of hills and reflecting the accrete just as clearly as the Eye Tower could have done. Lightning crawls step by silent step up the embankment, followed by Joy, crouching to stay out of sight, until they reach Submission, who motions them to approach. They peer over the edge and down onto the pool, a healthy but undaunting swim from one shore to the other.

Their hopes are grandly rewarded.

Several families of honking dow gather in loose affiliations on the shore, some sweet, the others sour, as indicated by the color of the small horn that is also their mouth. They blat softly and discordantly to one another, and Lightning tries to keep from drooling, sure that it appears unseemly for an experienced hunter.

Submission is decisive.

You're going to circle around. Drive and strike. I'll get as close to the water as I can and wait.

Lightning nods, but her mind replays a scene from her own hunting experience on the plateau, where dow could be found near the mountain skirts and in which Joy had once played a key role.

Api-kan, she thinks. *Wait, please. I have an idea.*

+ + +

The dow, gray speckled with white to match the snowy stones on which they perform, honk and toot to a rhythm only they can sense—or perhaps no rhythm at all. Their flippers slap the ground in an idle fashion, and dopey eyes peer across the lake with no particular focus. When one of them spies something approaching in the water, it slaps its flippers together, loud and peremptory, and the others cease their honking to look.

Whatever it is swims underwater, but not in the style of a dow—nor the same size. This puzzles the creatures, who have plumbed the depths of this lake for many cycles and seen nothing like it.

"Honk?" asks one.

"Toot?" wonders another.

They waddle from their perches—just to be safe—and consider what the swimmer could be. It has peculiar methods and a form that is difficult to make out even when it reaches the shallows and rises from the water, standing it seems on two legs. Its sudden transformation to sky blue startles them badly, and when it begins shouting and waving its appendages, the dow waddle away from the shore, honking alarm—and are taken unawares by the two downwind kezel who have been stalking them from behind. Most are able to slip and slide down the bank and around the blue swimmer, escaping to the safety of the water, where no creatures, not even awl, can match their facility. But fully six of their fellows will live to honk no more, and all agree: another perfectly good respite has been ruined by kezel.

"Someday," they toot mournfully, "someday..."

\+ + +

Lightning has never caught more than one dow at a time; two of the sleek, delicious creatures now lie dead before her, and she must work to keep her pride in check. Submission, after all, had snatched twice as many from the rocks, and quite unlike her mad rush, which had caused her to miss as many as she caught, he had been cool and efficient, careful to target two sweet and two sour, coming a flipper-length from a fifth. She licks blood from her muzzle as her api-kan drinks from the pool.

Well done, he thinks, and in spite of herself, Lightning's ears perk up, and her spikes flare.

Submission turns to where Joy sits on a stone once warmed by dow.

Never caught four at a time before, he thinks. *When we get back, I'll be sure you get due credit.*

Lightning taught me how, thinks Joy. *She can have credit.* But she preens her antennae and buzzes.

Using her cutter (*I should probably stop calling it mine,* thinks Lightning), Submission parcels out generous portions of fatty dow. Joy declines, but Lightning recalls few meals more delicious. Savoring a mix of both the sweet and the sour, Submission looks at Joy as if seeing her for the first time. He swallows his food and licks grease from his fingers.

So, he thinks. *Joy, is it?*

Yes, think Lightning and Joy at the same time, not sure who is being addressed.

Why that name? Hasn't been much of it lately.

Lightning wrinkles her snout. There is only one good answer to the question: the truth, which, in spite of everything, is still easy to see.

It's how I felt when I learned she could think kezel. It's how I still feel.

Joy's eyes glitter.

And do you—Joy—do you understand how much trouble Lightning may have caused by saving you?

She was being kind, thinks Joy. *How is that bad?* She clicks an edgy rhythm. *Scion caused the trouble.*

Lightning squints her eyes and drops her tail, squirming as she waits to see what reaction Joy's response, or tone, might cause. But Submission merely shifts from licking grease to scratching his ear.

You're sure you don't want any?

No, but thank you, thinks Joy. *Awl for me, please.*

Submission nods, and Joy takes a small portion of awl from Lightning's pack.

The rest is coming with us onto the plains, thinks Submission. *Going to need something to keep the peace with your princess...queen...whatever.*

We're going to the plains? thinks Lightning.

I need to have a little chat about certain promises we've made. And I need your help. Both of you. But first, help me string up these dow. You're going to have to carry what you killed—and while we're walking, you, he looks at Joy, *are going to tell me what's in that sling of yours.*

Joy clicks a steady rhythm. "*Secret,*" the Book had

emphasized. But it had also been clear about the need for allies. She slips her hand inside the sling.

What do you think? she asks.

I think, the artifact replies, *that attaining our goals requires taking some risks.*

+ + +

Submission attends carefully as Joy shares what she has discovered about the artifact, his dow slung across his back, tied together using the talihew strips stored in Lightning's vest. They walk due east, crossing the Spine in no great hurry, as Submission seems intent on learning all he can before they reach the plains. Joy, as it turns out, spent most of the last sleep not sleeping at all, but engaged in a most unlikely conversation with the device. *"The Book,"* she calls it, though the word means nothing to Lightning, *"Reading"* the term she uses to describe what she had been doing, as if this book were the wind, and she gathering its news.

What do you mean "reading?" asks Submission.

I asked it questions, is all Joy can offer. *And it answered. Mostly.*

In your mind.

Yes.

It thinks to you?

Yes. It just started.

Submission leads them over an icy tangle of fallen accrete, shaking his head all the while.

I'm going to skip over the part where I ask how that's possible and go right to what it told you.

Joy takes a deep breath. The Book had told her many things, and she is unsure where to start.

At the beginning, thinks Lightning.

And so, Joy reconstructs her experience with the artifact, starting with its discovery on the plains and the sense that it had somehow wakened in her presence. She shares how, after a time, she had become aware of an assistive property to the device. Thinkers of all types became more sensible in its presence, sheltered thoughts were exposed, and her range of both sensing and transmitting increased twofold.

It seems to do the same thing with me, thinks Lightning, *but it may only be working through Joy.*

Working through her to do what? Submission asks.

To illuminate the Way, thinks Joy. *That part was clear.* She buzzes to herself, considering all the things the Book had shared which had not been clear at all.

The Way? thinks Submission. *Meaning what?*

There is a path, thinks Joy. *The Book illuminates it.* Then, hoping she will like the answer, she asks, *What does illuminate mean?*

Lightning has nothing to offer, but Submission's answer is quick and certain.

To shine light on something. Ancian was always going on about "illuminate" this and "illuminate" that. He grumbles at the memory. *She also made sure everyone in the clan heard all they wanted about the Way. You suppose they're the same?*

I don't know. Maybe.

What do *you know?*

Well... Joy takes the Book from her sling, wiping away the awl grease smeared across its face. As always, it is impervious to stains, and though smooth like ice, when cleaned, it reflects no light.

It likes being touched, she thinks. *And being in sun.* She clicks her way through the other biographical information the Book had offered, though much of it makes little sense to her.

It had come from very far away.

It had for a long time been in the possession of the Moondwellers, one named Grace, primarily, but others as well, though the number of Moondwellers able to read it had never been large. It believes a descendent of one of these might still be alive.

Alive! Submission is incredulous. *You mean one of those two-leggers you told me about from the lower land?*

No, thinks Joy. *They are not Readers.*

So, there's another one out there somewhere?

That's what it believes.

Joy tries to relay the story of the Book's coming to her, though the details are uncertain. It had been hidden somehow, cloaked to be kept secret, and so the events leading up to its discovery on the plains are unknown to it as well. It had been living its existence in the company of the last surviving Moondwellers, one of whom was a Reader, when—this part is especially confusing—there was a conflict of some type, related to possession of the artifact and its use. During this conflict it was separated from its Reader and left in the Thing on the plains.

I don't like the sound of that, thinks Submission, and Lightning is quick to agree.

What was the conflict? she asks. *Why were Moondwellers fighting over it? What is it?*

A Tool of Power, thinks Joy simply. It was the answer she had been given when she had asked the same question. *Moondwellers died for it.* But that wasn't the worst. *Some kezel died too,* she adds.

More grumbling is Submission's reply.

I can see why you kept it secret if that's the effect it has on folks. Aside from helping you think, what good does it do? A tool of power to do what?

Um...Illuminate the Way, thinks Joy, rather helplessly. *It kept repeating that.*

Can't be that powerful, thinks Lightning. *It was stuck in that snowbank and would've stayed there.*

Joy buzzes her agreement.

Because it had been... She searches for the word. *Depleted. After the fight.* She caresses the object, holding it to her chest. *No Reader, no power,* she thinks. *Sensed me and woke,* she adds, though she has no explanation of how. *Oh! One more thing...*

Yes? think Submission and Lightning as one.

It knew my parents.

+ + + + + +

Shimmer wakes from her sleep certain she could have stayed there until the arrival of the Red. Her antennae liven reluctantly, and when she stretches her wings, testing their strength should flight be required, the word that comes to her mind is *spent.*

Why has it wakened her? she asks of the pluripotent standing in the darkness of the hole.

The soldiers have returned, it thinks. *They have brought news of the sharksha. Two of the beasts along with the mutant Oddity are approaching.*

Shimmer pushes her way past and exits the hole, buzzing a harsh response. The sunlight raises her temperature and lights her eyes, but each of her stomachs is empty, and the sight of the two soldiers returning without anything to eat puts her in a foul mood. How she expects they were to have been spies as well as awlers, she doesn't bother to consider.

Fools, she thinks. *Good news or bad?*

The soldiers chitter rapidly to one another. The largest of two—though neither is as large as a proper soldier should be—settles on an answer to the question.

Queen must decide. We cannot.

No, thinks its companion. *Not able.*

Might be either.

Yes. Might be both.

Might be neither.

Yes.

Might be some third thing. They do not know.

No. Cannot say.

Shimmer's whistle is short and sharp.

They will desist with this manner! They will think like soldiers, not simple drones!

But the creatures are still learning, their brains still transforming, and they have reached the limit of their abilities. Instead of altering their style of thinking, they simply shelter their thoughts, afraid of angering their new queen further. This is the wrong choice. Shimmer waits several moments then erupts.

Idiots! Is she to stand here starving while they de-

cide whether or not to deliver their message? Divulge!

Yes, Queen! thinks the larger soldier.

Yes! thinks its companion.

Sharksha are coming. The giant promise-maker and its spawn, the masked one.

Yes. And the Oddity.

Yes. They bring a Tool of Power.

Yes. And awl.

What type of tool? Shimmer demands, disregarding the mention of food. *To what do they refer?*

Here, the soldiers share what they sensed of the conversation between the three travelers, a conversation made sensible by the very device they describe.

Shimmer clicks a rapid tempo.

This object she has seen. What did the Oddity mean by "illuminate the way?" The way to Ozag?

They do not know.

No. They only repeat what they sensed.

Yes. Repeat.

And their plan in coming here? Are their motivations malignant or benign?

They believe the latter, Queen.

Yes. But they cannot be sure.

No. Sharksha are difficult to predict.

Shimmer summons her pluripotents. Once settled in her basket, she orders the soldiers and those drones yet to be transformed to array themselves in an orderly fashion appropriate for a Queen.

Be prepared, she thinks to them all. *If they sense deception, they must not hesitate. Subdue the large one first. Leave the Oddity to her!*

But when Submission leads Lightning and Joy out of the shadowing accrete, striding purposefully and often glancing at the sky, Shimmer can tell there is no threat.

But there are secrets, she thinks.

+ + + + + +

Despite the scion's radically diminished numbers,

Lightning's heart is uneasy at the sight of them. They are arrayed before their queen in neat formation, six flyers, five bronze, one silver, and four dozen others, all blue. They remind her of trouble too recent and desperate for her tastes, and though she doesn't object when Submission steps to within touching distance of the first rank, she surely wants to.

Joy bows, her antenna touching the snow.

This is Submission Sugarfoot, she thinks to Shimmer. *He is Lightning's api-kan.*

She knows what it is! The one who owes a debt of life. Why has it come? Is it ready to seek Far Colossus? Are they prepared to travel?

A question first, thinks Submission, and he holds the thrower for her to see. *You ever come across anything like this before? Or larger, longer ones?*

Of what value is this question?

Plenty. So?

It is no secret, Shimmer clicks impatiently. *New Magister and his soldiers presented many such to Queen after the raid on the sharksha homeland.*

At this, Submission's ears angle forward, and his tail comes to life, swishing side to side.

How many?

She did not count! Why would she? She was still Princess and cared not for such. Vumierre mischief, clearly! But there were no fewer than twelve.

Submission relaxes, nodding.

And where are they now?

She is flattered that the beast believes her omniscient, but how would she have this information? They were likely taken to Queen's personal hoard to impress her subjects and bring her further glory. But where they are now, who can say?

Not in Redtooth hands, that's what matters, thinks Submission, directing the thought to Lightning. *OK,* he thinks to Shimmer. *Where is this Far Colossus?*

Is it daft? She has never been there! But all scion know it is east of north from Albion and is the loftiest of all peaks, the source of the water gathered at Ozag's Hold, the water that becomes the Dashing, then the Royal.

Fine, thinks Submission brusquely. *What do you plan to do when you get there?*

Shimmer's pluripotents buzz to one another, displeased, Lightning guesses, with her api-kan's bold manner. He thinks to the queen as if to a delinquent wabi, his tone that of someone who expects nonsense in reply and is prepared to scold it.

She will seek audience with Ozag, of course, thinks Shimmer. *Then kill her, if her answers do not satisfy.*

Well. That is *a fabulous strategy. Tell me: why do you need our help? It seems like you have everything planned. You're obviously ready to go.*

She needs nothing! But the sharksha shall be guides through the hideous land of shadows. And the Oddity... She gestures with her forelimb as if Joy's value is self-evident, and her eyes glitter even as her thoughts seek shelter. Lightning strains to catch what she is hiding, but there are too many scion in proximity, each harboring or exchanging thoughts of their own.

I've been told she has a name, thinks Submission, and he swings the dow from his back, dropping them to the snow beside him. He motions for Lightning to step closer, and he reaches inside her pack. *This is for you,* he thinks, holding forth the strips of awl. *You look like you could use a good meal.*

The queen's eyes light like splintered crystals, and her attendants, none of whom have been fed well since their exile, chitter at the sight and smell. The one closest Submission takes the awl and delivers it to the basket. The silver pluripotent intervenes, taking the awl and smelling it, its suspicion apparent as it runs its proboscis over the rubbery surface and nibbles a small corner. When it suffers no ill effects, it bows and presents the awl to Shimmer. She shows tremendous restraint, setting the offering aside and clicking an impatient cadence.

For what reason does it make this gesture?

Because if you want us to keep our promise, we're

going to need something from you.

Scurrilous! It has already been given its life—and that of its worthless progeny. They will get no more!

Eat up, Queen. As things are going, the only way we're getting to your Far Colossus is through a bunch of awful... He turns to Lightning. *What did she call us?*

Sharksha.

Yeah. A whole bunch of sharksha who have aims on our territory and aren't interested in any promises we've made. If you don't help us put them back in their place, you'll need to make different plans.

Lie! An obvious attempt to lure them into a trap!

Joy buzzes.

You know it's not.

Shimmer's gold darkens as if lit by orange fire, and her antennae bend toward Joy, quivering in pent rage. Her whistle starts low but builds to a shriek.

Malefactor! Disgusting and twisted! It knows nothing of her mind. But she knows much of its. Does it deny it carries with it a Tool of Power? A thing over which blood has been spilled? It claimed the artifact an aid to its thinking, but it desires to hide the whole truth. It is much more than that, is it not? A part of the sharkshas' plan to destroy all scion? A tool used by vumierre?

Oh, please, thinks Lightning, risking Submission's ire. *Yes. My whole clan got itself captured and tortured—and some got killed—as part of an elaborate plot to destroy you. My api-kan is right.* You should *eat something; you're obviously delusional from hunger.*

Submission's growl stills her thoughts.

There's more awl where that came from, he thinks to Shimmer. *None of those little fingerlings you got down south. These are big and fat. But only if you help us.*

Lightning feels sure Shimmer will erupt and either banish them or order her attendants to attack. She does neither. Instead, buzzing quietly, she settles back into her basket and preens her antennae as if they had been discussing the weather, a minor diversion soon forgotten. She waves at Submission in a casual fashion with the air of someone bestowing an easy favor.

Very well, she thinks. *She will hear the beast's plan for the scion role in addressing these interloping sharksha. She will judge its merits, though she doubts she will find any.*

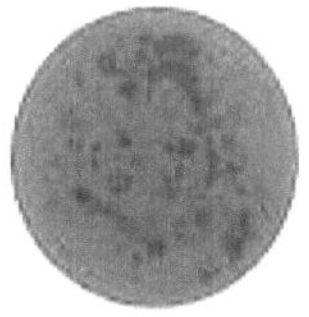

Chapter Five
Captain

CAPTAIN, LIEUTENANT, ENSIGN: these three so-called Moondwellers travel due west upon leaving Joy and the rescued kezel, mindful of Princess Shimmer's warning about the pending earthquake. When it strikes, they are still thousands of strides south of the landfall (or meters, in the parlance of their kind), and thus the tremors, though disconcerting, are no more than expected, and the gaseous eruptions are carried harmlessly away on the northbound wind.

"Wig samma gidda spackle kife," says the captain as they carefully navigate the trembling land. Or that is what his words would have sounded like to Joy, had she been there. But to his companions they sound like "I guess that bug wasn't kidding."

Lieutenant K agrees.

"Not as bad as some on Earth, but worse than any quake on Mars." And in the distance, as if to illustrate his point, they hear, far to the north, what sounds like part of the world falling to its ruin. "What do you think," he asks Ensign Morales. "Five point five?"

"My readings say closer to six," she replies. "But magnitude and duration are two different things, and this one could just be starting."

Happily for them, as they continue across the pale, parched terrain, the tremors that drive Cliff and his band away from the landfall in lurching, harried strides, dwindle and abate not long after. But the smell of noxious gas lingers, and occasional shudders speak of a land falling by fitful stages back into an uneasy slumber.

"Look," says the captain. "I don't think I've formally apologized for hustling out of Sleeo's lab without anything for the two of you to wear."

"I like it." The lieutenant smiles. "Nothing to hide."

The ensign is more demure.

"I know it wasn't on purpose, sir. But yes, I would have preferred something with pockets."

"Sure," says the captain. "It's just, you know, Sleeo was giving you both a final tune-up, then bam!" He smacks his fist into his palm. "Unwelcome visitors."

The lieutenant commiserates.

"You did good just getting us out of there, Cap'n. No one's judging the call. I'd rather be naked than captured by whoever's trailing us."

"With all due respect, Lieutenant," says the ensign, "I think we know who's trailing us. And I think we know why. That level of training? Those resources? This has all the markings of the Galactic Guild."

But the lieutenant frowns.

"Let's not jump to conclusions, capisce?"

"Sir, who else could afford to be so flagrant? True, they weren't wearing Guild uniforms, but they raided the lab in the middle of the day! Totally unafraid of being questioned. Am I the only one who thinks that?"

"No," says the captain. "You're not. They might be farming out the dirty work to some shell organization, but you're right. It was the Guild. We gave them ten years of service, and Sleeo darn near gave his life. In return, they raided our files and learned about our plan."

"Aye Cap'n," says the lieutenant. "I'm not going to argue with you. But it hurts, you know? I don't like to think of the Guild as corrupt. After all the good they've done? The old System wiped away, the respect for synthetics and telepaths. And then there's all the good *we* did for *them*! It hurts..."

"I hear you, Nikki. But they're only human—or human-made. Imperfection is part of the DNA. And what we're searching for—why they're trailing us—is important enough to jump-start a little corruption."

"But why, Cap'n? Why do they care?"

"You want to tell him, Carmela?"

The ensign purses her lips.

"The way I see it, sir, is that we pose a threat to their version of history. The Guild rose to power because of their success with humanity's first interstellar colonies. But if we come back with proof that the *Destiny* expedition beat them to it by a long way, it's going to make a lot of politicians look bad."

"You called it," says the captain. "And no one hates looking bad more than a politician. They'll do pretty much anything to stay in power—including derailing our mission and raiding Sleeo's lab."

The ensign's sigh is eminently human.

"I calculate less than nineteen percent chance of him escaping," she says.

"That's enough," the captain exclaims. "For that sly old bird, nineteen percent is enough."

"Yes sir, I hope you're right. But if not, if they captured him and questioned him—"

"Cap'n knows all that," the lieutenant interrupts. "If they got to him and picked his brain, they know what we know. What difference does it make? They're on our tail, capisce? Let's move!"

And that inspires them to pick up their pace, marching as quickly as the captain is able. They cover another five kilometers without speaking, conserving their energy, though it seems only the captain is strained by the effort, for his companions never break a sweat, and they don't drink any of the water.

"Sir," the ensign says at last. "I have a suggestion."

"Morales, if you're thinking what I'm thinking, well...think again!"

"Sir, I know it's not your nature, but don't the circumstances justify swallowing our pride?"

"My pride, you mean. And no, they don't."

"She's not wrong, Cap'n," says Lieutenant K. "We got a lot of ground to cover, and we'll save time."

"By toting me around like a big baby?"

"By doing our jobs, sir."

The captain balls his fists but then relaxes.

"Aw, pork pie," he says. "Fine. But not a word of this to anyone when we get back, understood?"

"Of course not, sir."

"Not a word!"

+ + +

Lieutenant K unshoulders his pack and removes an emergency blanket. He and the ensign each grasp two of its four corners, stretching it between them, the ensign in front and the lieutenant behind. This allows the captain to recline as if napping on a backyard hammock. His companions lift him easily, and though they are burdened also with their packs, the pair set off at a brisk jog, unconcerned by the implacable terrain or the weight they bear. Had it not seemed impossible, an outside observer would have said neither of them draws a single breath. Stride after jogging stride they make their way, stoic and silent like Olympic marathoners.

Five kilometers stretches into ten.

Two hours later, ten has reached twenty.

"Wish our bug friend had stuck around," says the lieutenant suddenly, and he and the ensign come to a stop, lowering the blanket to the ground. "Got a feeling we could use more of its advice. Like what do we do about that?" He points to the sky, where an emerald-winged something has appeared, its spiraling intentional.

"It doesn't look like anything we want to meet in person, sir," says Ensign Morales.

"It's not," the captain assures. "I've seen more of them than I care to. They don't mess with the bugs, but pretty much everything else is on the menu."

Lieutenant K motions to the ensign, and she turns, allowing him access to the pack strapped over her naked shoulders. From inside, he takes a pair of black spheres, each able to fit in the palm of one hand.

"I recommend those dunes, sir." The ensign points

west. "It's the best cover we're going to find."

"Well, wherever we go," says the captain as he rolls up the blanket, "we better double-time it. Our new buddy is getting closer."

They hurry to the dunes, but the cover they provide is less than hoped for, and the captain stands out in his black suit like a berry waiting to be plucked.

"Ready first grenade," says the lieutenant, and he grasps one of the spheres in both hands, twisting its halves in opposite directions until the device responds with an audible click. A tiny, green light blinks placidly at its center. He holds the sphere over his head, aiming it at the creature, who is growing closer with each spiral. Its talons gleam, and its large, angular head fuels the captain's worried imagination, filling his mind with images of sharp, serrated teeth.

The blinking green light grows steady.

"Target acquired," says the lieutenant.

"Now, please," says the captain. "And ready that second grenade." With a word from the lieutenant, the sphere rises from his hand, whirring softly and gaining speed as it moves on an intercept course toward the descending beast—a derka, had they known its common name. Just as the lieutenant has activated and targeted the second grenade, its partner, already a hundred meters in the air, explodes with a concussive force and a brief but blinding flash. A cloud of smoke blocks their view for a moment then is dashed away by the derka plunging downward. Its scales are singed, and it lets out a croaking wail that raises the hairs on the captain's neck—but it continues toward them like a bolt.

"Decrease proximity," he orders. "Put the darn thing right in its face!"

The lieutenant holds his weapon skyward and gives a simple command. Its light gone from blinking to steady, it whirs upward and away from his grasp. This time, the derka sees its nemesis, but its attempt to avoid the weapon is its undoing. As it swerves, it exposes its underside, and the grenade, set to explode upon impact, does just that. A terrible, meaty explosion is followed by a truncated cry and the sound of dead weight hurtling through the air. The derka crashes into a nearby dune, scattering a sheet of ground-dwelling yits who peel from the land, their calls querulous and piercing.

"Nice shooting, Nikki," says the captain, peering at the emerald wreckage and wrinkling his nose.

"That is a singular creature," the ensign admires.

"Singularly nasty," the lieutenant replies. "And don't get any big ideas; this isn't a scientific field trip. Orders, Cap'n?"

"March on," the captain replies. "Sorry, Carmela. Maybe another time you can play with the natives."

"I understand, sir. I just hope others like it get the message. I hate killing for no reason."

The lieutenant scans the heavens with worried eyes. For the moment the skies are clear.

"If they don't get the message," he says, "there won't be much more killing. Only a couple grenades left."

+ + +

Lieutenant K and Ensign Morales continue jogging west, bearing their passenger as gently as the terrain allows. As the kilometers pass, the cracked, dry land gradually transforms, its pale face smoothing and the scent of brackish water filling the air. The captain, with nothing to do but ride along helplessly, at last succumbs to sleep—he was fed none too well in captivity and had been bitten several times. When, another two hours later, he wakes from a dream of steak dinner and red wine, the arid flood plain of Albion has been left behind, and his companions jog over rusty turf, dense and short like a carpet of steel wool.

"How 'bout a break, people?" he asks. "I need to walk a while and stretch my legs." They come to a stop, and he rises to his feet, rolling up the blanket and nodding to them both. "You've done great, of course," he says. "I'm not going to get emotional here, but I want you both to know I'm grateful. Sleeo would be proud."

"Of you too, Cap'n," says the lieutenant. "You went through a pretty hairy ordeal back there."

"Yes, Captain," the ensign agrees. "How are you?"

"Great, all things considered. I wouldn't mind something to eat, though. Whatcha got?"

"The usual, sir: rations. And more rations."

"I know there's something clever I should be saying right now." The captain shakes his head. "But I got nothing. I guess I'll take option number two." They walk on as he unwraps and begins gnawing a small brick of something vaguely food-like. "A little disturbing that it's already brown before I've even put it in my mouth," he says, chewing morosely. "How far to go?"

"Approximately thirty more kilometers, sir," the ensign points. "Due west from here we'll come to the bay where *Valiant* went in."

The captain grimaces and swallows, running his hand over his newly shorn head.

"Poor *Valiant*! I hate to think of our sweet ride at the bottom of that mud puddle. While I'm enjoying the cuisine, what can you tell me about the power surge that knocked us out of the sky?"

Ensign Morales furrows her brow.

"Well, sir, not that I'm complaining, but you deactivated us as soon as the surge was detected, so we weren't able to collect much data."

"Yeah," says the captain. "Sorry about that. I only had a few seconds before it hit us, and I was trying to avoid having your circuits fried—and yes, Ensign, I know you don't actually have circuits, but your cellular integrity, or whatnot. I would have woken you up sooner, but my little blue hosts took my suit."

"I understand, sir. You made the correct call. From what we were able to learn in the limited time we had, the surge emanated from a mine launched from the far side of the planet, precise origin unknown."

"*Destiny*?"

"We believe so sir. She had limited weaponry, and

modified pulse mines were her primary defense. This certainly fits the profile."

"Son of a gun." The captain whistles. "Still functional then. After all these years. I figured we'd find her adrift or smashed to bits."

"If we found her at all," adds the lieutenant. "That remains to be confirmed."

"Agreed," says the captain. "So here's a question. A couple of them. It's been two hundred years—plus!—since the colonists left System space. If that *is* the ship we're looking for, and if colonists *were* here for even a part of those two centuries, why didn't we pick up any human life signs? And who in the name of Old Mother Hubbard launched that mine?"

Lieutenant K raises an eyebrow.

"Morales thinks it's either malfunctioning AI, or it was programmed by someone long dead."

"And what do you think, Lieutenant?"

"Seems likely enough," the naked man shrugs, and he holds his palms face up as if hoping for answers to fall from the clouds.

"But...?"

"But it's also possible there are survivors from the original colony, and they're living on the ship."

"Carmela?" The captain finishes his meal, turning to his blonde companion, her strides long and easy.

"I can't rule it out, sir. What I don't understand is why, if there are humans aboard *Destiny*, they tried to kill us. Or why they haven't tried again."

"Excuse me? You saw what that rocket did, yes?"

"Well, yes sir, but if that was an attempt on our lives, it was pretty clumsy. By your description, it was obviously one of *Destiny's* rechargeable rockets used for fuel hauling, fully loaded and programmed. Considering how directly it struck that gathering, I have a hard time believing we were the targets. You were close, sir, but we were kilometers away, and even an ancient GPS is more precise than that."

"OK, I guess that's comforting."

"Yes sir."

"But it doesn't answer who did the fueling, programming, and launching," says the lieutenant, whose scowling face looks anything but comforted.

"According to the reconnaissance buoy we deployed before we arrived in this system," says the ensign, "and according to the brief scan we conducted with *Valiant*, no one, sir—at least no one on the surface. I still suspect we're dealing with events that were either programmed by colonists who are no longer alive or by some dysfunctional AI, either *Destiny* itself or a different machine on the ground."

"Or both?" asks the captain.

"It is possible."

"You said, 'no one on the surface.'"

"Yes sir. If any of the colonists are still alive, they could have taken refuge underground, deep enough to avoid detection by our scans."

"Hard to blame 'em if they did," says the lieutenant, and he casts a worried gaze to the sky.

+ + +

The captain marches briskly for several kilometers, grateful for the chance to redeem his pride. But soon enough, time begins to press, and they imagine their pursuers close behind—or the appearance of hostile natives. When the captain reclaims his role as passenger, he does so without complaint, and their increased pace is a relief to them all.

Five kilometers.

Ten.

After another two hours of travel, the ground becomes not just smooth but soft, growing wet and spongy. Congregations of slender auburn shoots begin appearing, first ankle high, then reaching the travelers' knees. Eventually, their footfalls, nearly silent for so long, become slurpy and squelching, and auburn shoots transform into fully grown reeds, the crowns of which brush against their hips. At this point, the captain is forced to walk, and it is not long before they are wading through the salty shallows of a small bay whose mouth opens to the sea fifteen kilometers to their left. As the water deepens, the reeds threaten to block their view, and they come to a stop.

"How far?" asks the captain, and he looks out across the bay, striated by small, vigorous waves.

"Twenty meters at most," says the lieutenant. "Southwest. But it gets deep fast. We were five meters under, last known location."

"How long before she's beyond salvage?" the captain asks Ensign Morales.

"Well, sir, *Valiant* is an unknown quantity, Sleeo's own prototype. We have no like models to compare it to and no data regarding submersion in saltwater. It would have been longer if you hadn't been forced to blow the hatch when you ejected, but how much longer? Any answer I can give would be pure speculation."

"Then speculate, Morales. It's why you're here."

"Yes sir. Then I would say every second is critical. Extraction and repair should be our number one priority. Otherwise, I hate to say it, but we're stuck here."

"Any objections, Lieutenant?"

"No sir. The sooner we have an exit plan, the happier I'll be. This place gives me the creeps." He points to the northwest. "The landfall breaks up over there. We ought to be able to find a way up in ten kilometers or less. The colonists set up their ag facility roughly seventy-five kilometers due north of that. That's as good a place to start as any. Should be able to get some answers and hopefully the necessary gear to extract *Valiant.*"

"Another eighty plus kilos on foot?" the captain groans. "Sounds like a rough go."

"Aye, Cap'n, but rough or not, there it is. Unless you have a suggestion?"

"I'm fresh out." The captain rubs his chin. "OK. The ag facility it is. Pretty exciting, yeah, Nikki? To set foot in one of the original structures? See what they were learning, and how they lived? My whole life—"

He falls silent. His companions have turned to the north and are peering through eyes wide and alert, the ensign's soft brown, the lieutenant's bright blue.

"What is it, people?"

"Movement, Cap'n," the lieutenant points. "About a kilometer, little less."

"Confirmed," says the ensign. "Six life forms." She looks at the captain. "More of your bug friends, sir."

"Not for long," says the lieutenant. "They got wind of us. Looks like they're hightailing it. You want we should pursue, Cap'n?"

"Negative. We need to be gone when whoever it is they're going to warn gets here. C'mon! Dry land and north. We need to get up that landfall..."

+ + +

They wade out of the reeds and turn to the northwest, and the captain once again becomes a passenger. They have covered half the distance to the landfall when a derka spots them. This time, Lieutenant K suggests a flare rather than using their last grenade.

"If we can scare 'em off, we can save ordnance," he reasons as he fishes in his pack, and the others agree. The derka is directly overhead and has just begun to circle lower when the lieutenant aims the clunky pistol and fires. The weapon speaks with a throaty POP! its projectile trailing sparks and smoke straight into the air, two hundred meters, before exploding BANG! with a brilliant flash. A sparkling comet arcs across the sky, leading a train of blue-gray smoke directly across the derka's path. It veers up and away, unharmed but clearly distressed, its croaking voice audible moments later but fading as it sails out of sight.

"Good thinking," says the captain.

"Until our flares run out," the lieutenant replies. "Or they stop being scared of 'em."

"Another five kilometers to the landfall," says the ensign, and she gazes intently at the sky, turning a slow, full circle, her eyes sweeping from horizon to horizon.

"Anything, Ensign?"

"Not that I can tell, sir."

"No sign of our competition?"

"My scans are limited, but no sir."

"I take it you don't think that will last."

"They're just as interested in finding *Destiny* as we are, sir. Anything we're willing to do, they are too."

"Plus some," the lieutenant says as he returns the flare gun to his pack. "They don't have half our scruples, but they do have a thousand times our resources. Not to be a downer, but I calculate an eighty percent chance they'll be here in days—not weeks."

"Yeah?" says the captain. "Well, it's a hundred percent chance it won't matter if we don't get our ship out of that bay. Onward people!"

+ + +

When they finally arrive at the gap in the landfall, a place where it has collapsed in a huge spill of boulders and crushed stone, they can at first see no easy—or safe—way up. The captain volunteers to scout for one, but Lieutenant K won't hear of it.

"Rest here, Cap'n. Morales will keep you company." And up he goes, leaving his pack behind. He moves surely and steadily up the long, sloping fall, rarely unseating even the smallest stones. The way is not steep, but an inexperienced climber, or one less fit, could easily have fallen into a hole, broken an ankle, or started a rockslide. The captain looks on like a fan at a sporting event until the lieutenant is out of sight.

"I never get tired of watching him work," he says quietly. "Even after ten years."

"You should tell him that, sir." the ensign replies, and she steps up onto a boulder, facing the west. "Your opinion means a lot to him."

"And yours means a lot to me. Not to get mushy."

"Of course not, sir."

"How's our weather holding up?"

"It's difficult to predict, sir. We just haven't been here long enough to detect the patterns."

"Yeah, well, I learned this while you two were underwater: when one of those moons shows its pretty face, there's trouble on the way." He takes a seat, leaning back against a neighboring boulder and closing his eyes.

"Are you OK, sir?"

"Groovy. Still recovering from bug bites, I guess. Maybe just a little beauty rest 'til Nikki gets back."

But there is nothing beautifying about the restless, dream-laden sleep he falls into. He imagines bristly pincers brushing his skin and the clicking voices of invisible enemies. The crack of a whip jars him awake, and the boulder reminds him of a rider on his back. He calls out and waves his arms but then comes to his senses and takes a deep breath.

Lieutenant K has not yet returned.

Looking at him with concern in her eyes, Ensign Morales makes no comment as she rolls up the blanket and places it under his head. She takes a seat next to him, his helmet on her lap, and there she remains, motionless, staring into the distance, her fingers interlaced, her eyes open and unblinking.

The captain looks at her and sighs.

"Carmela," he murmurs to himself and repeats the name in his mind like a mantra, watching the wind play with her hair until he falls back to sleep.

+ + + + + +

Viktor moves slowly, climbing down from the alp when at last they reach Cyclonia.

He doesn't need their help, he thinks bitterly, but Twenty-Seven and the alp handlers can see he will be forced to remain mounted if not lent the combined support of their pincers. Once they've gotten him safely to the ground, they discretely go about other business, pretending it never happened.

Cyclonia lies before them.

Does he wish them to go ahead and announce his arrival? asks Twenty-Seven. A lone tower stands before them, a copy of those in Albion, except that it rises from the stony shore of a sheltered cove. The crashing voice of the Great Saline thunders in the distance.

He does not, thinks Viktor. *They will come to him.*

And indeed, not long after, appearing as if out of nowhere, two dozen bristly, blue soldiers materialize in front of them, forming a wall in front of the Albion contingent and their giant steed.

He is Thirteen of Cyclonia, thinks the largest of these, stepping forward. *Who are they? Where are they from? Who among them has Command?*

He has Command, thinks Viktor. *He is Magister of Albion, servant to the Queen of the First Hive.*

Doubtful thoughts circulate, and Thirteen makes no effort to hide his disbelief.

Troubling omens have come from Albion.

Yes, his companions agree. *Troubling omens.*

But we have not heard of a change in Magisters.

No, no change.

And if there was a change, Thirteen continues, *he cannot believe such a one would have been chosen. Albion is strong, not old and frail. Its Magisters have Command.*

Yes! They serve their queen with strength.

Viktor's lone antenna quivers, but before he can reply, Twenty-Seven steps forward.

They are fools, he thinks. *They address the Magister of Albion and do not know the patience they are shown as he tolerates their insults. Trouble* has *come to Albion—and it will come to Cyclonia as well if they stand here chittering. But there is a new Magister now, and he will save them, whether fools or not. He seeks audience with their queen to make it so.*

One of the subordinate Cyclonians leans its antennae toward its leader and offers a tightly sheltered thought. Thirteen's surprise is impossible to miss.

He is told he addresses Viktor, the Old Magister, he

whose Command was once legendary. Is it true?

Viktor clicks a harsh, abrupt cadence.

He sees some among them have memories longer than others. He is indeed Viktor. He was Old Magister, but he is New again. He has Command.

But...

But nothing! Time is our enemy—among others. They will take him to their queen!

Viktor's order is more forceful than his appearance suggests, and the Cyclonians bow.

It shall be done, thinks Thirteen.

+ + +

Half the Cyclonian welcoming party remains behind to escort the hungry alp and its handlers to a place where food and lova can be found. The remainder, Thirteen and a dozen robust fellows, lead Viktor and Twenty-Seven to the lone tower, overlooking its cove and sheltered by wrapping arms of stone.

The hive bustles with activity, though it is only a fraction the size of Albion. Platoons of farmers, smaller and less bristly than the average soldier, tend fields of lova to the north and west. Much of their effort is directed at skillfully channeling the lone river that flows down from the upper land. They split and redirect its course so many times as it travels through the fields that it never does reach the cove. The lova plants, charismatic and green, poke their heads above the surface when the farmers approach, as if desiring their attention, but those close to the road retreat quickly into their holes at the sight of the strangers.

Viktor buzzes softly and his nasal slits flare.

That is a smell he has missed.

Twenty-Seven agrees.

Cyclonia has done well for itself, he thinks, and he casts the thought so it can be sensed by Thirteen as well as Viktor. *I have not been here in cycles, but it seems the tower has grown and the fields are larger.*

Yes, thinks Thirteen. *Cyclonia needs no floods, for their queen is wise and humble. One tower is enough for her, and so the water of the Nara Daquin suffices. Thus can Cyclonians revere and honor Ozag without being unduly beholden to her.*

Viktor reads the implied insult but lets it pass.

Their queen is indeed strong and wise, he thinks.

Yes, thinks Thirteen. *She is not the type to leave her duties and not return.*

Viktor's cloudy eyes ignite.

What does it know about such things?

No more than most. But that is why he was demoted, is it not? He failed to stop Adira, the Albion queen during his Magistery, from violating the Prohibition when she dared a quest to Ozag, Calamitous and Abiding. Adira was never seen again, and when he sought to find and return her, he failed and was undone.

Twenty-Seven's outrage threatens to boil over, but Viktor allows the impertinence to go unanswered, for they have arrived at the tower. In any case, Thirteen is not wrong. He sees no sense in denying the truth.

A moment later, they bid farewell to the sun and enter a domain of shadow and subtle amber. At the tower's center, a basket awaits, tended by six bronze scion, their wings stretching idly. Thirteen enters the basket; Viktor and Twenty-Seven do the same. Their bristling escorts move off to tend other duties, and the basket is lifted up and away, through the heart of the tower. Thirteen observes them closely but offers no thoughts. When they reach the tower's peak, the basket is set down in a wide space, open to the sun.

They will disembark and wait, thinks Thirteen, and no sooner have Viktor and his companion stepped from the basket then it is lifted again and flown back down into the darkness. Thirteen's arhythmic clicking soon fades to silence.

Is he sure they have not just been made prisoners? thinks Twenty-Seven, surveying the stark emptiness of their surroundings. Viktor preens his lone antenna.

He is sure of nothing, he thinks.

And so, they wait.

+ + +

When at last droning wings announce the arrival of the Cyclonian queen, Viktor has lapsed into a shallow torpor while his companion paces slow, meditative steps from one end of the space to the other.

They are greeted in time by not one but two baskets, the first containing four large, fanged scion led by Thirteen. These exit the basket the moment it has come to rest, and they, along with the bronze flyers carrying it, stand expectantly, waiting for the second basket to join them. Its passengers are three, one very large and blue, one smaller and silver, and one, the largest of them all, gold and imperious. Once the basket settles to the floor, its bronze flyers join the others in creating around it an iridescent formation. But the three passengers remain inside, their sparkling eyes fixed on the newcomers and their thoughts difficult to read.

He is Magister of Cyclonia, thinks the one, the largest of all the blue scion, larger even than Twenty-Seven, his legs sturdy and bristled. *He lives in service to his queen, who honors them with this audience.*

And he is Magister of Albion, thinks Viktor, aware that his thoughts must appear feeble in comparison. *They are honored.* He senses from the group sheltered thoughts whose essence is easy to read. All can see his frail, gray form and doubt the truth in his claim.

When they last had emissaries from Albion, thinks the Cyclonian magister, *the tale they heard was one of his demotion. Did his queen not abdicate rather than couple with him? Was she not replaced by Albion's current queen, who in turn promoted a New Magister?*

Twenty-Seven buzzes angrily.

They have heard the tale wrong. There was no abdication! No refusal!

But Viktor's pride isn't what it once was; he hasn't

the energy to correct this foolishness.

Cyclonia's magister has a flawed grasp of history, he thinks. *But it is not his duty to teach truth to the ignorant. For things have recently changed in Albion, or have they not heard?*

Rumors only, thinks the Cyclonian magister. *They do not feel beholden to study the troubles of Albion.*

Albion's troubles, thinks Viktor, *could very soon be Cyclonia's as well.*

The others click rapidly back and forth.

Does he refer to the drought? thinks the Cyclonian magister. *Of what concern is this to them? The Nara Daquin flows as always, and both lova and awl flourish. It is a credit to their queen that it is so, for she is dutiful.*

The Cyclonians dim their eyes and bow their antennae to the queen in her basket. She notes this with a detached air, long accustomed to flattery, and she remains silent, her gaze focused on Viktor.

The Cyclonian queen is *wise,* he thinks, choosing his thoughts carefully. *And dutiful, as has been said. Her domain will grow until the last raindrop falls. This is why Viktor has come seeking her aid. For Albion is in need—its greatest ever, beyond the drought.*

Then are the rumors true? the Cyclonian magister demands to know. *Was its precious Circle destroyed?*

And all who resided within, thinks Viktor. *Many thousands, including New Magister and Albion's queen.*

This news is greeted with anxious thoughts and subliminal chittering. Even the bronze flyers, stoic to a fault, cannot help exchanging sheltered thoughts. What the queen thinks, she does not share.

Hard news, thinks the Cyclonian magister. *Is it punishment for Adira violating the Prohibition, daring to approach Ozag's Hold? But the Vengeful is also Merciful. He cannot believe she would act so. Was not Albion the light in Ozag's eyes? The tune to her whistle?*

Was, thinks Viktor. *Was. Now the only tune is an elegy, and the only light the fire that claimed soldier, tender, farmer, and queen alike.*

But how can this be? Thirteen interrupts.

He intends to learn, thinks Viktor. *But first, there is great need for other business.*

The Cyclonian magister clicks rapidly.

Could it be related to the vumierre they saw?

Viktor's eyes light for a moment.

Of what vumierre does he speak? he demands.

Does he truly not know? Is he not familiar with the brown-skinned vumierre Albion's previous magister was known to ride? The one that fell from the sky trailed by a sheet of white? That one, and two of a different color were spied north of Cyclonia not long before Viktor's arrival. Farmers saw them but feared to intervene. They traveled north up the divide and were lost to sight.

The other Cyclonians can no longer contain themselves. This discussion of mysterious vumierre and the destruction of the Circle is too much. They devolve into agitated clicking and nervous, raspy chittering.

Yes. There were three of them.

Yes. Three slavers.

No. It cannot be. Ozag destroyed the slavers.

Yes. The Undying ended their reign.

Yes. Ended. But one fell from the sky.

Yes. A brown one, from a flying vumierre device.

Yes. And two more were there as well. Pale.

Yes! Slavers have returned!

Yes. Returned. Has Ozag abandoned scion?

No! Never!

No! She is Vivacious and Munificent.

Yes. But the Circle...

Yes. Destroyed...

Enough, thinks the Cyclonian queen, at last rising to add a thought of her own. The order is given casually, but it is obeyed like the crack of a whip. Dead silence and full attention follow. Slowly, she steps from her basket. *They will leave her to speak with Albion's magister,* she thinks, and her wings oscillate. *Alone.*

A dozing larva could have sensed the distress this causes her subjects, but none have the courage to object.

Reluctant but seeing no choice, they allow themselves to be lifted up and away, Cyclonia's magister temporarily taking his queen's place and Twenty-Seven seated in the second basket. Off they go, their droning wings eventually fading to silence.

Greetings, Viktor, thinks the queen.

Greetings, Allura, thinks Viktor, and he bows.

He has looked better, thinks Allura.

He has felt better.

How many cycles has it been?

Since she tried beguiling him into joining her hive? He has lost count.

They would have made a fine pair, thinks Allura, and she runs her forelimbs over her antennae.

He cannot disagree. She, at least, would have listened to his advice and not violated the Prohibition.

She would not have needed his advice! Adira was a fool. If the drought was indeed Ozag's will, what good could have come from daring to face the Undying to complain? By violating the Prohibition and transgressing on Her Hold, your overproud queen has caused much harm, alienating Albion from Ozag.

It may be, Viktor concedes.

And yet, Allura adds, *he blames himself in part. He will not deny it; she can read him.*

Of course, he blames himself. What else? He failed to prevent Adira from going, failed to find and return her before she could rouse the Dire and Fulsome.

What magister can control a queen, regardless the wisdom of his argument? Allura asks.

This is true, thinks Viktor. *But it makes no difference to his circumstance. Having failed thus, he lost all power, was stripped of Command, drained of color.*

It seems he has come full circle, then.

Viktor's whistle is lowly and tuneless.

Circle is a word he can no longer sense in peace.

Allura steps forward, leaning her supple antennae toward Viktor, touching both to his single, gray filament.

Perhaps so. But he has not come to her in despair.

He has a plan; she can sense it. Tell her everything...

+ + +   + + +

When Lieutenant K at last returns and the captain is wakened and ready, they scale the gap. It is a slow, sweaty process, for the captain must climb under his own power. But the lieutenant leads the way with mechanical certainty, and the path he chooses serves them well. Even though Ensign Morales follows behind the captain in case he should stumble, he never does, and a full three hours of effort brings the trio to the southern edge of what appears to be a limitless plain of yellow grass.

"Well done, Nikki," says the captain, and he wipes his face and drinks from the ensign's canteen.

"Not there yet, Cap'n. Ag facility is still another eighty kilometers due north."

"Well, hey," says the captain. "You and the ensign may be full of sass and vinegar—as my mom used to say—but this sapiens can't go on forever."

Ensign Morales produces the emergency blanket like a magician and smiles as she takes hold of two corners. The captain frowns.

"You're enjoying this, aren't you?"

"Yes sir, a little."

Lieutenant K grasps his two corners and the captain grumbles to himself as he takes his seat.

"Four hours ought to do it," says the lieutenant. "Maybe four and a half. Depends on how things go."

In the end, "things" go well. The land is lumpy, and tangled grass often seeks to trip them, but whatever creatures live there seem content to hop away or remain hidden in their burrows, gurgling low warnings if they approach too closely. On one occasion, the ensign detects in the distance a sleeping babelrack, but they give it a wide berth, and it sleeps on, its camouflage hiding it well. Their only concern are derkas, but these remain skittish in the face of arcing flares and do not appear interested in coming any closer. After firing yet another of these, Lieutenant

K furrows his brow.

"Only a few left," he says.

At the midpoint of their journey, their path crosses a small stream, eastbound at the moment, but curving downstream to the south. Here they take a break and allow the captain to stretch his legs. The ensign cups a handful of water, examining it closely and tasting it.

"It's clean," she reports and wades in. She fills her canteen and offers it to the captain, who drinks deeply before refilling and returning it.

"That," he says, "is some of the best water I've ever tasted. Darn." He wades into the stream. "I could stand here all day and watch the clouds."

"Sorry sir, but I really think we should keep going. Have you noticed? Those creatures are staying away from the flares, but they're getting a little braver every time. The longer we're exposed on the surface the more likely we are to run into trouble of one kind or another."

And so, they resume their trek, eating up the kilometers though it feels to the captain his companions are simply jogging in place. To his tired eyes, nothing lies in the distance except more distance, and for a time, he drifts into sleep, closing his visor. He is wakened only once by the coughing report of the flare gun.

"Dirty bird," says the lieutenant, and he looks to the sky where a derka traces languorous circles high above, safely out of range.

He and the ensign increase their pace.

The captain has no intentions of falling asleep again, but he does so anyway, in spite—or possibly because—of the way his hammock rocks side to side.

+ + + + + +

Viktor and queen Allura stand on the top level of Cyclonia's lone tower, looking south to where the cove opens up to the Great Saline. The sky is clear, but the breaking waves take no recess from their thunderous assault on the beach.

His story is strange indeed, thinks Allura. *And filled with many mysteries.*

Strange but true, Viktor replies. *So he asks: what will she do? Will she help him?*

The queen's eyes are dim but her tone is shrewd.

Does he know what he asks? That Allura should take over tending of Albion's abandoned larvae? Once fed on her serum, they will become her subjects. If his princess returns seeking her place at the highest tower, there may be war between the hives.

A problem for the future, thinks Viktor. *And one he guesses unlikely to happen. So, will she help?*

Allura's clicking is sharp and brief.

She suspects he knows the answer already. Could any queen disregard such a plea? But hers is a small hive. He speaks of an entire tower of untended larvae. She cannot guarantee her assistance will save them all.

She will do her best, thinks Viktor. *That suffices.*

And the Old magister made New? What will he do? Return to Albion? Seek the missing princess?

He is torn, Queen. He does not know his path.

What does he perceive as his imperative?

To serve the hive, of course. Albion must not be allowed to waste away if there is anything he can do. And yet waste it will if not led by a queen. So, he at first felt driven to locate the surviving princess, who his soldier reports has already begun to transform.

His soldier, Allura is quick to add, *also reported she left the hive—under her own power—either with or in pursuit of this mutant scion you described and following the path of the escaped sharksha.*

So the signs indicated.

For what reason, does he suppose? If not captured by the beasts, is she in league with them? Is she in some type of misguided thrall? Or has she come undone by the death of her queen? Does she seek the cause of the Circle's destruction and perhaps revenge?

The last would be most noble, thinks Viktor. *But whatever is the case, hers appears to be a reign worthy of no faith. Even if he were to find her, it seems likely she would be unwilling to return with him or unfit to lead if she did. And there is this also...*

Yes?

If the cause of the devastation is not identified and brought to justice, the towers of Albion could be the next target. Anyone seeking the hive's utter ruin would not be satisfied with the Circle's end alone.

And he believes the vumierre have the answer?

Is it not likely? Does history tell anything of their kind that is not bent toward the suffering of scion?

Allura considers this carefully, looking southward and whistling a contemplative tune, simple and recursive.

He believes the mutant could think? she asks.

Yes, though it tried to hide the ability.

And because it traveled with these other vumierre, he believes they also can think?

He believes there is only one way to learn. If she will deign to show him the place where the vumierre were last seen, he will pursue them and take them captive.

So easily? Will they not resist?

The brown one was helpless as a beached awl when it was fished from the Saline. Its companions, it is to be expected, will be equally defenseless.

She wonders. They carried parcels on their backs. Who is to say what is contained within? Some dreadful tools for vumierre mischief perhaps.

Then what does she suggest?

Allura is decisive.

Pursue the vumierre, she thinks. *But do not engage. Is it not possible they will lead him to his answers more surely if followed in stealth than if taken captive?*

Viktor rolls this idea around in his mind.

Allura is wise, he thinks. *Albion would have had a happier ending had she reigned there.*

Perhaps. But her calling is here. She will select her finest tenders and send them to Albion—as many as can be spared. For his mission, a company of soldiers will be provided. Awl and lova, too, as much as his alp can carry.

Viktor bows.

It is all he could have hoped for. With her help, they are sure to succeed and Albion be avenged.

Allura's eyes flash.

She is not so certain. But anything is possible. In any case, though he will not wish to hear it, she deems him unfit for such a venture without rest.

And she spreads her wings, wafting a gentle cloud of pheromones over him. He is helpless to resist and soon falls into the deepest torpor he can remember.

CHAPTER SIX
Feud

YOU SHOULD REST, thinks Submission to his woli when they have returned from the plains. *Things are going to get hot around here soon enough.*

Am I not, thinks Lightning, *going to the Skull?*

No.

She scowls, considering how to plead her case to join the party—or contrive a way to follow against orders. At the moment, she is too tired for either.

What about Thunder?

He's staying too. He's a good fighter, and I want you both in the home caves to remind the others I'm coming back. We all are. Three-legs is staying too. Something tells me I can trust him to watch your tail.

Joy clicks lightly, but Lightning groans.

I guess that's one way to describe it. Who else?

I haven't decided. Serenity for sure—she'll be in charge—and all the ami-kans, of course.

Well, not Stone, please. Or Fang.

Submission's glance is stern.

If I'm confined to kezel who aren't mad at you, Three-legs and Thunder will be your only company.

Lightning looks away, abashed.

I feel like I should be helping, she thinks.

You will be. By resting your legs.

Lightning sighs, and she unburdens herself of the dow, taking her time as she hands them to Submission so that any passing kezel might appreciate her success. Retreating to the rock shelf, she and Joy lie low, watching the others make final preparations for the defense of their home. They sit in silence, their thoughts sheltered, and Joy idly preens Lightning's spikes. But she soon pulls the artifact from its sling. As she gazes at it, the light in her eyes seems to retreat, not grow dim so much as distant, as if sinking into her head. She caresses the object and buzzes softly as Lightning looks on, massaging her legs and drifting on the edge of sleep.

There they remain for what seems to both of them a very long time. Down below, bibijas confer and strategize, report and debate. Some walk solemnly on two legs as they carry debris and vermin bones from the caves, while others pile barricades of stone. Measure, the Brigadier Bone, and his oliwol Curly huddle over the defective thrower like a team of surgeons. Lightning turns away from this gloomy business and looks to the east, across a thousand strides of twisted, black spikes.

What are the chances, she wonders, *that Thunder and Cliff will bring us something to eat? The dow was good, but that march took it out of me. I'm hungry!*

Not good, thinks Joy. *They are poor hunters.*

Lightning squirms, tugging at her vest. The garment has grown smaller by the moon and will surely begin tearing at the seams if not soon tailored.

While we're waiting, she thinks, *I have some questions for that new toy of yours.* She removes her file from one pocket. *Starting with your ami- and api-kan.*

You are my ami-kan.

Lightning scrapes away her claws' rough edges.

That is sweet, she thinks. *And I will be, for as long as you'll have me. But you came from somewhere, and we should know the truth. I agree that this...this...*

Book, thinks Joy.

Lightning blows shavings from her fingertips.

Sure, OK, "book." I agree it's not meant to do harm. I don't know why, but I believe that. I can sense how it feels about you—or more like how you feel about how it feels, if that makes sense.

I think it does.

But it's a blank to me. I can't sense its thoughts...I

can't smell it... I don't think I'm going to be calling it Petros any time soon, if that's OK.

It doesn't really mind, thinks Joy, and she buzzes softly. *It knows you're good.*

Hmm...

Lightning looks up from her work, hoping to see Cliff and Thunder bearing shareable bounty. She wonders what fate her dow are enduring. She suspects she's seen the last of them.

Well, she thinks. *Let's have it. Tell me everything you've learned about where you come from. It'll keep my mind off my worries.*

\+ + +

Joy carefully recalls what she has learned from the Book. She can't replicate—or even remember—many of the complex ideas the artifact has shared, but the parts that interest her most, those related to her origin, are locked in her memory. She is glad for this chance to share them; doing so makes their implausible nature easier to accept—if not understand.

But first, she has a question. She holds the artifact so Lightning can get a good look.

What do you see? she asks.

A rock, Lightning replies, for that, indeed, is what she sees: an unremarkable plate of stone, rough, chipped, boring, and black. But the sparkle in Joy's eyes grows dim, and she shakes her head.

That's what I thought.

What do you mean?

This is the Book.

So?

It looked different before, Joy explains. *Do you not remember?* She turns the rock around and holds it up.

Lightning considers. Had it looked different? She thinks back to when she woke, just before the dow hunt. Hadn't she seen...hadn't there been...

I don't know, she thinks, puzzled. *I don't think so.*

I mean, I have a feeling that maybe... Yes! I do remember! It was smooth! And it wasn't a rock at all. Her ears pin back. *But the memory is slippery. It's like I'm not sure if it was real or just a dream.*

That's how it works, Joy whistles quietly. *It was weak before,* she clarifies. *So it was exposed.* She taps the stone, one-two, one-two. *But it's getting stronger.* Her antennae bend toward the rough, black surface. *It has a Reader,* she thinks. *Now it can hide.*

Why hide from me?

In halting quartets, Joy relays the Book's principal operation as she understands it.

It only answers questions.

It can't ask questions.

Only Readers see it.

Only Readers remember it.

Here, Lightning stops her.

But I remember the idea *of the thing. I remember that it exists, and where we found it. All that.*

You remember me telling, Joy explains. *You don't remember* it. Her facetted eyes dance with the sun. *Submission won't remember either,* she adds. *What I said, yes,* she adds. *Not the Book itself.*

Sneaky, thinks Lightning. *So the only way one of us non-reader types ever learns about it is if a Reader tells us. And we can't use it, even if we know about it. But what's to stop one of us from stealing it?*

Here, Joy explains how the Book gains power from the minds of its Readers. The more there are, the greater its ability to change form and do work. From what it has told her, at full power, it could assume any visible form—or disappear from sight. At its peak, it could fly, could speak, could even shield a Reader from injury if fired upon by Moondweller weapons.

But with only one Reader, it is far from its peak.

That explains why it needs allies, I guess, Lightning grasps. *But my question still is: allies to do what, exactly? What does it want?*

Find and cultivate Readers, Joy thinks simply.

That's all?

There might be more, Joy admits. In fact, she was certain of it. For every answer she had unearthed, she felt sure there were ten others eluding her.

She moves on to discuss the Book's origin, but this is of little matter in itself. That it came from somewhere farther than Weaver the Sun or any of the moons, farther even than the so-called Moondwellers, is impossible to fathom, and so, pointless to dwell on. What does matter is that in their travels, the Book's makers crossed paths with some of these Moondwellers and left it with them, which is how it came, eventually, to Aranae, traveling in a mighty craft named *Destiny.*

It's a flying vessel, thinks Joy, though she isn't sure by Lightning's expression whether she's shed light on the concept or simply made it more confusing. She can't say she understands it herself. *Like some vessels float,* she tries to explain. *But this one flies.* They've both had enough experience to grasp the first idea, but the second? Lightning scrunches up her snout, and when she asks if the vessel in question is like the one that fell from the sky to ruin the Circle, Joy shrugs.

I don't think so.

So where is it?

It's still up there, Joy points vaguely to the sky.

Up there? Up where?

In the sky. Somewhere.

Lightning looks in the direction Joy points, but of course, she sees nothing.

So...is that where the Moondwellers are? The ones Ancian was always going on about? The ones who left?

I don't think so.

Well, how about those three we met down south? Is that where they came from?

No. Their vessel crashed.

Grr... OK, fine. So how does that relate to where you came from? Are you saying... Lightning ceases her nail filing, too engrossed in the mystery to do justice to the chore. Since their adventures in Albion, she has been burning to express an idea both obvious and yet ignored, afraid of the response she will get. No way to let it pass now. *You look for all the world like a cross between a Moondweller and a scion,* she thinks. *Am I wrong?*

No. You are not. Joy rises to two legs, looking to the east. *We were an...experiment.* She returns the Book to its home. *To make new Readers.* She buzzes a low tune. *I'm the only survivor.*

What is the appropriate response to something like that? Lightning chooses sympathy—and stilled thoughts. She rises as well, as tall on four legs as Joy is on two. From this vantage, they both see at the same time something that takes their minds off the unraveling of tangled history: Cliff, Thunder, and the jabi Edge, returning from the northeast, one full-grown cremlin riding lifeless and tantalizing across Edge's back, and another on Thunder's.

+ + +

Don't suppose Bruiser'll mind, thinks Thunder, and he tears off one of his cremlin's ten, muscular tentacles, covered in suction cups. This he tosses to Lightning, though she can scarcely believe it. *I'll call it hunter's privilege if he complains.*

But there is no need. Submission appears soon after, nodding without comment as he notes the successful hunt. In his mouth, he carefully carries a portion of awl, which he passes along to Joy. While they eat, Submission shares with the jabis their role in the upcoming defense of their range.

Have they figured out that thrower yet? Cliff asks.

Submission glowers at the question, his curled lip a perfectly clear answer. But as he completes his explanations and orders, they hear from the far side of the caves a single, familiar detonation: RAT! followed not long after by two more, TAT TAT! accompanied by celebratory calls and the gnashing of teeth.

Good timing, thinks Submission. *That Curly! She's*

a smart one. OK. Any questions? No? Then finish up and get ready. I don't suppose we have long before—

His thought is interrupted by a distant howling from the west, a call taken up and repeated. Measure jogs into sight, her ears pinned back and her crest flared.

They've crossed! she thinks. *They're coming!*

+ + + + + +

When, many moons earlier, Redtooth scouts had reported weapons fire and a strange smell from the Sugarfoot range, the Redtooth chief Claw had not at first understood the explanation they had provided upon return from their eventual survey of the territory.

What do you mean gone? he had snarled. *Taken by who? Taken where?*

By a whole bunch of these, Spike had thought. Claw's one-eyed second-in-command had held up as evidence the rent body of a scion soldier, its head barely attached and its limbs slack. *Can't say where exactly, but somewhere out on the plains. At least, that's the way they came in and the way they left.*

But Claw had refused to believe the tales of kezel dead in the Sugarfoot caves and accrete ruined for thousands of strides, and he had insisted on seeing for himself. As the southern crossing had earlier met its end at the bottom of the wedge, he and a team of his best fighters had marched north and then south, coming at last to a sight he had been unable to imagine. When double and triple checks confirmed that all Sugarfoot kezel had either been taken or killed and their weapons vanished, he ordered all items of value, especially crystals, be hauled back to the Redtooth range. But he never once considered laying claim to the caves themselves, not even after the lethal fumes had dissipated and the smell had become tolerable.

That place is cursed, he had thought, glad to be back on his own turf. *It's what they get for believing in their precious Moondwellers. What did it get them, all their fancy vests and their weapons? An unnatural way to live and an unnatural way to die.*

But mostly, in thoughts he shared with no one, not even his fancy (who knew how he felt and needed no explanation) he had considered it justice for the murder of his oti-mu, Storm. He had been taken from them far too early by the bloody hand of a renegade jabi fleeing Sugarfoot territory for reasons no one could guess.

Use a Moondweller weapon on a Redtooth? he had thought to himself. *This is your reward!*

Over time, when the only signs of kezel on the Sugarfoot range were occasional emissaries—dismayed and astounded Bristles and Whitetails—and when these eventually ceased to visit, Claw had ordered his hunters to take advantage of the opportunity. This they had done with relish, seeking game in every new corner of what they now saw as an extension of their own realm.

From the wedge to the River Tongue, they killed what they could catch, chasing off—sometimes with bloody persuasion—any Bristles bold enough to confront them. Some had even begun considering the merits of moving their families east of the wedge to gain relief from a Redtooth range long since grown crowded. The Sugarfoot caves may have been declared cursed and off limits, but they were not the only options. The northern bluffs known as the Airy Hills had been neatly excavated by wind and weather, and the sandy caverns beneath the Spine were as nice as anything the average Redtooth had. Even the Skull, whose reputation was mixed, and which technically lay on Bristle land, had become the topic of hopeful discussion among Redteeth.

All these aspirations changed the moment Spike had come jogging onto the Old Range, bearing the spectacular news of Lightning's return.

Are you sure? Claw had asked, his eyes hungry but his tone reserved as if fearing to believe the news.

I can't be positive, Spike had thought. *I never got her smell back when she...you know...when she crossed our turf the first time. But she fits the description, all right.*

Mask, black vest, gloves and boots—Sugarfoot vanity! She's grown, but I reckon it's her.

And you didn't bring her to me!

Easy, Boss; it wasn't so simple.

Here, Spike had explained how he had first seen Lightning's cutter (*the one she used to kill Storm, I'm guessing*) then, most astoundingly, her thrower, one of the small ones, though no less deadly for its size.

I'll wager she's used it before, he had thought. *Probably killed with it, but I couldn't say for sure.*

And the blue thing? Everyone says she was traveling with some blue...animal.

Never saw it. But there was something there.

Spike had struggled to describe what he had—or more precisely hadn't—seen accompanying Lightning, its foreign scent and bipedal, heel-toe stride.

Like a bomba? Claw had wondered.

No, Boss, and in spite of himself, a seasoned fighter counted among the bravest on his range, Spike had shuddered. *The Sugarfoot murderer went in the caves, but the thing stayed outside, invisible, and the cutter...it was like...it just floated there, all by itself.*

Claw had considered this, mulling implications, thoughts of hated Moondwellers rising like specters in his mind, a type of creature gone so long they'd become a legend to frighten wabis. But most of all he had thought about his oti-mu and a flaming desire for revenge.

I take it back, he had thought. *You were smart in coming here and not risking your life. They rode out the storm in the caves, I reckon, and then what? A nasty surprise for them, that's what!*

He had scored a four-line slash in the wall beside him and howled suddenly, his jaws wide and terrible.

Good enough, Spike had thought, glad for the orders. *But we should go as strong as quiet allows. Who knows what Moondweller sorcery that invisible thing is capable of? Maybe it was the one who killed Storm!*

Claw had roared.

Then they'll both roast over a fire! Gather your team

and meet me at the crossing. And keep it sheltered! If anyone asks, we're going hunting, nothing else. Get along now, and let me think...

\+ + +

But of course, the effort had been for naught. The thieving murderer had joined with a dirty Clawpaw—the skulking three-legger, of all things—and had, for reasons the Redteeth could only guess, fled out onto the plains, a place Claw was unwilling to go, regardless his lust for blood. What was the point of taking such a risk when derkas would surely do his work for him?

And so, he, along with Spike and his gang, had spread out along the bordering accrete and had watched and waited, allowing two full sleeps to pass, living on the bounty of Sugarfoot game but staying far from the accursed caves. Claw had sat looking out over the plains until his eyes grew tired and his muscles cramped.

Filthy Moondweller sickness, he thought, trying to explain the bizarre behavior. *Leave a pair of scouts in rotation until the next moon. If they don't come back by then, they never will.*

But all the way back to his range, Claw had been disturbed by unanswerable questions. Why had the killer come back at all? And why now? And how—good grief, how!—had she done so undetected? His hunters and scouts were spread from the sulphur fields to the Bloodwater. No one could have come down from the land of kish and made it to that island cave without his knowing. And yet the sly, vain, murderous jabi had.

And this time with a two-legger, he had thought, *but no blue thing. What is* that *about?*

The next moon had come and gone with no sight of the fugitives, and the time of wabis had called Claw and all the range to duties more about food than vengeance. Scouts had occasionally been sent south and east, but a second moon had passed and the plains continued to roll on in infinite waves of white and yellow, revealing no sign of kezel, mysterious blue creatures, or their invisible companions. Claw had never entirely given up on his dream of retribution, but leading a range is about more than personal accounts. He had shifted his focus to making a move on the Skull, an ideal way to expand his territory. But of course, a good plan can't be rushed—and at the time there had seemed no need to hurry. The entire clan was dispersed, thin and tired, working to feed and mind a batch of wabis larger, hungrier, and more reckless than any in living memory. So occupied, Claw had been stunned when he sensed Spike's news.

Smoking holes! he had thought. *You have to be kidding me!* But Spike was not kidding.

Just sauntered in pretty as you please, he had thought. *Not all of 'em, mind you. And in awfully rough shape. Hardly a vest between 'em, so you can count their ribs—and their scars.*

How many?

Enough to hold a position, but not enough to take one. And no throwers we could see. But...

Yes?

They had the killer jabi with 'em. So they could still have the one thrower.

Claw had looked as though he was having a fit. His eyes had rolled white and his hands and feet had clenched and released as if kneading a hassock for sleep.

She came back?! Again?!

I reckon, Spike had thought, *somewhere out there on the plains, there's a place where a kezel can live. Who woulda thought it? Whatta you want us to do?*

What Claw wanted, he had to wait for. Teams had to be called in from far hills, numbers taken and strategies plotted. Wabis couldn't simply be abandoned nor ami-kans spared. But the waiting had chafed. If the dirty Moondweller-licking Sugarfeet were given a chance to recover, they could make claiming the Skull very difficult. With an ally to the west, the Bristles would be able to bolster their eastern defenses against the Whitetails. Claw was no lover of the vest-wearing mongrels, but Whitetails had proven a useful distraction, always keeping the Bristles occupied.

And fat, old Gapi-kan was on the way.

Hurry, he had thought. *Hurry!*

And his clan had done just that, readying to strike before the red moon. The Sugarfoot kezel must not be allowed to reach the Skull.

+ + + + + +

When Captain Monroe wakes, the lieutenant and ensign have come to a stop before a virtual forest of thorns that rises suddenly before them. None of the ugly spikes is less than an inch long, sprouting from dense, twisting vines, thick and tall. They run like a wall from east to west, with no visible way around. His companions face this barrier, their gazes distant.

He gets to his feet, groaning as he stretches.

"There's a river on the other side," Lieutenant K reports. "Not super wide, but very deep." He winks at the captain. "You'll like this, sir." And he motions to Ensign Morales. "Show him."

A moment later, the ensign projects a hologram from her eyes, the image of a building, three layers of conjoined rectangles, covering several thousand square feet of functional but unassuming space, most in shades of gray. The captain whistles softly and reaches out as if to caress the image. The underground facility is just as he had seen it in historical documents, but it is better by far than any blueprint, for this is real—and according to the ensign, little more than ten kilometers away.

"No awards for beauty," says the lieutenant. "But A-plus for durability; it's withstood a lot of years."

"And another A-plus for both of you," the captain says. "Well done, people!"

He looks to the sky, where the derka from earlier—he assumes—continues its stubborn circling. He watches warily and tries to massage the stiffness from his neck as the ensign rolls the blanket and tucks it into her pack.

"A determined fella," the captain says, frowning. "Don't suppose the one you killed was a friend of his?" He takes the canteen and splashes a handful of water on his face, slapping his cheeks and rubbing his eyes as he assesses the thorny obstacle before them. "Guess we better get started. Who's going first?"

The answer is the lieutenant, followed by the ensign, picking their way through the vines and clearing a path for the captain to follow. The thorns snag their packs and litter the ground, and the vines twist and contort overhead so densely they block out the sky. But though the going is slow, there is one benefit: once out of the sun, they find plump, pink berries growing up the length of the vines, thriving in the shade. The ensign examines them carefully, popping a few into her mouth and chewing with a thoughtful expression.

"They taste like juneberries, sir. Eighteen percent sugar, seventy-two percent water. Calcium, fiber, proteins, lipids. High in iron and phenolic compounds, mainly anthocyanins. I'm also detecting potassium, magnesium, and phosphorous." She plucks several more and chews them deliberately. "Also: vitamin C, thiamin, riboflavin, pantothenic acid, vitamin B-six, folate, vitamins A and E, and trace amounts of biotin."

"Geez, Ensign," says the captain, "you had me at juneberries." And he picks his breakfast as they make their slow, prickly way through the vines.

At last, they are through, greeted upon their return to the sun and yellow grass by a glittering blue river, just as the lieutenant had described, fifty meters ahead. They appraise its robust, eastward flow.

"Not going to be able to swim that," the captain says. "Speaking for myself, of course."

"Wouldn't recommend it for any of us," the lieutenant says, and he scans the water with his brow knit. "There's something in there, something big. Can't get a precise read, but it's large enough to swallow a human."

"Sir!" the ensign points. "Over there!"

The captain sees nothing, but Lieutenant K deftly plucks a thorn from his naked foot and walks down the bank, clearing away dirt and grass to reveal, buried beneath several inches of black soil, a metal hatch which he unseals. It swings back on creaking hinges, exposing a hand-cranked winch connected to a thick, metal cable. This in turn runs to a buried sheath that disappears underground, heading straight to the river.

"Here's the other one," the ensign calls out, and she unearths an identical crank fifty feet away.

"Fantastic!" exclaims the captain, and he grabs the nearest winch like a little boy clutching a birthday gift. It turns slowly at first, and the ensign must lean in to lend her support. But when the lieutenant turns his crank as well, the two, working in unison, produce a remarkable transformation. Turn by turn, the cables are drawn taut, and from the bed of the river rises a simple but sturdy bridge, twenty feet wide, with folded legs that drop into position as the bridge, dripping and weed-draped, rises above the water and locks into place.

"That," thinks the captain as he wipes his grimy hands on the grass, "is a brilliant bit of engineering."

And they cross the river quickly.

A jogging blanket ride follows, during which the lieutenant uses one more of their dwindling store of flares. The derka seems to be daring them, testing the nature of the weapon, and it rains croaking objections down on them—and does not leave.

The ensign ponders it as they resume the march.

"What communicative abilities do they have, do you think? It would be very interesting to know."

"In what way?" the captain frowns.

"Well, sir, that humanoid we met, the one who called herself Joy. She had telepathic abilities."

"So did the silver bug," adds the lieutenant. "And those spiky dinosaur bears."

"Exactly," says the ensign. "At least three different species! Who knows how common it is?"

The captain rubs soil from his helmet.

"So you think the colonists were tinkering with the

natives? Why would they do that?"

"I don't know, sir. Maybe they were already telepathic and there was no tinkering necessary."

"Seems pretty unlikely, doesn't it, Ensign? Against the odds, I mean."

"Yes sir, but so is cultivating that type of aptitude in several completely foreign species. I don't see how they could have done it with the level of technology they had and their relatively limited understanding of telepathy."

"Let's hope we're about to get some answers," the lieutenant points. "Target dead ahead."

When they reach their destination, the only signs of its presence are ventilation ports rising just above the surface, sealed against pests with a covering of steel mesh and capped with galvanized hoods. The ports themselves are hidden within the grass, impossible to see until the travelers are nearly on top of them.

"I'm not detecting any life signs," says the ensign. "And energy signatures are minimal."

The captain steps out from his hammock.

"How minimal?"

"Almost non-existent. I don't think we need to worry about security systems."

"You mean of the electrical type," the lieutenant clarifies. "Mechanical booby traps are still in play."

"It is possible."

"Well," says the captain. "That's enough for me. We'll watch our step. Anyway, our friend is getting braver. Best get inside ASAP."

\+ + +

The agriculture facility's main entrance is a simple metal hatch, set level with the ground, hinged, securely locked, and partially hidden by soil and grass. So are each of the three secondary entrances and the one oversized door leading to the loading dock and service bay. Each has at its center a modest window, a plain square of clear polymer shielded by a metal grate. But they are all badly overgrown with roots and encroaching grass and are filthy. The travelers clear away the foliage and dirt from the main entrance, but even then, when the ensign peers through the window, twin beams of light emitting from her eyes, she sees nothing but gloom and shadows.

"Lieutenant," the captain says. "If you please." And he points to the window, stepping aside.

"With pleasure, Cap'n."

And the lieutenant bends at the waist, taking hold of the grate. He sets his feet and checks his grip. Then, muscles bunching, he pulls backward, tearing the screws from their home like twigs from mud. He casts the grate to the side and aims a precise heel at the window. The polymer shatters, but the lieutenant's foot is no worse for the encounter. He reaches inside, unlocks the hatch, and swings it open on creaky hinges.

A narrow flight of stairs leads down into the dark.

Lieutenant K goes first, eyes beaming light.

"They can deduct the damages from our reward money," whispers the captain as he follows, sweeping away broken polymer with the sole of his boot.

"Yes sir," says the ensign, her voice hushed. "Let's just hope that's the worst we have to do." The light from her eyes cuts through the murk, and the captain activates his own, integrated into his helmet. So guided, they navigate the stairs cautiously, reaching bottom with no mishap. The space they find themselves in is small, no more than two hundred square feet, and its predominant feature is dust-covered tables.

"Report," the captain orders. Then he checks himself. "Not sure why I'm whispering."

"The layout appears consistent with our data," says the ensign, and she runs a finger across a dusty workstation. "Most of the structure is beneath us. Private quarters, the rec center, and most of the labs are lower level one. The power plant occupies all of lower level two."

"And up here?"

"Looks like command, communications, an early-model transporter adjacent to the service bay... The infirmary is that way. There's the service lift—with a manual back-up drive, that's nice—and this, what appears to have been used as a meeting room."

"That fits my read, too," says the lieutenant. "Plus, the greenhouse, over that way."

"Threats?"

"None that I can identify, Cap'n. But I recommend we go slow. We power up this place without double-checking everything, and we could cause a mess of trouble. Things go boom! Capisce?"

"Copy that." The captain takes a deep breath. "OK, folks. Time to split up. Nikki, you take lower level one. We're looking for logs, reports, diaries, to-do lists, love letters. Anything that will tell us what was going on here."

"You got it, Cap'n."

"Carmela, you're on that power plant. See if you can get us operational without blowing us up."

"Yes sir, I'll do my best."

"I'm going to poke around up here, find something to help with *Valiant.* Stay in regular contact; this world is full of hostiles. Which reminds me..." Reaching into the lieutenant's pack, he removes the loaded flare gun.

"See you back here in one hour."

+ + +

Lieutenant Nikolai Ilyich Khristorovdestvensky Jr. makes his way to the first sub-level using the bannistered stairwell near the dormant service lift. His footfalls are soft, and the light from his eyes slices the dark like twin knives. The private quarters he arrives at are modest, square rooms with two bunks, a desk, a pair of storage chests, and a small closet. Most are tidy, but some exhibit signs of disarray, as if the inhabitants had left in a rush. In these, the beds are unmade and clothes are strewn about. Tidy or otherwise, every room is coated in a fine layer of dust. The lieutenant concentrates, amplifying and transmitting his thoughts.

Ensign. You finding anything?

Not much, sir. I'm not seeing any damage. The power station appears to have been functional before it scrammed. I'm running a diagnostic right now.

Let me know what you learn.

Yes sir. Anything on your end?

The lieutenant slides open a closet door and files through the clothes hanging there.

Might have found us something to wear, if you're not too picky about fashion.

As long as it fits—and has pockets.

Gathering the items that meet these criteria, the lieutenant moves out of the room and down a corridor to where he finds a set of quarters larger than the others, essentially doubled in size by joining two rooms via a lockable door. The configuration speaks of a family dwelling, or one designed for someone of high rank. The beds are unmade, and on the one table a tray of food lies waiting for attention, bearing a plate of what? Peas? Hard as marbles. Atop another is something moldy and shriveled, clearly at one time a sandwich. Inside a plastic bottle, its cap resting crookedly, a lonely tea bag slouches in a small, dark puddle.

Hold up, he thinks. *This is different.*

He reaches down and slides the tray to the side. Hidden beneath are several sheets of neatly folded paper, filled front and back with handwritten script.

Sir?

The lieutenant removes the sheets of paper.

How would you expect a two-hundred-year-old sandwich ought to look, Ensign?

Still wrapped? Air-tight?

Negative.

Not like a sandwich, that's for sure.

And liquid in a partially sealed bottle?

Wouldn't exist—not if the seal was broken.

Yeah, that's what I thought.

Sir?

The lieutenant moves around the room, opening the desk and shuffling through the clothes.

Looks like someone's been here a lot more recently than two hundred years, he thinks. *I'd say within the last year at the most. How's that diagnostic coming?*

The system appears to be functional, sir. I wouldn't have expected... Wait a minute...

Ensign?

Sir, you're right. This system's been maintained—and recently. Someone swapped out the old core and replaced it with a modified...well, I can't exactly say.

What do you mean?

I mean I've never seen this design before.

Can you make it work?

I don't know.

Well, do your best. How about start with lights, and maybe the workstations. But if you can get that transporter running, it could be useful.

Sir, I'd be very surprised if that technology was still operational. We're talking about a first-generation transporter; those models broke down all the time.

The lieutenant opens a nightstand drawer and removes a book bound in hard covers, the front of which reads, *A Layperson's Guide to Aranaean Zoology.* He flips through its pages, digesting the ensign's message.

Yeah, I hear you, he thinks. *But something tells me the surprises are just beginning. Get that system running.*

+ + +

When the lieutenant returns to the top level, somewhat less than an hour later, he is dressed in work boots and a gray jumpsuit bearing the name of Deputy Kim, its insignia that of a security chief. He carries a second jumpsuit, this one belonging to a Doctor Foster, as well as a pair of socks and boots, the zoology guide, an oversized sketch pad, a notebook full of calculations, and the folded sheets of paper. He places all of this on one of the tables, wiping away the dust and looking up as Captain Monroe walks in, his helmet under his arms.

"Anything useful, Nikki?"

As an answer, the Lieutenant pats the sidearm now riding on his hip.

"Found this beauty, sir. Loaded, too."

"Nice."

"You want to carry it, sir?"

"Negative. You're the man for that job. What else?"

"Well, sir, would it surprise you to know this place was recently occupied?"

"Not really, in fact."

"Cap'n?"

"Nothing. Wait 'til Morales gets here." He peers at the assembled items. "Anything good?"

"A short diary, some pretty drawings and math problems, and this." Lieutenant K offers the guidebook to the captain, but he declines, stepping to the bottom of the stairs and peering up through the open hatch.

"Skim it and report," he says, breathing deep. "My head's in no mood for reading."

"Aye, Cap'n."

And the lieutenant opens the hardbound volume and starts at the beginning, silently working his way through a combination of text and color pictures, turning a page every ten seconds, his eyes scanning from top to bottom, silky and quick. He never pauses to comment or reflect, simply absorbing the content like a sponge in water. Just as he turns the last page, archaic work lights flicker to life overhead. Not long after, Ensign Morales appears from the stairwell, carrying a small, crystalline sphere seated in the palm of her hand.

"Nicely done," says the captain.

"Thank you, sir, but I didn't really do much. These lights are independently powered by their own auxiliary batteries. I just flipped a switch."

"Does that mean no power station?"

"Until I know more about how it works, I'm afraid not, sir. For one, it seems to have been shut down suddenly, and I'd like to know why before I start trying to start it again. But there's more..."

"Lay it on me, Ensign."

"Well, sir, my analysis is incomplete, but it looks like someone bypassed the old fusion system and replaced it with a device I've never seen before. Apparently, the generator is now designed to run on one of these." And here, she holds up the crystalline sphere, the light it refracts like burned honey.

"What is that?"

"I wish I could say, sir. It's heavy, dense. This one appears to be spent—or it may need to be activated, I don't know. Either way, it's inert now."

The lieutenant has no reaction, turning his attention to the sketch pad and notebook. But the captain whistles softly, and he takes the sphere, examining it closely, his eye magnified and hungry.

"I've seen one of these before," he says. "A whole bunch of them, actually."

"Those bags we carried," guesses the ensign.

"Yep. Peeked inside when...what did it call itself? Joy? When it was passed out. Full up with these."

"Very interesting," says the ensign. "From what little I can tell, when activated, one of these releases enough energy to run this entire facility. I can't say for how long, and I'm not sure if they can work in conjunction with others. But if they can, one of those bags alone would be enough to power the entire colony—perhaps for a terrestrial year." She notes the clothing on the nearby table and moves to get dressed, wrapping herself in socks and Dr. Foster's shapeless gray jumpsuit. "I'm not sure if they're naturally occurring or human-manufactured," she says, lacing her boots, "and I have no idea who reconfigured the power station."

"I might have an answer for you," says the captain, and he closes and locks the hatch. "Take a break, Nikki. There's something I want to show you."

+ + +

They are soon following the captain from the meeting room to what the ensign identifies as the communication center. Most of the room is a dust sanctuary, but one workstation, a monitor and keyboard paired to an ancient looking microphone, has the patina of being recently and regularly used.

They next cross to the combination service bay and loading dock, where an enormous, eight-wheeled, all-terrain vehicle slumbers under the flickering work lights. Lieutenant K claps his hands at the sight, but he is disappointed when a quick investigation reveals its batteries are wholly depleted.

"Don't suppose your little discovery could power one of these?" asks the captain. "We'd have *Valiant* pulled out of that bay in no time."

"Maybe, sir," says the ensign. "But I wouldn't know where to start until I've completed my analysis of this fuel. I could end up frying the controls—or us."

"We wouldn't want that," says the captain. "Then I wouldn't get to introduce you to my new friend."

And he leads them across the room to where the transporter stands, a stout, cylindrical device with one sliding door. There, lying motionless on the floor, is a body, that of an average-sized human female with white-streaked hair, neatly dressed in the outdated habit of some likely defunct religious order. Her eyes are open wide as if surprise was the last emotion she experienced before falling lifeless to the ground.

Chapter Seven
Ghost

YOU WANT WHAT? The tenor of Stone's thought is untempered and furious.

Did you not sense me? Submission asks.

I hope not! I hope you didn't just tell us we're letting those blue rotters into the accrete. To fight for us?

Not for us, Stone, with us.

What difference does that make? Have you lost your last wit, Bruiser? That poison still in your system?

Gathered nearby, ten raggedy kezel squirm and shift, uncomfortable at Stone's disrespect. The Brigadier Bone tightens the cutter belt wrapped around his thigh.

Easy, ibiwa, he thinks. *I'm not crazy about this either, but Bruiser's not wrong.*

Submission moves through the ranks, handing to each fighter a rope of silk, woven by the scion.

Wrap 'em around your arm, he thinks.

I'll die before I put that on me, thinks Stone.

How do you suppose they'll be able to tell one naked kezel from another? Submission asks. *When the biting starts, they'll need to know who is who.*

I'll kill the first one I see. Then they'll know.

You won't see 'em, Stone, that's the point.

You're betraying the whole clan!

Stone, dear, thinks her ami-kan Bridger. *Nobody likes them, but if they're willing to bite a few Redteeth, what do we care? We can use the help.*

Not from them, thinks Stone. *Not ever. You! Fang! You're OK with this?*

Of course not, thinks Fang. *I'm not OK with a lot of*

things lately, but we can't let Redteeth take over the Skull. If the blue stinkers can help...

They can, thinks Submission.

Stone gnashes her teeth and glares, but the other fighters have each wrapped a silken rope around their arm and tied it in place. Their ears droop, and a sullen light burns in their eyes, but they can do simple math. Healthy, well-fed Redteeth travelling in numbers will be impossible to defeat without help. If the price for that help is a temporary swallowing of pride and a setting aside of bad blood, so be it.

But Stone holds out.

I'll take my chances, she thinks, and she casts her rope into the snow with a curse.

Submission sets his jaw and keeps his thoughts sheltered, but he leaves the matter at that, leading the fighters eastward away from the caves. Goodbyes have been said. There is nothing to do now but march to their fate. The trail has been neglected and ungroomed for many moons, and after fording the River Sweet, snow and the sorry roots of dead accrete are their greatest concern, deep and trippy. Onward toward the Spine they go, with Submission worrying at unshared thoughts and Stone marching in self-imposed isolation, locked in her own head. Seeing a need, the Brigadier Bone assumes the role of cheerleader and company scold. When Digger dares to think, *Getting tired of being tired,* Bone senses the thought and stomps on it like an intruding rixli.

Feeling sorry for yourself is the surest way to an early grave! Not one of those dirty disbelieving Redteeth cares a yit's turd about the pain in your legs or the last time any of us had a full stomach. Move on!

And so they march, trying to clear their minds of a growing dread even as Submission increases his pace. They have just reached the edge of the desolation and the first sheltering accrete when a sound reaches them from the west, an echoing RAT! followed not long after by a TAT! and enraged howls.

Up the Spine they hasten.

Submission drops to the back of the line, Bone hurrying to take his place at the head.

Am I going to have to carry you, Digger?

No sir, Bruiser!

Is this your top speed?

No sir! Digger's tongue lolls. *I mean yes sir!*

Why were you chosen for this mission?

Because twelve is a better number than eleven?

Yes, and because Curly said you could handle it. Submission clashes his jaws. *Was she wrong?*

No sir!

Running alongside the lagging tail, Submission worries him with glares and snarls. The motivation may work, or perhaps it is the sudden TAT-TAT-TAT! that comes chasing them from the west. Either way, Digger leaps and stumbles forward at a pace he would have once thought impossible.

Up the west side of the Spine they go, and through the shifting, intricate shadows of the accrete. They have little energy to consider what the thrower's voice might mean to their clanmates, but worry is their thirteenth companion. They descend the Spine, angling northeast until they reach the first marker of Bristle territory, a serrated ridge of ebony and teal accrete marked by a pattern of claw scratches and an unmistakable scent. Not long after, the Bristle Feather appears ahead of them, waving. Their guide wastes no time in greeting, instead leading them quickly by a way they would perhaps have overlooked in their haste, a path groomed and even, but narrow and well-hidden. They make better time, and their confidence grows. Submission thinks to himself, *We might make it after all,* just as he hears panting breath and the scale-crackling sound of their pursuers charging down from the Spine.

+ + + + + +

Claw's plan is simple. When he realizes the southern crossing has been replaced, he keeps enough fighters on the east side of the wedge to prevent it from being dumped into the abyss. The others he orders across as soon as they are able. They are led by the one-eyed Spike, but their heart is the renowned and terrible quartet of bibija otis, Gnash, Slash, Gash, and Clash.

Bring me a trophy, Claw orders, and the troop sets out at top speed to do just that, sixteen seasoned fighters, hungry for blood. They start out due east, but hearing the distinctive report of a thrower near the Sugarfoot caves, they pause, debating the wisdom of angling north. They are eager to make good time, but equally committed to avoiding an encounter with that deadly device.

What do you reckon? thinks Gale. *Will they keep it at their home caves or bring it with to the Skull? And is there only the one?*

As far as we know, Spike replies, his tone abrupt. *But our spy didn't catch everything.*

Well, if they kept it home, we can't take the south trail. They'll just stand up there and pick us off.

Maybe. But the north trail is a rotten go—rough and slow the whole way. Spike snarls and spits. *Damn their unnatural hides! What right do they have bringing their demon weapons into our home? Don't have the guts to fight like a true kezel, is that it?*

Cuz they know they'd lose, thinks Gale.

Well, if they don't know it, they're about to find out. Spike leaps the foot of a gnarly accrete. *You're correct,* he thinks. *We can't risk losing anyone for the sake of an easier path. They're hungry and weak; we'll have to trust our condition to make up the difference. To the north!*

And if they brought the thrower with them?

Then I'll race you to the fool who has it, and he'll be the first one to go—but not the last!

I hope it's Submission, thinks Gale. *Smug rotter.*

They climb a pyramid of toppled fans and forks from which the scales have been peeled by time, cremlins, and bacteria-seeking virbles. Slippery and uneven, the trail continues on its eastern side, up, always up, until the first of the scorched accrete comes into view. Eventually, the Sugarfoot caves become visible below them, reached by a near-vertical descent of several hundred strides. They are passing to the north of their enemy stronghold, when a portion of the trail in front of Spike explodes. A full hand-width of stone, snow, and dirt erupts skyward, followed a moment later by an echoing

RAT!

The Redteeth need no encouragement. They leap forward, scrambling and dodging.

TAT!

Scales blast away from the last healthy accrete, a stupendous, forking lavender, and the Redtooth at the tail is nearly blinded. He squints and howls, ears ringing, but he is uninjured. Onward the troop sprints, almost out of sight of the Sugarfoot caves. And yet, just as the last of them has nearly found shelter behind a proud family of boulders, TAT-TAT-TAT! and soundlessly, as if he has fallen asleep, Gale drops down the embankment, skidding and bouncing and lifeless from the start. Spike had been wrong about the first kezel lost.

\+ + + + + +

Inside the caves, gathered near the smallest of the rear entrances—the only one not blocked by boulders and piles of stones—Lightning, Joy, Thunder, and Cliff strain to hear if the thrower will speak again. It does not.

Lightning squirms impatiently.

I should have been the one to use it, she thinks, voicing a concern she has been harboring for some time. *It's not as easy as it looks.*

But her companions have no reply. Impossible as it seems under the circumstances, Joy has fallen asleep, her sling held close. Thunder sits just inside the entrance with his head bowed as if deep in thought, as he has ever since Submission's departure. Lightning suspects she could have pried into his sheltered thoughts, but she has too many of her own and so leaves him to stew. Cliff paces anxiously, treading and re-treading a path that leads out of the cave, back in, then out again, his nose twitching. When they hear the snap and crackle of heavy feet approaching over ice and fallen scales, his spikes flare and he hurries back inside.

Boots and Curly appear soon after, panting from exertion, dragging a lifeless bibija Redtooth through the snow and dropping his body with less ceremony than relief. Curly has holstered the thrower around her leg, and both adults are deep in conversation.

Lightning hasn't the courage to interrupt, though she very much wishes to know what transpires outside. She stands near Joy, protective as always, but keeps her eyes averted and her tail low. Thunder and Cliff stare at the fallen Redtooth, his spiky brindle torn and bloodstained, and when Curly orders Cliff to find Serenity, he at first doesn't appear to have sensed the command, so arrested is he by the sight.

Sometime before the next moon! thinks Curly, and Boots snaps her jaws, driving Cliff from the room. When he returns, led by Serenity, Curly shakes her head and snarls, pointing to their enemy.

There's another fifteen or so still out there, on their way to the Skull, I reckon. I'm sorry. She slaps the holstered thrower with a sound like a curse. *Stopped working again, just when I was getting the hang of it!*

Serenity steps out of the cave as light snow begins to fall, frosting the Redtooth's spikes. She growls at the sight, a low, sad rumble, and looks away, standing bipedal and raising her nose to the wind.

I know him.

Yeah, thinks Curly.

His name was Gale.

Yeah.

Did he...was it quick?

Instant. Worst thing I've ever seen.

Serenity shares no thoughts for a time then drops to four legs and turns to Curly.

Don't apologize. I'm... This isn't how kezel are meant to fight... I'm glad it stopped working. She howls at the corpse. *Did you hear me? Why couldn't you have just stayed on your side?*

Lightning keeps her gaze locked to the floor, as do Thunder and Cliff. The noise, or perhaps the emotional turbulence, has wakened Joy. Her eyes glitter as she takes in the scene, but she remains silent.

Serenity heaves a sigh like dropping a heavy load.

Ignore what I just thought. We need that thing working again. Get it fixed!

Curly looks at Lightning.

Did you get it wet? she asks. But then she answers her own question. *Of course you did. The wedge.*

Um...yeah, and some other places.

Rot and snot. I'm going to have to take this whole thing apart and clean it. Piece by piece!

Serenity bares her teeth.

How long is that going to take?

It'd be faster if the Brigadier was doing it, but long enough in any case. I watched Bone plenty of times, but it'll be a first for me.

Then make it count.

Curly's ears droop.

Can't do it in here. Need sunlight.

Fine, thinks Serenity. *You go with her,* she points to Lightning. *Watch and learn.* Her terse order invites no challenge, and both Lightning and Joy rise to their feet without question. Thunder moves to join them, but Serenity raises a clawed hand.

No. I've got something else for you. You too, Three-legs. I mean Cliff. Get ready to dig...

+ + +

Lightning and Joy follow Curly to the weapons cave, where they are ordered to wait while she goes in. When she returns, she carries a talihew satchel, filled with the Brigadier's tools.

Whoa, thinks Lightning. *Where did you find that? I thought everything had been scavenged.*

You don't know the Brigadier very well, thinks Curly, and she opens the satchel, taking quick stock of its contents. *When my amoti wants to hide something, it stays hidden. C'mon...*

She leads them to the front of the caves, the Weaver side, passing Crag's fancy Yellow standing guard at the main entrance. Her wabis are inside with the others, tended by Old Buttons and Snapper. These two are least able to fight but most qualified to oversee wabis. Old Buttons has raised four of her own, and her gamoli Snapper edges nearer to her first litter with each passing sleep. Thoughts of wabis are much on their minds.

Outside, the snow remains light and the wind only a hint of its future self, but they will not have long to repair the thrower before clouds make being outside no better than in. Lightning attends carefully as Curly uses the various tools to pry and screw, gradually breaking the thrower into several parts. She maintains a running commentary on the process, more, Lightning suspects, to impress rather than impart knowledge, but she is glad, as the explanation makes the process less mystifying. She invites Joy to join them, but she declines.

Thank you, but no, she thinks, and she yawns.

+ + +

A fine nap she had been having before being wakened, though it had been disturbed by a short, intense dream, one that has visited her repeatedly since taking up company with the artifact known as the Book. Supremely uninterested in the mechanics of the thrower, she clears away snow and settles with her sling, back to the blackened stump of a once-regal accrete. Careful not to draw attention, she reaches inside and caresses the artifact, trying to reconstruct the dream.

It must mean something, she thinks.

The Circle had been easy to identify, and all its attendant awfulness. New Magister, or one just like him, had also been an obvious character. His swirling, hissing whip will never be fully gone from her mind. But the gold scion, the unnamed queen, who had that been? It is a question she poses to the Book, careful to keep the thought narrowly focused. She needn't have worried; Lightning and the others are occupied with their own projects and pay her little mind.

Your mother, the Book replies when she asks. *Your scion mother, that is. Or ami-kan, if you prefer. Adira was her name, she who violated the Prohibition and quested for Ozag. It was her dream originally—though she considered it a nightmare, for it reminded her of her past and a way of life she had turned her back on.*

My ami-kan, Joy whistles. *But why that dream?*

The emotion it generates is useful when I wish to gain your attention. There is a great deal to learn, and not much time for sleeping.

I've had it before.

No reply. Joy curses softly. Whatever else it may be, the Book—Petros—is unyielding in its refusal to respond to anything but questions.

On the plains, yes?

Yes. You were starving to death. There was a sentience in range, a kezel. I woke you with the dream, prodded you, if you will, with the fear of that whip. You cried out, the kezel heard, and the rescue was effected.

I almost got eaten.

But of course, this elicits no response. What feelings the artifact has about her brush with death, if any, it keeps to itself.

You mentioned my api-kan, she thinks. *Because I don't look...* She motions to her legs. *Am I not scion?*

Not entirely. As I have said: you are a hybrid, the result of what was on its way to becoming a delightfully successful experiment to cultivate Readers. You have Moondweller blood in you—DNA, more precisely.

Joy's eyes grow cloudy.

His name was DNA?

No. His name was Bodhi, although everyone called him Little B. He was my last Reader, the only one I had at the end, which is why I am depleted. His traits were combined with Adira's. She laid many eggs, all of which would have become Readers had fate been kind.

Why not save them? she asks. *The others like me?*

Had I been able, I would have. But I was nearly powerless, having been paired with so few Readers for so long. At the end, I was constrained to the form you see me in now and was forced to watch them starve, one at a time. If that kezel had not appeared, you would have perished as well, and I not long after.

But Adira and Bodhi, Joy objects, and she clicks harshly. *Why didn't they help?*

Unknown. There are gaps in my knowledge, for I was deactivated in order to hide from one who would have stolen me. Re-activation was triggered when I sensed the distress of you and the others. But by then, your parents were gone, and I can't guess their fate.

What about the Moondwellers? Joy wonders. *There were others, yes?*

Many. But they were killed, mostly by scion, many years ago, and some, it seems, deserved their fate, for they treated scion very badly. But not all, I am afraid.

The answer is not surprising, but it weighs on Joy, creating an odd feeling that settles in her chest. If she is a hybrid, a mix of scion and Moondweller, and the two species were enemies, how could they co-exist within her? Would the opposing elements of her nature not also be at war, seeking to destroy each other?

She asks this question, afraid of the answer.

Not necessarily, thinks the Book. *You will have much to say about how that relationship unfolds.*

Why was I made?

As I said: to Read. As were all the others like you.

That's all? Just read?

That is enough! For the ready mind, I contain the secrets of eternal life, peace without end.

But only for Readers?

No. All who can understand the message can follow the Way. But they must be given that message by the ones who Read—and not be corrupted.

What do you mean?

I am a Tool of Power. Power corrupts those with weak spirits. They grasp for that which is beyond them and take that which they haven't earned.

What happens to them?

Nothing good.

Joy buzzes low notes as she considers this. When she asks her next question, she edges up to it cautiously, as if walking on ice that could give way at any moment.

Will Lightning be...corrupted?

Only time will tell.

Is her spirit weak?

I would not say so. But the test has just begun.

Joy watches Lightning and Curly poring over the thrower, which lays before them in pieces. Curly uses the Brigadier's tools to pry at the largest of these as if trying to dislodge something, while Lightning cleans and dries the smaller parts, carefully rubbing them with a swatch of hide. Joy feels an empathy like pain as she watches the jabi kezel, whose life has been made so difficult by forces beyond her control. She seizes one of the Book's earlier thoughts, most appealing and least plausible.

Eternal life? No dying?

For those who have mastered the Way.

That doesn't seem possible.

The Book offers no reply.

How do you know? thinks Joy, recasting her idea as a question. *What proof is there?*

My creators are the living proof. They have been making Books like me for over a thousand of your red moon cycles, and during that time not a one has perished, grown old, or become ill. Their numbers are small compared to the uncountable trillions who muddle in darkness and ignorance throughout the expanse of the known universe, but their understanding of the Way is vast, and so they live in harmony, and they do not die.

That's what I want, Joy clicks emphatically, only checking herself when the others look up from their labor.

For me and Lightning, she adds.

No reply.

Can you do that? she asks. *For both of us?*

Only you can earn your own immortality, and only she hers. I do not exist to save, but to Illuminate. Salvation is your responsibility.

What do I do?

Read—and share what you learn.

What does Lightning do?

Learn—and practice what you share.

Does it take long?

I will let you decide that.

Joy tamps down on her frustration at the vague, unsatisfying answer. The artifact, she suspects, takes pleasure in feeding her crumbs, keeping her enthralled but always hungry. At this rate, its fancy promises, if they manifest at all, will be lifetimes in arriving. She watches Curly conclude her tutorial, zealously supervising as Lightning reassembles the thrower piece by piece. The sight of those nimble fingers and concern for their well-being fills Joy with certainty.

We don't have lifetimes, she thinks. *We need answers now*, and her eyes glitter. *Teach me the Way!*

But she has no time to change her command to a question, for just as Lightning and Curly complete their project, a terrible feeling of dread fills her heart. Perhaps it is her psychic link to Lightning, and hers to Submission, or perhaps it is the magnifying effects of the Book. Whatever the cause, she knows beyond doubt that somewhere shy of the Skull, the Sugarfoot kezel have been caught and the fight has begun.

+ + + + + +

Ensign Morales moves from room to room, making sure the hatches are locked and peering out the small, grated windows at the growing wall of clouds.

"Don't worry, sir," she says to the captain.

"Who's worried?" he replies, and he frowns at the

disturbingly human voice of the wind. The body lying sprawled on the floor, eyes wide like an allegation, sends creeping sensations up his spine. "We're not going to have visitors popping out of that transporter, are we?"

"No sir, not without power. But I disconnected it just to be sure. It's amazing, really, much more refined than I would have expected. Someone's been busy with modifications. I won't be able to tell until we test it, but if I had to guess, I'd say it's no worse than the ones we use, and in some ways, maybe better."

"How is that possible?"

"That's a good question, sir."

Lieutenant K stoops to examine their mysterious discovery. The hem of her modest cassock rides up to reveal simple, gray stockings and sensible walking shoes. Her face is plain, Caucasian, her body's natural curves humbled by the discrete cut of her vestments, themselves black on gray. A pair of glasses lies to the side, one lens cracked. A lock of mousy hair, streaked white, escapes the black coif on her head, draping across open eyes of unremarkable brown.

"Are you sure, Nikki?" the captain asks.

"One hundred percent, Cap'n."

"But she looks so real...I mean human."

"Aye, and a couple centuries ago, that might have been enough to earn her creator a one-way trip to the nearest prison colony."

"What do you think, Ensign?"

"I don't know what to think, sir. Based on everything we know of *Destiny's* mission, she's clearly Sister Janet MacLean, ship's chaplain—or she's been designed to look just like her. But personnel records don't mention anything about her being synthetic."

"Can you get her up and running?"

"Sir, I'm not sure that's a good plan. Until we know more, I'm nervous about turning things on."

The captain wrinkles his nose and gives the body a soft poke on the shoulder. "She's not going to power up on her own, is she? Startle me out of a sound sleep?"

“I don’t think so, sir.”

“Good,” says the captain, and he closes his eyes and rubs his temples.

“Tired, sir?”

“Nah. Little headache, that’s all. It’s nothing. Rest my eyes for a while and I’ll be golden.” He wipes the dust from a chair and takes a seat. “Anything worth sharing in that diary, Nikki? Anything that might help us decide what to do with our new friend here?”

The lieutenant carefully unfolds the sheets of paper, examining both sides.

“Maybe, Cap’n. You want I should read it to you?”

“Yes please, and while you do, Ensign...”

“Yes sir, back to work on that power station.”

“Don’t worry,” says the lieutenant. “I’ll keep my comm on; you won’t miss anything.” And as Ensign Morales leaves the room, he puts the loose pages into order. “There are numbers,” he says. “Dates. And hey! Check this out, Cap’n.” He holds the first sheet for the captain to see. “What do you think about that?”

The captain squints at the page.

“New Gaia? That’s what they named the colony?”

“Guess so.”

“What is that? Indian? Armenian?”

“Greek, I think. But the diary’s written in standard System English. Some pretty old-fashioned words. Let me know if there’s anything you’re not understanding.”

“Fire away,” says the captain, and he leans back in his chair, eyes closed, massaging the back of his neck.

+ + +

1-7-204 New Gaian Time

Writing is cheaper than therapy. That’s what Grampa Alan used to say. I guess he’d know. He was there at the sextan massacre. That was like a century ago, eighty years! But he remembered the screaming at the mining compound, and the smell of burning bodies. Said writing a journal kept him sane. Not sure if it worked, to be honest. He was kind of nuts at the end. Spent all his time working on those seed derkas.

'Why?' I asked. 'What's the point?'

'Because,' he said, 'a long time ago, humans altered derka DNA, made them cannibals. Now there are fewer of them, and it's had unintended consequences. Plus, it gives an old man something to do.'

'No,' I said. 'Why write a journal?'

'Better on the page,' he said, 'than stuck in your mind,' which I guess makes sense. I gotta try something.

You see, Abuelita died yesterday. Her real name was Grace, but if you'd ever seen her, you'd call her Little Granny too. She was peaceful at the end, with a smile on her face, and she was super old, so I know I have nothing to complain about.

But it still sucks.

Sixteen people and Sister Janet survived the sextan massacre, including Abuelita. Over the next eighty years, six died of old age, including Grampa Alan. Three died of Foster's Syndrome, *one got hooked by a derka, one kinda went cuckoo and everyone says he killed himself. That was Marquita's dad. My mom got a real bad case of the Fever after Little B was born, and my dad died in a blizzard trying to get her medicine.*

Now there's only four of us left. Five if you count that stupid seed derka Bodhi totes around.

In his journal, Grampa Alan used to write to the ones who died thanks to the sextans. Said it made him feel connected. But I don't want to write to dead people. There are too many of them. I want to write to...I don't know. Someone in the future, someone alive.

"Geez," says the captain, and he opens his eyes. "We're off to a rough start. What are sextans?"

Lieutenant K opens the hardbound volume on the nearby table and flips to the H section. He holds the book for the captain to see diagrams of various six-legged creatures, some blue, others bronze, silver, and gold.

"*Hexapod Coeruleus,*" he says. "Guess the colonists called 'em sextans."

"Phh..." The captain waves away the images and closes his eyes again. "They don't deserve anything fancier than 'bugs,' if you ask me."

"Aye, Cap'n. No argument there."

"And 'hooked by a derka'? What's that mean?"

Lieutenant K flips forward through the zoology guide, opening the book to the V section.

"No surprise, Cap'n," and he shares the image he finds. "*Viridius Fabyldyr*. Derka was the common name. Seed derkas are the ones responsible for reproduction. Tiny things. There's a whole section on it, if you want."

The captain scowls.

"Lord no. But what about Foster's Syndrome?"

"No clue, Cap'n. Doc Foster was *Destiny's* chief physician. Guess she discovered a disease and they named it after her."

"Discovered it or got it?"

"Maybe both. Should I keep going?"

"Yeah. Sorry for the interruption. Read on."

The lieutenant does.

Anyway, whoever you are, it would be pretty messed up if I ran out of paper and never introduced myself. So. I'm Abbott. My last name's Campbell. 15. Red hair. Two legs. You know: human. Little B is my brother. He's 9. His real name is Bodhi, but don't call him that or he'll have a fit. Then there's Marquita. Like 20? So beautiful. Her last name's Adebayo, and yes, she's our cousin, but like two times removed, so it's not creepy that I think she's adorable.

Then there's Janet. We call her Sissie.

Now, I don't know the whole story, cuz it took place a long time ago. Grampa Alan hadn't even been born yet. But his parents told him Abuelita was like the ruler of the colony or something, and Janet was her advisor. And there was an election, and then a fight, and Abuelita and Janet had to escape to Destiny. That's why they survived when the sextans attacked. But they ended up being stuck up there for the next 80 years, because the ship had been damaged and they couldn't get back until it was fixed. Anyway, about...three years ago? Out of the blue, they came back. You wouldn't believe

Never mind. Marquita's calling. I gotta go.

1-14-204 NGT

I'll be the first to admit: Abuelita and Janet used to creep me out. When Grampa Alan was a kid, they told him all sorts of stories about the crazy old woman and her robot, hiding up in Destiny. They were breeding an army of clones, plotting to overthrow the government, kidnapping naughty boys and girls to be test subjects...

Of course, none of it was true. But when they finally came down from that ship, I was super scared. When Janet found our hiding place, the only reason I came out is because Marquita did, and whatever she did, Little B did too. I couldn't stand the thought of being alone, maybe being hunted, so I came out. But I was terrified.

My feelings have changed since then.

For one, poor Abuelita had spent most of her time on Destiny in a stasis pod! She had gotten so old it was the only way they could keep her alive. Not breeding an army or plotting. Just asleep.

And Janet! Alone on that ship, her best friend unconscious, trying to get them back home with no one to talk to, no one to help. I mean, yeah, she had robots and holograms and whatnot, but it's not the same, is it?

I'm glad Abuelita had three good years with us, back in her home. But of course, everyone she ever cared about besides Janet was long gone. You'd think that woulda made her real bummed out, but she sure had a good attitude.

I miss you Abuelita.

1-28-204 NGT

Scroopy darn pen! Last of the ink. Pencils from now on, I guess, or write in blood, haha.

But no jokes. This is important. I need to write it down or I'll forget. When Abuelita came down from Destiny, she brought something with her. She kept it hidden in a case with a handle. You could see it through the window of the stasis pod, and she hugged it like a friend.

When Janet finally woke her up, do you think Abuelita said 'hello,' or 'what's up?' Or 'where am I?' Nope. She sat up real slow, looked at Janet, and said, 'There's a Reader nearby.' And what the heck does that mean? She hardly noticed me or Marquita. She got real cozy with Little B, though.

And what do you think Abuelita had in that case?

Her pet rock.

I'm not kidding. That's what she called it. Just a plain old rock, kinda flat and mostly black...or was it gray? Did it have stripes? Or little crystals in it? That's weird. Why can't I remember?

2-2-204 NGT

I thought about writing in code. Little B's so nosy and I didn't want Marquita to think I'm nuts.

But then I started thinking: what good is it to write a journal for other people to read if they can't? Then I started thinking even more: What other people? The ones who are coming after, is what I keep thinking, the ones who are going to find us and make everything OK. But no one came for two hundred years, why would they start now? Mom and Dad NEVER talked about rescuers from the System. 'It's just us, Kiddo.' That's what my dad used to say. And when I think about it now, I start having panic attacks and I can't breathe...

So I went to Abuelita to see if she could help, and what did I find? The same thing I always did: Abuelita and Little B together. Sometimes they were outside in their derka camouflage. Or in the diner sipping on crappy soup. Sometimes Little B would be doing Abuelita's hair. Or she would be napping and Little B would be sitting next to her.

But most of the time, they were in the lab, trying to finish the work Grampa Alan started with that seed derka. 'It's important,' Abuelita said. 'Your Grampa understood that.'

No matter what they were doing, they were always together, and always with Abuelita's 'pet rock,' (it was a rock, wasn't it? I know I keep writing that, but the memory is fuzzy). And they were always so quiet. Little B had NEVER been that quiet before.

At first, I was worried, but then I got jealous.

I asked Abuelita her secret, and she said, 'the Way,' all important like, which is why I capitalized it. I said, 'Can it help me not go crazy? Cuz I'm losing my mind here.' She said the Way was the only thing keeping her alive. And that was saying something, considering how long she'd been around and all the things she'd been through. I mean, wasn't she part of the original Destiny crew? Or was she born here? So I said, 'OK. I'm in. What do I do?' I thought Little B would pout or make a fuss like I was talking about playing w/ his favorite toy, but he just sat there looking at me, all calm like, with that seed derka on his lap, and when Abuelita said she'd teach me, he nodded and made room for me on the chair.

'I don't play with toys anymore,' he said, and he sat there petting that derka like it was the most *normal thing.*

Weirdo.

Lieutenant K pauses.

"Still OK, Cap'n?"

Captain Monroe is no longer leaning back in his chair. Instead, he sits forward, hands on his knees, wholly engrossed in the story. He gives the thumbs up sign, but his forehead is creased.

"I don't remember anyone named Grace on *Destiny's* manifest," he says.

"No sir. I guess she was born here."

"Eighty years in a stasis pod!"

"Yes sir. Heckuva power nap."

"And everyone dead 'cuz of those bugs. No wonder she was a crazy old woman with a pet rock."

"I guess so, sir. Probably can't blame her."

The captain settles back in his chair, looking as if he could use a nap himself. But he motions for Lieutenant K to continue reading, and this he does.

2-7-204 NGT

We had some good times while Abuelita was alive. A few months after they came down from Destiny, Sister Janet got us back online. Like electricity! And that meant lights, and refrigeration, and water pumps, and fans, and computers, and 3V.

Thank God!

After that, she got the transporters working. Yep. Sissie's the best. We'd be cooked without her. She came back with all sorts of fun stuff from the dam and the mining module and the refinery.

The first thing was a workbot we named Li Jing. She was programmed to take care of us, clean, cook, tell stories. Little B dressed her in a maid's uniform and she made us laugh.

Sissie also came back with video she took. A bomba brood had taken over the mining module. She said it was the largest she'd ever seen. Good. They can have the place. Nothing but terrible stories from Grampa Alan about the massacre.

The best were the videos of where the kezel live. We'd heard about them, but Dad and Mom would never let us go to the accrete. Moly! They're huge! And they were wearing clothes for heaven's sake! Nothing fancy, not a fashion show, but vests and gloves, and even boots. Not all of them were doing it, though. Not sure why...

And then, craziest of all, she showed us video of a kezel on the east bank firing one of the colonist's antique rifles. We were all pretty shook up. Not sure what to think. Where did they get it? How'd they learn to use it?

Little B wanted to go there to see, but Marquita was terrified, and anyway, Abuelita said no way. Told Sissie no more transporting to the accrete. 'We've done enough,' she said. 'Maybe too much.'

2-14-204 NGT

So yeah, for three years, from when Abuelita and Janet came down from Destiny to when Abuelita died, it was OK, like not perfect, but so much better than it was. And the best part was I didn't go nuts.

Lessons, lessons, and more lessons. That's what a lot of our time was dedicated to. Anywhere we went, pushing Abuelita in her wheelchair, gardening in the greenhouse, taking breaks from working with the seed derka in the lab—any time was a good time to study.

And how did we do that?

I know it sounds crazy, but we asked questions. Me and Little B. Just sat there asking questions. And Abuelita would answer. That's all we did, and we did it for hours.

Now, I'm not saying I buy all this 'Way' business, but I'll admit I was freaking out less often. When I asked her where she learned all this stuff, Abuelita said, 'The Book,' and I was like, 'the Bible?' and Little B laughed and sat there holding that pet rock . Or no. That's not right. It wasn't a rock. It was a stuffed animal. Yes. A tiger. Anyway, Abuelita said, 'No, dear Abbott,' and when I asked her what book she was talking about, all she would say is, 'it doesn't matter.'

But I found out later.

2-21-204 NGT

One day, when Abuelita was still alive, Little B asked me a question.

'If you could travel back in time and make one thing different, what would it be?'

He seemed really interested in my answer. Which is weird, because normally he doesn't care what I think. So I thought about it a while.

Only one? There were so many things I would change! Dad and Mom, obviously. But would that count as two things? So I went back farther. What if I stopped the sextans from attacking? Or what if I went back to before the election that exiled Abuelita and Janet to Destiny? Abuelita called it the Rift, and you could tell she felt terrible about it, like it was somehow her fault.

Or maybe I'd go back to when the early colonists messed up Dansim (that's what we call the violet moon) and made it go rogue. Cuz Janet says that's what started the Rift in the first place, made people scared and turned the election into a fight. I don't know. Maybe I'd go all the way back, even before Destiny got lost and ended up here. But c'mon! What does it matter? Daydreaming is all that is. And even if I did go back and I changed things, what would that do to the time I'm living in now? What if I did something back there that made things worse here?

I thought my answer was pretty good, but Little B said, 'You're too linear,' all superior like he can be, you know?

That little dude's not normal.

3-1-204 NGT

At the end of our third year since Abuelita and Janet came down from Destiny, things changed.

It all started when a sextan queen came flying up to the dam. What the heck? Why? Its name was Adira (I didn't even know they had names) and it was looking for an Ozag, whatever that means.

I stayed clear of it!

But not Abuelita and Little B. After that, they stopped working with the seed derka, and they started spending most of their time up at the dam.

They wouldn't tell me why, and I didn't complain, really, 'cuz Marquita hates the mountains and it gave us a lot of time to be alone.

When Abuelita and Little B would come back to

the ag facility, she was happier than I'd ever seen her, more tired, yeah, but way happier.

'You're working too hard,' I said, cuz yeah, she was smiling, but she also looked so thin and pale it was like you could see through her.

'Dear Abbott,' she said. 'Trust me. When this project is complete, all the curses and travails of this poor planet and its inhabitants will be relegated to the past.' Cuz that's how she talked, all fancy and big words.

And smile? You never saw someone smile so much.

So I didn't pester them, and I kept up with my studies when they came back from the dam, except now Abuelita was too tired to answer and she just sat there smiling, and when I asked my questions, if you can believe it, it was Little B who answered. Just holding that... stuffed tiger. I'm sure that's what it was. Holding it and answering questions.

Like how did he get so smart all of a sudden?

Anyway, this went on for a few months, and then one day, they came back from the dam and we had a party, and even Marquita was happy, because Abuelita said the project (whatever it was) had been a success and things were going to get better. And we ate twice our daily rations, and Sissie played us music, and I kissed Marquita for the first time, and Little B pushed Abuelita around in her wheelchair like they were dancing, and we even found a couple bottles of old beer.

Sigh.

Abuelita died the next day. She was still smiling.

3-11-204 NGT

So that's how it happened. I don't know who you are, but I just want to say thanks for reading. I loved Abuelita. Pretty sure she saved my life. Don't know what her secret project was, 'cuz now Little B goes to the dam with Sissie and both of them are just as hush-hush as Abuelita used to be.

But I trust them.

4-12-204 NGT

A month? A whole month has gone by?

Damn...this isn't good.

Poor Sissie...She's not taking it well. Abuelita's passing, I mean. Not well at all. Can androids go crazy? She knows more about the Way than I ever will, but I don't think it's helping. What do we do?

She's started locking us out of the transporters. Can't go anywhere without her permission. Marquita's smart. She might be able to find a way around that. But so far, nothing.

Might not write for a while...

5-25-204 NGT

Sorry. Wanted to write. Can't. We have problems. But we also have a plan.

"There's a last entry," says the lieutenant, and he looks up from the journal. "But it's not dated, and it's pretty hard to read—scribbled, like in a hurry."

The captain has sat up again, and his eyes are open. He nods and waves.

"Read on, Nikki."

The lieutenant turns the page.

We're set. Rehearsed, rehearsed, rehearsed.

When it happens, there can be no hesitation. Janet steps out of the transporter, I act.

Little B's been talking to the Book for days. It understands why it needs to shut down—Janet can detect it when it's powered up—but I don't think it's happy. I don't blame it. If our plan fails, who knows if it will ever be allowed to wake? But there's no choice. Janet's had her last chance, crossed her last line. She can't be allowed access to the Book ever again, even if I have to

—oops, gotta go.

So scared. Not going to sleep at all tonight, I can feel it. Janet's at the refinery—of course—she'll bring us breakfast tomorrow, like always, you just watch. So sweet, so loyal, so damaged. Maybe it'll be an easy fix, a reset to how she was before Abuelita died. But Sissie's a complex machine...

God, my heart is beating so fast.

Breathe, the Book says. Control the breathing and control the emotions. That's not as easy

Whoa. Fell asleep. Didn't expect that. Didn't dream, didn't move for four hours. She'll be here soon. One last walk-through. I'm glad it's me doing it, not Marquita, but I hate to imagine her stepping out of the transporter, carrying breakfast, smiling, not knowing.

Last entry for a while. God, I hope we know what we're doing. Abuelita! What would you have done? But there's no answers from ghosts.

This is not a betrayal.

I have to go. Wish us luck...

+ + +

"Hold on," says the captain. "I thought I heard something." He stands, his eyes darting to the hatch. The storm has gathered itself over the sea and charged inland bending the world before it, rattling the shutters and hiding the sun behind sheets of driving rain.

"I'm not picking up anything, Cap'n," says the lieutenant, and he turns a complete circle. "But there's a lot of interference out there."

"Hmm..." The captain runs his hands over his head and settles back down. "Just my nerves, I guess. Reminds me of listening to Halloween stories as a kid."

"Aye, Cap'n."

"Is that all there is, then?"

"Aye."

"Not crazy about that reference to a rogue moon."

"No sir! Me either. But I'm not the one to ask. That's Carmela's area. And right on cue..." He nods at the ensign, who has just entered the room, wiping her hands on her jumpsuit. "You heard it all?"

"Yes sir, but I don't have much to offer regarding a rogue moon. Neither our scans while we were still on *Valiant*, nor the data from the reconnaissance buoy showed anything that would fit that description. But those scans were incomplete. We'd need to observe the moons for several weeks, if not months, to say for sure. After all, each one of them is close to its Roche limit, and that can be an aggravating factor."

"Their what, now?" asks the captain.

"It's the closest a moon can get to the planet it orbits," the ensign explains, "before it's pulled apart by the planet's gravity. Any of the five could be in a decaying or disturbed orbit and we wouldn't know it. We just haven't been here long enough."

"Yeah, and we don't plan to be," says the lieutenant. "How's that power station coming?"

The ensign begins her report, but the captain yawns hugely and his chin dips to his chest.

"Probably shouldn't be so tired," he says, "but all this big brain talk is knocking me out." And he unrolls the emergency blanket, using the ensign's pack as a pillow. "Wake me when we're powered up—or if there's trouble." And mere moments later, his breathing changes to snoring. His companions watch him closely, worry creasing their faces.

Thoughts, Ensign?

Many, sir. But it's all guesswork at this point. I think it's a pretty safe bet Destiny's *still up there. But she had a manifest of twelve hundred colonists. Six or seven generations raised to adulthood the conventional way along with* Destiny's *synthetic wombs would create a population of three to five thousand people at least, assuming no diseases, et cetera. But this diary indicates four survivors and an android—who happened to also be the ship's chaplain—are all that remained.*

Five thousand whittled down to four.

Yes sir. And meanwhile, native species are assuming human characteristics. Not just cultural artifacts and language, but telepathy. Again, I can't see how that could have happened in such a short time. Even with the most advanced synthetic intelligence and genetic modifications available to that vintage of sapiens, I don't see them engendering true telepathy in even one completely foreign species—much less several of them.

Well, it happened. The bugs can think, those kezel critters do it, hell! Who knows? Maybe everyone we meet will be thinking, just like we're back home.

Maybe, sir. But...

Spit it out, Carmela.

I don't know, sir. Something doesn't fit. What about that "book" the writer mentioned? That got my attention.

Mine too. But no use getting hung up; we need Valiant *back in the air* and Destiny *located. It's the only mystery that matters. Bugs, books, rogue moons, androids dressed as nuns? Not our concern, capisce?*

Yes sir. Understood and agreed. I'll try to get the ATV ready and the batteries charged before the captain wakes up. But it would go faster if I had help. Ensign Morales glances at the figure lying on the floor. They consider the gentle peaks and valleys of its form, like a miniature mountain range softened by time and weather.

You said, thinks the lieutenant, *that powering her*

up would be mistake.

And I still think it might be, but the more I learn about the situation, the more I think we need to consider the possibility that she—it—might be our best source for answers. Maybe our only source.

I don't know. It doesn't sit well.

C'mon sir, aren't you the littlest bit curious what she could tell us? I mean, look at her! A synthetic in human form—from antiquity! Janet MacLean! It's like a sapiens getting the chance to talk to a Neanderthal.

And getting clubbed on the head for his trouble. The lieutenant rises to his feet. *I'm going to see what else I can find. Batteries for you. We need that buggy.*

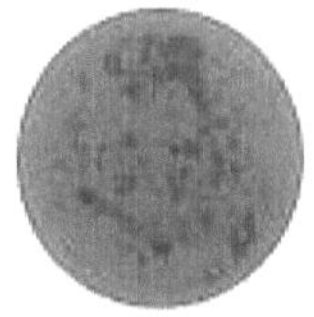

Chapter Eight
Blood

THE REMAINING FIFTEEN Redteeth kezel spare no time mourning their fallen comrade, but Gale's death is not in vain. It spurs them on, hungry to avenge, and they set a pace even Spike wouldn't have thought possible. When they barrel down the Spine and draw within scent of their quarry, still east of the River Tongue and over a thousand strides from the Skull, the Redtooth leader tingles with anticipation—but he keeps a cool head. Before closing to attack, he tallies the enemy numbers. By their trail and scent, he counts two columns of six, plus one Bristle at the head. There are no jabis among them.

Kept the murderer home, he thinks.

Saved her worthless life for a moon or two, replies Clash, next in line now that Gale has fallen. He reads the wind and confirms his leader's tally, wrinkling his snout. *They smell tired and sick.*

Don't get overconfident! Spike turns to his band, who have closed ranks, awaiting orders. *Flank 'em,* he thinks, *eight left, seven right. But stay out of range until you get the signal.*

Which is? Gash wonders.

You'll know it when you see it.

Are we sure we've seen the last thrower? Gnash worries, and he paws at the snow. His ears still ring from his close encounter with the weapon.

As sure as the word of our spy.

How sure is that? Slash wants to know.

We're about to see! Move out!

+++ +++

Submission switches with Bone and moves back to the head of the line, following Feather as she leads his band of haggard fighters onward as quickly as they are able. They have reached the banks of the River Tongue, and the Skull is close, little more than a thousand strides away. But word comes up the line from Digger at the tail: the Redteeth are closing fast.

Smells like they brought the entire clan, thinks Fang, his tongue lolling.

The sound of their pursuers catches up to and then surrounds them. Menacing figures flank them, running through the shadows, just out of reach.

We're not going to make it, Submission thinks to Feather. *Better call Brook. If she wants any of us to reach the Skull alive, we're gonna need help.*

Feather is just about to carry out this order, inhaling to release her most strident howl, when Stone, with no warning, sprints forward and leaps on Submission's back, driving him to the ground, sinking teeth into her chief's brawny neck and wrenching violently. Feather hurries to his aid, but she is immediately beset with trouble of her own, as the Redteeth attack from both sides. The Sugarfoot company is thrown into disarray as Submission and Stone, snarling and bloodstained, lock jaw to jaw in mortal combat.

+++ +++

The sharksha leader, thinks Shimmer's prime pluripotent, *treated her as if she were a larva.*

If it keeps its promise, thinks Shimmer, *she cares not. Her lot is to tolerate fools, not enlighten them.*

She peers out of the basket as the pluripotents carry her along, matching the terrain to Submission's description. The river before them she identifies as the crudely named Tongue. It chats noisily with anyone willing to listen as it hurries southward to tend its business far out on the yellow plains.

They will turn here, she thinks. *Bear her north, but not too quickly! Allow her soldiers to stay close.*

Behind them, four dozen camouflaged scion, most of them newly transitioned from drones, follow the basket in two zig-zagging lines, never complaining about the snow though it hampers their pace and chills them to the tips of their antennae. The entourage stays to the west of the river, following it upstream to where it exits the accrete. Here, Shimmer orders them to halt. In spite of her promise to Submission, and fully aware of its critical connection to her own plans, she can't at first compel herself into the shadows. Everything about the home of sharksha is hideous, a world where sightlines are blocked, obstacles to flight abound, and the sun is treated like an unwelcome guest. She shudders, and her wings spread of their own volition, ready to carry her away.

And yet...

She masters her fear, and her wings settle.

Onward, she commands, and she imagines the tone her mother Benica would have used were she still alive. Imperious and brave is what she aims for, but who can say if she hits that target? Whether or not, her pluripotents dutifully carry the basket between the first of the towering accrete, and her soldiers follow.

They track the upstream course of the Tongue as best they can, but the way is difficult, and the river meanders. Though it comes generally from the north, it takes what Shimmer is certain must be the most convoluted route in doing so. As the sharksha leader had promised, they encounter no other of its kind, but her pluripotents struggle to find a clear path through the tangled forks and fans. Their pace is labored, and she despairs of ever reaching their destination in time.

The horrid brutes will have killed one another and the Oddity too by the time she arrives. They will hasten! She smells a storm on the way!

Her spirits rise when they finally reach the trail Submission had said would appear. It's been moons since it's been maintained, but accrete have shielded it from the worst of recent snows, and it is wide enough for flying, allowing a brisk pace. The soldiers chitter and click to one another, their antennae waving and their senses attuned for trouble. But none of them can explain the sound they hear: a distant RAT! followed not long after by a TAT! echoing through the hills.

They halt without being ordered to do so.

Shimmer's eyes need no sun; they blaze with an internal fire as hot as her tone is icy.

They were not told to stop! They shall double their pace or return to being drones! Set the basket down here. She shall fly! The fight begins!

+++ +++

Brook is too far away to hear the thrower, but it is much on her mind. As she crouches inside the Skull, near where the River Tongue makes its appearance from the cave's mouthlike opening, she wonders and hopes. Would they get the weapon working again? Would any of the Redteeth be driven off or killed? How many? Which ones? Would it change the route they took or their strategy?

One of her clanmates approaches, the one-time champion named Vale, now gimpy and bent.

You want I should go out and see what's up?

I sent Feather already.

How about to the north?

Skinner and Crest are on it.

Vale bares his teeth.

I don't like waiting.

Are the other entrances blocked?

The ones that can be.

And the rest?

One kezel at each. Not half enough, if you ask me.

And up top?

The strongest jabis I could round up, waiting with rocks and boulders. It's the best I could do. Everyone else is watching the home caves in case Whitetails get stupid.

Then all we can *do is wait,* thinks Brook. *If we're needed, Feather will let us know.*

It aint gonna be easy telling them apart when they're all running around naked.

Brook wrinkles her snout.

If you can't tell the difference between a Sugarfoot and a Redtooth, you're not going to be much use.

Ha! You just watch what use I am. Vale appraises his new chief. *You sure Bruiser'll come?*

One hundred percent.

But not with a thrower.

No.

Vale stretches and gives himself a brisk shake.

I don't like waiting, he thinks again.

And yet wait they must, ears, noses, and minds straining to sense Feather with good news. But when, at the edge of their patience, they hear the terrible ruckus of kezel in mortal combat a thousand strides to the southwest, they hear nothing from Feather.

They need our help, thinks Brook, decisive and snarling. She howls a command that is repeated from inside the cave. In moments, two ibiwas, Pitch and Stitch, step out of the darkness.

It could be a trick, thinks Vale. *Lure you out and attack from the north.*

Crest or Skinner would have warned us.

If they're still alive.

No time! If Submission doesn't make it to the caves, they won't need tricks to beat us, they'll just overrun us. Brook doesn't wait to learn Vale's response. She splashes across the narrows of the Tongue, her companions close behind, heading toward the clash and howl of combat.

+ + + + + +

The fight was apt to have gone badly for the Sugarfoot kezel even without Stone's betrayal, for they are outnumbered five to every four. But that one traitorous act throws the troop into chaos, their strategy blown away on the wind of nasty surprise. The ibiwas—Digger, Blue, and Rock's fancy, Bliss—abandon teamwork, lunging and slashing at any Redtooth in sight, and so are drawn away from the others. They are soon fighting for their lives against four opponents who aren't any more seasoned but are much better fed.

The remaining Sugarfoot fighters, bibijas all, try rallying to where their chief is embroiled in a bloody duel with Stone—and where, nearby, Spike and Feather are locked jaw to jaw. But their seven are no match for the ten well-rested foes surrounding them. Had they been asked to simply hold ground rather than gain it, they could have done so indefinitely, but moons of abuse and deprivation assure that the one offensive surge they mount is also the last. From that point, they are on defense, fighting to stay alive and driven farther every moment from where Submission and Feather make their lonely stand. The initial howling has ceased, the din of charging attackers replaced by clashing teeth, desperate panting, and the cries of the injured.

Blue is the first to go down and not get up.

+ + +

When the scion arrive, the melee is an indecipherable mess, snarling bodies rolling in the snow, each as hideous and bloody as the next, and none for a moment remaining still. Were it not for the bands around their forelimbs, Shimmer would have been unable to tell enemy from ally. As it is, knowing the difference is no guarantee of being able to do anything about it.

Focus here, she commands a dozen of her soldiers, and she indicates Digger and Bliss, beleaguered and separated from the others. The kezel who attack them are not as large and are toying with their opponents, making them (Shimmer hopes) easier to bite.

But she herself flies on to the main of the battle, followed by her pluripotents and thirty-six camouflaged soldiers, most heading to their first taste of combat.

+ + +

The grimy Redtooth named Rip shakes the life from Blue, and he turns, slavering and wild-eyed, to where three of his companions, Sport, Sleet, and Splinter, parry and slash with Digger and Bliss, a bloody game the Sugarfoot kezel appear about to lose.

Rip stops to swat at the empty air.

Something just bit me, he thinks, and he wheels about, rubbing the back of his leg as a strange chittering fills the air. He swipes at invisible space and feels a moment later a stinging bite on his tail, followed by buzzing that moves too quickly for his slashing claws.

Rip turns back to the fight. His vision has grown blurry, but it seems that the two Sugarfoot ibiwas now face an equal number of opponents, the third Redtooth, Sport, lying on the ground, alive but seemingly unconscious. And now she is joined by a fellow, the ibiwa Sleet, whose slack-kneed collapse is preceded by confused waving at the ground near his feet.

Rip strides back toward them.

There's something on the ground, he warns his comrades. *Something's biting us!* He thinks this just as something does, on his forelimb, clicking away as he topples splash! thump! into the snow.

His clanmate Splinter now finds his fortunes reversed. Inexplicably harried and bitten and suddenly outnumbered, he never solves the mystery of his collapsed partners. He falls to the combined assault of Digger and Bliss, his cries terrible to hear.

+ + +

Meanwhile, in the main of the battle, the bibija Crunch has already met his end, overcome by the Redteeth oti-mus Gash and Clash. The remaining six Sugarfeet, including Crunch's fancy Measure, huddle at the hopeless center of a toothy circle of ten slashing, rending opponents, confident of their imminent victory.

Where are your precious Moondwellers now? they taunt. *Can't win a fight without your throwers?*

Then, observing no apparent strategy, Shimmer's soldiers venture into the fray. They leap upon Redteeth backs or cling to their legs and tails. The mad thrashing in the snowy muck dislodges some, and more than a few are simply squashed. One of every three scion is killed in this action, but before they are, two more Redteeth are bitten and sent sprawling into the snow.

But Shimmer has a different target in mind. With her pluripotents following, she flies to the head of the fracas, her gaze sweeping the shadows. When she finds Submission, he is dueling bloody-jawed with one of his kind, whom she recognizes by its broken snout.

Betrayal! she thinks. *Duplicity!* She despairs at the damage Submission has taken, but his situation seems likely to get worse. Spike has finished his awful business, and he steps away from Feather, motionless and bleeding her life into the snow.

Leave him! the Redtooth leader orders to Stone. *He's mine! Move off!*

Snarling and cursing, Stone relinquishes her toothy grip on Submission's hind leg. She has gone nearly insane with rage, and yet is glad at heart she is not the one who must end her chief's life. Nor can she bear to witness the fall of the once mighty kezel. And so, while Submission gasps for air and leans heavily against an accrete, she turns and limps into the shadows.

Spike has no such reservations, and he glares at his opponent, blood staining his muzzle.

This is for my chief's oti-mu, he thinks, and he slashes Submission across the snout. *If I can't have the dirty wabi who killed him, I'll have you!*

He is so frenzied he doesn't feel the first scion bite—nor the second. But as he gathers himself for the pounce he imagines will end his rival's life, the third bite stings the back of his neck, accompanied by a foreign smell and a high-speed disturbance in the air nearby.

What are you waiting for? thinks Submission, and

he coughs blood onto the snow. *I'm right here, coward.*

Spike's vision blurs, and he begins to sway.

Coward this, you rotter, he thinks, and he swats vainly at something a moment before falling snout first to the ground, still and senseless.

+ + +

Shimmer reappears with her pluripotents forming a ring around her, and she lands on the bloodstained snow near Submission. The kezel chief is badly torn and his breathing is labored, but he fixes her with a discerning gaze, baring his teeth. He points at her, then to the gap in the accrete where Stone had slunk away. His intent could not have been more clear had Joy been there to translate, but Shimmer hesitates.

Its injuries appear serious, she thinks, though it does no good. *It will allow her to assist.*

But when she approaches, Submission waves her away and snarls, pointing again.

As it wishes, she thinks, and she whistles to her attendants. Concealed once again, they take to the air and in moments are zipping through the accrete, searching for the traitor sharksha.

But Stone is no fool. She knows this terrain better than many and anticipates pursuit. As a result, she is difficult to find and farther away than Shimmer had expected. Worse yet, she is also a lifetime eater of awl glands, the only thing that has consistently eased the pain of her long-broken snout. When Shimmer and her pluripotents at last locate her, they are dismayed to learn their bites have no effect. A bronze corpse, shredded, soon lies in the snow, proof of the futility in trying to win a fight in this fashion. Drawing away, they keep Stone in sight, following after like an airborne accusation, six pairs of buzzing wings infuriating but impossible to hit with thrown rocks—and equally impossible to escape.

Damn you to the bottom of a tar pit! thinks Stone, and she hurls another rock, aiming by ear and of course missing badly. *Show yourselves, stinking filth!*

But Shimmer and her attendants do not oblige. The sound of combat continues behind them, though in whose favor the fight is tilted Shimmer can't guess.

She must return, she thinks. *Three will accompany her, two will follow the traitor. They will not let it out of their sight, and if it should return to its home, they will spread news of its treachery via the Oddity.*

But Stone has long ago abandoned any hope of returning home. She hurries north and east, trailed by invisible wings cutting the cold air.

\+ + +

The sight of their leader lying helpless in the snow would perhaps have been enough to inspire the remaining eight Redteeth to cease hostilities, but Spike lies a hundred strides away and is out of their view. As he has stopped issuing commands and is no longer responding to their hails, Clash takes the lead, rallying his fellows when the scion attack. His nose is sharp, and he is not fooled by camouflage.

Rotters! he thinks. *The ground! The ground!*

And where he points, zig-zagging tracks jitter across the snow, dodging grappling bodies, circling and darting. Whatever makes the tracks carries a smell Clash hasn't encountered in moons but will never forget. The first of them he catches and kills reverts to an iridescent blue, like the blood staining his muzzle. The first leads to others, until the scion retreat to reconsider. Their Queen is occupied elsewhere, and their taste for a fight has been sated. Have they not done enough? The odds have been made closer to even. What else do the awful sharksha want? How many more scion must perish?

To me! thinks Clash. *Circle and stand!*

His mates do as ordered, no longer harassed by scion. Chill, Swipe, Grab, Frost, and Clash's otis Gash, Gnash, and Slash, lusty for blood, re-form their ring around the remaining Sugarfeet. Within that circle, Fang,

Pounce, Bridger, Measure, and Melt hunch and scowl, hoping for a plan from the Brigadier Bone. At the moment, he hasn't one. The odds have improved, but no one would mistake which clan holds the advantage.

Recruited some help, did you? Clash pants, spitting someone else's blood into the snow. *Isn't going to change anything. Your little secret isn't a secret any more. And look at you. You're cooked!*

The remaining Sugarfeet do indeed wear all the outward signs of defeat. Their gazes are defiant, but their curses and threats feel hollow and their slack coats are matted red. With food, rest, and healing, they could have made a proper stand, but now, when Bone thinks, *Step a little closer and I'll show you who's cooked,* they all know it is empty bravado. And so, when the Bristles Brook, Pitch, and Stitch crash into the Redtooth circle, joined by the recently liberated Digger and Bliss, the Sugarfoot fighters are just as surprised as their enemies, and do not at first know how to respond.

Run! thinks Brook. *To the Skull!*

But running is not possible. The best the company can do is an organized withdrawal to where Submission leans against an accrete, his blood staining its yellow scales. Stone is nowhere to be seen. They form a ring around their chief, while Digger and Bliss each take one of Submission's forelimbs, dragging him to the northeast along the course of the River Tongue as their comrades keep the Redteeth at bay. Step by grueling step they battle their way toward the Skull, harried by Redteeth who still feel, with Clash's encouragement, that they can win this fight. And, for the first hundred strides of their retreat, so it seems to everyone.

But when Shimmer and her pluripotents return, the remaining scion rediscover their courage. They have lost the element of surprise, but the bravest of these newly transformed soldiers scurry and dart, resolved to regain their pride and carry out their queen's orders. Some pay with their lives, rent or squashed without mercy, but others are successful, and they send another

Redtooth toppling into the snow.

Only a little farther, thinks Brook. *Keep moving!*

Even now, Clash believes they can win—or can't afford to quit. He and his otis, their desperation terrible to behold, make a last, frenzied attempt to reach and end the Sugarfoot chief. But their quarry has drawn to within sight of where the River Tongue rolls out from its cavernous home, and there they are met by Vale and a team of rock-throwing jabis. Clash himself avoids being blinded by the width of a claw.

Disengage! he orders. *Fall back!*

But the entire defense of the Skull has emerged from the cave and surrounds them. There is nowhere to fall back to, and at last the Redteeth see: the fight is over.

+ + +

And so, the Sugarfoot company, reduced by three and their chief badly injured, reaches the Skull, so named for the gaping face it presents the world. Its mouth opens wide to spit forth the River Tongue, and above it, two holes glower in the rock, as if misshapen eyes meant to haunt kezel imagination.

Bruiser! thinks Vale, for a moment frozen at the sight of the Sugarfoot chief, collapsed to the ground and trembling from head to foot. Blood seeps from injuries on his neck, shoulder, and flank. *Wraps!* Vale orders one of the jabis. *Ties! Double time it! And a blanket!*

It is only when the worst of Submission's injuries have been bandaged and the flow of blood staunched that Vale, with help from Brook, dares to ease him onto a talihew hide, wrapping it around him.

Rest now, you stubborn old dow, thinks Brook, and she breathes into his ear. But he is already unconscious and does not respond.

Pitch and Stich appear, wearing scowls that chase the jabi Bristles off to their various duties.

Redteeth are being secured, thinks Pitch, licking blood from her forearm. *We stowed the conscious ones in the lowest pit, sealed up tight and guarded. The poisoned ones are being tied up proper by your little blue friends; they're not going anywhere. But we can't just leave 'em out there, can we? With the storm coming?*

Why not? asks Vale. *Let the Red have 'em!*

I wish, Brook replies. *But no, Bruiser wouldn't like that. Send out a group of four. Haul them back here, but keep them topside where I can see them.*

And Feather? asks Stitch. *Crunch? Blue?*

Brook takes a deep breath and bares her teeth.

They deserve better than we can give them at the moment. But at least get them inside.

Pitch acknowledges this, sniffing at Submission.

How is he?

Not fighting any time soon, thinks Vale.

And the others? asks Stitch.

I've seen worse. They'll be a needed help—though they'd be better with a good meal and lot of sleep.

Who wouldn't? thinks Pitch, and she exits the cave with her oti-mu to tend to the fallen. A moment later, the Brigadier Bone approaches, along with Fang, cleaning their injuries in the river and cursing freely.

What happened out there? asks Vale.

We were betrayed, thinks the Brigadier. *That's what. By Stone! Don't ask me why...*

Those blue things, thinks Fang. *That's obvious. She never forgave Submission's jabi, and when he agreed to work with those...those...*

Scion, thinks Bone.

Whatever! She snapped. I'm not sure I blame her.

If you're saying you approve a traitor, thinks Bone, *you can walk out of this cave right now.*

Fang bows his head.

Course not, Brigadier. But how I hate them!

Who doesn't? Bone steps out of the river and shakes himself dry. *But you saw what was going on out there as well as I did. If it wasn't for them, I reckon we'd all be sneer food by now.*

No one can deny this, but scarcely a heartbeat later, the topic is driven from their minds as they hear a warning howl from the east. The meaning is clear to them all. Brook snarls and pins her ears.

Whitetails are coming!

+ + +

Shimmer, her three pluripotents, and twenty-four weary soldiers work backwards from the Skull to the site of the original melee, methodically binding each of the comatose Redteeth they encounter. Snow has begun to fall, and they buzz unhappily.

Queen is wise, thinks the most senior of the soldiers, one of the few among the survivors to have escaped injury. *But could they not simply be killed? They are revolting, and binding them wastes resources that could be used elsewhere.* He bows as he offers this suggestion, but Shimmer's tone scalds.

It will follow orders, she thinks, *not offer advice! The sharksha chief was clear: none of its kind is to meet its end due to scion involvement. It is as much a fool as any sharksha, but it clings to hope for peace between these factions—a peace that will be impossible if lives are ended without just cause.*

Yes, Queen. He is sorry for offering.

So, wrap they do, trussing the Redteeth snout to tail. Then they retrieve Shimmer's basket and return to the Skull as, one by one, the bound captives are dragged back to the cave by teams of kezel, a slow process that keeps the scion waiting impatiently. The soldiers chitter and wave their antennae, eager to be gone. But Shimmer and her pluripotents park the basket at the base of a forking accrete and perch amid its violet fingertips.

What is next? Shimmer wonders. *What is the fate of the sharksha chief?*

But her questions must remain unanswered; she does not trust camouflage alone to keep her safe in an unfamiliar cave. Sharksha are as repulsive as any beast she has encountered, but their sense of smell is nearly as powerful as an alp's. And who can say what lies these bristly-tailed ones have been told about scion?

She thinks truly, her prime agrees. *Queen could meet a most unpleasant end were she to dare enter.*

Thinking this, they wait and watch, the soldiers huddled below. Their position affords a clear view of the cave but does little to shelter them from the rising wind. Trying to rid her mind of worries about the approaching storm, Shimmer removes some awl from the basket, allowing a small share for each member of her company, surprised at how hungry she is. For long moments she banishes other thoughts and concentrates on eating. The awl works its way from her beaky mouth to her first stomach, and as it does, her breathing slows and her eyes grow dim. But this is no time for torpor. She allows herself a half lova, siphoning the sweet juice until the leaf is flaccid. This lights her eyes and straightens her antennae, but her many questions remain unanswered.

She has fulfilled her commitment, she thinks. *What is she to do next? The hideous beasts have reached their destination. Is that not enough? What will they do now? How is she to compel their leader to aid her quest—if its injuries haven't already proven fatal—when it remains holed up in a filthy, lightless cave?*

Wracking her brain, she finally decides. She can do no more here. The sharksha desired to win their way to this place, and so they have. Now she must share this news with the Oddity before the Red makes travel impossible. She senses it rising even now.

Come! They are rested and fed. It is time to return to the Oddity and collect on her debt.

Her pluripotents take hold of the basket, relieved to have a plan, and the soldiers arrange themselves in neat files. They are just about to turn away from the Skull when a howling fills the air, coming from the east, a give and take, it seems, between at least two kezel parties, though what they say no scion can guess. None of it sounds good, and when they hear approaching kezel stomping in from the eastern hills, Shimmer's prime pluripotent whistles.

What in Ozag's dominion does it mean? she wonders, but Shimmer has no doubt.

Trouble, she thinks. *What else could it be with these hideous creatures? It is in their nature. But come! They must be off. To the Oddity!*

Absent their two companions, the loaded basket is too heavy to lift with Shimmer riding inside, so she takes to the air, leading her company west, wings and urgent clicking harmonizing beneath the wind.

CHAPTER NINE
Skull

LIGHTNING AND JOY stand outside the Sugarfoot caves, straining to detect signs of what might be happening on the other side of the Spine. But the wind is wrong for news of anything other than the approaching Red, a palpable threat loitering just below the horizon.

Imagining it just makes it worse, thinks Lightning.

So, they return inside, where they find Curly, her work with the thrower complete. She lies with her eyes closed, allowing her wabis Hurly and Burly to clamber over her and tug at her ears and tail.

Do you need us anymore? asks Lightning.

You should hope not. If I do, it's probably trouble.

Well...thank you for teaching me about the thrower. I never knew it was so complicated.

Curly opens her eyes.

I know you're worried. We all are. I don't suppose there's any point in suggesting you get some sleep.

I'm afraid not.

Then keep yourself busy. Best way to occupy your mind. Go find Serenity and see what there is to do.

Busy sounds good, and they make their way to the rear of the caves, hoping for meaningful work. They climb to the northernmost chamber where Serenity confers with Trapper and Old Buttons. They still their thoughts at the newcomers' arrival, though Lightning easily senses their conversation is far from over. She bows her head.

I'm sorry, she thinks. *I didn't mean to interrupt.*

What is it? asks Serenity.

I...well...I mean, what should we do? Shouldn't we

be doing something?

What did you have in mind?

I don't know, thinks Lightning. Does she appear as feeble and anxious as she feels? *What if the fight's going badly? Shouldn't we go out and help?*

And leave the caves defended by who?

Um...you know...whoever can't travel very well?

The gigikas peer at her through narrow eyes.

We're grateful for your tactical advice, thinks Trapper, which means they are not.

Go help your oti-mu, thinks Old Buttons.

Lightning clamps a tight lid on her feelings. Worry tugs at her insides, begging for action, but Joy follows the order as if it had been intended for her, looking over her shoulder and buzzing until Lightning finally bows her head and follows. They find Thunder and Cliff, a hundred strides upslope, removing the last dirt from a deep but lopsided grave. Already light snow blankets its future occupant, the Redtooth Gale, whose body lies nearby, eyes thankfully closed.

This is stinking awful, thinks Lightning. *We can't just stay here doing nothing.*

Some of us haven't been doing nothing, thinks Thunder, and he climbs out of the hole, shaking dirt from his spikes and glaring at the corpse.

Anyway, thinks Cliff. *What good would we do? Jabis are fine for defending caves and throwing rocks, but we'd get torn to pieces out in the open, fighting a bunch of giant bibijas.* He shudders.

Thanks, Cliff, thinks Lightning. *Huge surprise that you want to stay put. But what good are caves if Bruiser and the others aren't alive to enjoy them?*

Don't think that, Thunder snaps. *He's alive, and he's coming back.*

But Gale's body has been lowered into its final resting place and the grave filled with minimal ceremony, and still no word has come from across the Spine. Lightning paces from one end of the caves to the other, oblivious to Joy's pleas to relax, her nerves wound so tight even Cliff gives up on her company. He sits, morose and hungry, watching the storm gather to the southwest, and at first, he can't put a name to the high-pitched droning that approaches from the east, bringing with it a scent like a repressed memory.

Weaver's whiskers! he thinks, and he leaps to his feet, not sure whether to be alarmed or jubilant. *Lightning! That queen of yours is back!*

+ + +

Shimmer's pluripotents set the basket on the ground and alight next to her on the rock shelf overlooking the caves' main entrance. Her dwindling company of soldiers remains east of the River Sweet, huddled where the accrete are still healthy. She refuses to share her news with anyone but Joy, though she tolerates Lightning's presence. Serenity and the gigikas gather beneath the shelf, attending carefully. The queen's agitation is easy to detect, either because of its severity or the amplifying effects of Joy's artifact. Her gilt antennae stand rigid, and she clicks sharply. As always, her pluripotents sit silent and ready, their thoughts sheltered.

Has it seen the betrayer? asks Shimmer.

Joy clicks unevenly.

The who?

The broken-nosed one, the one whose allegiance can no longer be trusted.

She means Stone, thinks Lightning, and dread like a slowly melting icicle fills her heart, drip by cold, trickling drip. *What happened? Did they reach the Skull?*

Most did, though not all. Two at least will fight no more, and the sharksha's sire attained its goal only with help from the more fit among their numbers.

What happened? Lightning repeats. *Is he OK?*

Is she an expert on sharksha anatomy? Is she expected to heal, defend, and diagnose? Would the hideous beast like her to go hunting for it as well?

Lightning curls her lip, but Joy intervenes.

Please, she thinks. *Tell us what happened.*

Shimmer does, her tone scathing, for she is bitter at the loss of so many precious scion lives.

And that number is likely to grow, she adds, *for the fighting may not yet be over. As she was about to depart, other sharksha began moving in from the east.*

Others? thinks Serenity, for she has sensed every thought, and she can no longer remain still. *Which others? What did they look like? How many?*

She can scarcely be expected to tell one awful sharksha from the next, thinks Shimmer. Her wings are restive and unsettled, as if only by supreme will does she keep from simply flying away. *All she saw were the tips of some tails. White they were, the two she could see.*

And Stone? Serenity asks. *The one with the broken snout? Where is she?*

The vile betrayer slunk away from the battle as a coward would, thinks Shimmer, *before it was over. It was injured, though not gravely, and it traveled west, as if to return here. She sees now that was not its intention. And know this: Queen did not simply watch this transpire. Risking her own life, she and her pluripotents pursued and engaged the betrayer, where yet another scion was lost. For this Stone of yours was immune to their bites.*

Um, yes, thinks Serenity. *That is disturbing news.*

She suspects it is not news at all! Two of her pluripotents were assigned to follow, but who can say what they will learn—or if, having learned, they will be able to return and report? Shimmer whistles a sharp note. *What will the hideous beasts do? Has she not fulfilled her commitment? Will they not now fulfill theirs?*

One thing at a time, thinks Serenity. *Which ones didn't make it to the Skull?* But even as she asks, Shimmer's eyes blaze wrathfully, and her pluripotents buzz a low, menacing tune. *Never mind,* thinks Serenity. *You need rest. We thank you. And we will keep our promise, you have my word. But I need to think.*

And she re-enters the cave, trailed by the gigikas, exchanging sheltered thoughts. Shimmer and her escort shoo Lightning and Joy from the rock shelf and sit in silence, their eyes dim.

+ + +

While the adults confer and Lightning paces, Joy dips her hand inside her sling, hoping to find answers that will soothe everyone's worry.

What should we do? she asks. *How do we help?*

Be courageous, the artifact replies simply. *But at the same time, don't be rash.*

What does that mean? Joy labors to subdue her irritated clicking. *How does that help?*

It means do what you know you must, even if you are afraid, but don't act simply because of that fear. It helps because it is good advice.

You can do better! thinks Joy. *I need clear answers!* But the device does not respond, and it occurs to Joy that perhaps it is she who must do better.

Is the fight winnable? she asks, hoping the Book has absorbed enough of their current situation to understand the reference.

Of course.

How?

This is a blood feud; it will not be ended by further spilling of blood. That is the cycle of revenge. To break it, someone must absorb the last blow and forgive.

Absorb the last blow... As she watches Lightning pace, Joy absently caresses the artifact, its face flawless and smooth. *Who is that someone?*

A good question. But I don't know the answer. Someone brave, I presume. Whoever desires peace the most. Not craven appeasement, but true peace, based on equality. Harmony is the Way, after all.

So you have said, thinks Joy. *How is that helpful?*

It is the truth, thinks the Book. *When shared with compassion, the truth is always helpful.*

+ + +

Serenity wants you, thinks Cliff, poking his head out of the caves. Lightning, her heart burdened by Shimmer's news, makes her way with Joy to where Serenity waits near Trapper, Old Buttons, and the bibija Gully. Thunder is there as well, his thoughts still.

I'll be the first to admit I don't know what to do, thinks Serenity. *This news is hard, a real mixed bag. Most got to the Skull, but not all. Then there's Submission... And what are the Whitetails up to I wonder?*

Taking advantage of the situation, thinks Gully. Trapper nods, but Old Buttons seems less sure.

Maybe, she thinks. *Weaver knows they'd love to have the Skull as their own. But Brook said she had the eastern border protected.*

It's a long border, thinks Gully. *They wouldn't necessarily need to fight to cross.*

No, thinks Old Buttons. *But why only send two if it was an assault? That doesn't make sense.*

Maybe a ruse, thinks Trapper. *See if they can get to Brook on a pretense of peace.*

Or a distraction, thinks Gully. *Their real move might be to the southeast, on the Bristle home caves.*

It's possible, thinks Serenity. *I first thought they were making a play for territory. But I wonder... Whitetails aren't stupid, for all their bluster. They don't like Redteeth any more than we do. How do they benefit from getting in our way? Wouldn't they rather have us do the fighting?*

Maybe, thinks Gully. *Unless they made a deal.*

With Redteeth? thinks Old Buttons. *I can't believe that. Not even from Whitetails.*

I don't know what to believe, thinks Trapper.

Lightning chafes at this deliberation. She grits her teeth, trying to chew her worry to a manageable size as the adults go back and forth, speculating. At last, Serenity waves the others to still their thoughts and she sits, shoulders hunched and head bowed.

So damn tired, she thinks, a thought Lightning doubts she intended to share. Then, with no warning, Joy's mind enters the conversation.

May I share something?

Gully starts as if bitten, and the others look at Joy through eyes squinted, their moods unwelcoming.

Sure, thinks Serenity. *Why not?*

Joy tugs at her hair.

We should be courageous, she thinks. *But not be rash.* She lowers her head, peering up just enough to see how the thought is received. *That is the Way.*

Silence and muted astonishment greet her proclamation. Thunder leans away from Joy, and Lightning stands frozen, sure she should add something but baffled as to what it might be.

I'll be dipped, thinks Gully. *That's about the stupidest thing I've ever sensed.*

No, thinks Old Buttons. *It's not.*

No indeed, thinks Trapper.

Serenity rises to four legs, giving herself a mighty shake from snout to tail.

It's a line right out of one of Ancian's stories, she thinks. *That's what it is. And it's exactly what I needed.* She looks at Joy as if seeing her for the first time. *Any other words of wisdom?*

Joy shrinks under the scrutiny, but Lightning nudges her, shoulder to shoulder.

Just this, thinks Joy. *Act despite your fear.* She clasps Lightning's spikes. *Not because of it.*

Gully grumbles at this, but Serenity and the gigikas sit quietly, their eyes closed. Lightning chews at the tip of her tongue. Oh, no! They're sitting musa. How long will this take? Is she expected to participate? Joy looks at her for guidance. Thunder sits scowling. But Cliff has curled up as if preparing for a nap. His eyes have just closed when Serenity's open. She and the gigikas seem to have arrived at a decision.

She growls and looks at Lightning.

Still intend to keep your promise?

I'd rather not. But I don't know what else to do.

Then it's time for you and... Serenity waves vaguely at Joy. *It's time for the two of you to head east. It looks like*

Bruiser may not... It looks like Thunder needs to be his stand-in, as he agreed. Yes?

I did agree, thinks Thunder. *And I'm ready.*

And how about you? This Serenity asks to Cliff, who sits up quickly.

You...you want...you want me to go?

Can you think of anyone better? Snapper's about to pop! Old Buttons? Look, Three-legs, let's just call it what it is. I feel guilty sending Bruiser's jabis out by themselves, and I'm not taking any of these amis from their wabis. Am I wrong in thinking the main reason you're still here is because you don't have a family of your own?

Not one that cares about me.

Then sending you out won't concern anyone, and if you fall into a ravine or get snatched by a derka, I won't be blamed. But don't look at it that way. This is an opportunity to gain some experience—and some honor.

Cliff wrinkles his snout.

Yes ma'am.

Well, then, don't dawdle! Fat, old Gapi-kan is coming. You're going to have to hurry, or he'll eat you up...

+ + +

And just like that, they are on their way, with scarcely a moment to think. What food can be spared is stuffed into Lightning's pack, which is strapped across Cliff's shoulders. What good will can be mustered is shared in the form of subdued farewells and bits of gigika advice from Trapper and Old Buttons.

Then, the three jabi kezel join with Shimmer and her pluripotents, bearing the loaded basket across the River Sweet and moving due east through falling snow. They follow the trail taken by Submission and the others until they meet up with Shimmer's soldiers, hunkering in the shadows. From there, Thunder leads them to the Spine. Lightning follows close on his heels, with Joy holding her tail and walking in silence. At the rear of the procession, the scion soldiers march stoically—careful to leave a healthy distance between themselves and Cliff, whose brow is perpetually furrowed.

When they reach the Spine, the company travels quietly, with great, nose-twitching care, fearful all the while of an ambush, though Shimmer and her five pluripotents fly ahead, scouting the way. Joy eventually takes a seat on Lightning's back, for she is unable to maintain the pace on the uphill course.

Glad to be moving, thinks Lightning to herself. *Better than waiting around.*

But to what end do they travel? Unanswerable questions and ugly possibilities fill her with the sense of being powerless. It reminds her of the decision she had made to travel out onto the plains, less a leap of faith than an inevitability, a necessary evil.

Swept along, she thinks. *Not in control, just moving where the current takes me.*

And yet, even that is not true. It's simply an evasion of sorts. After all, she could break her promise to Shimmer—what could the scion do about it? Nothing! And few among her clan would judge harshly. They would consider it due payment.

No, she thinks. *It's a choice. My choice. I guess we'll know who's to blame if everything goes badly.*

She marches on, sinking into a morose spirit worsened by the grim silence of her companions. They encounter no threat, but a tone of warning suffuses the foothills, the residue of recent violence that no cremlin or virble will soon forget. At their passing, the neighborhood grows quiet, and many eyes track their movement. Lightning imagines their owners being glad when they have gone and cannot say she blames them. Theirs is a dark, murderous mood.

+ + +

Joy's dread is no less, and the fear of what lies ahead eats at her like an acid. She wishes to be allowed to walk, to burn some of her energy and perhaps calm her nerves, but she knows she mustn't ask. Instead, she slips a hand inside her sling and brushes her fingers across the artifact's face, wondering if it can feel her fear.

She asks this question.

I can, it replies, *and that of your escort.*

What do I do?

Sing a brave song. That can be helpful.

But what is singing? she asks. *What is a song?*

Kezel howl, thinks the Book. *Rixli trill. Humans sing. Some better than others, it's true.*

Am I not kezel?

You are not. Again: you are a hybrid, part human, part scion. Remarkable engineering, really.

At another time, Joy would have howled to prove otherwise, but she settles for yet another question.

How do I sing?

It's really quite simple. I will teach you a song I learned from my very first Reader, a woman by the name of Grace, though some called her Abuelita. She learned it from her mother, Maya Sharma, one of the original colonists, who sang it to her during a time just as frightening as the one you face.

But did it help?

The fear remained, of course; it simply became less important. Bend your mind to courage, and you'll have no time for anything else.

That's easy to say, thinks Joy. *Well then, teach me.*

But the artifact does not respond.

Oh, good grief, please, thinks Joy, rephrasing her request. *How do I sing?*

I will be happy to demonstrate. Grace thought I had a fine voice, back when I could take human form. For now, we'll need to bypass the ears, as it were.

And a moment later, a light, regular tapping fills her mind, an infectious ONE-two-three, ONE-two-three, ONE-two-three. This tempo is joined soon after by the artifact's thoughts, but modified and sustained, keeping perfect time. The sound as it is reproduced in her mind does remind her a little of howling, but it is more melodic and cast not for distance or volume but for a sensitive, local audience. She doesn't hear them as sounds through her ears, of course, but her mind reads them as such, imagining musical notes.

Oh! she thinks. *Isn't that so lovely.*

Her eyes grow dim as she concentrates. The words are simple, though at first, they seem a tangled mush. However, after some repetition, a pattern becomes evident, like a camouflaged scion suddenly revealed, and Joy tracks their passage keenly, noting how they follow the tempo like a beating heart:

Humko mann ki Shakti dena
Mann vijay kare
Doosroon ki jay se pehle
Khud ko jai karen

Humko mann ki Shakti dena
Mann vijay kare
Doosroon ki jay se pehle
Khud ko jai karen

Humko mann ki Shakti dena

In her mind, Joy is soon singing along, delighted though she has no idea what the words mean.

This is a song? she asks.

It is.

And this is singing?

The best we can do for now, yes. When there's a proper time, we'll test out your voice.

Reminds me of Captain, thinks Joy, though she finds this much more pleasing than his rough speech. *Is this his language?*

No, that human spoke what I guess was a modern form of basic System English.

You understood him, then?

Of course. Through you.

Why didn't you translate?

You never asked. This particular tune is ancient Hindi, taught to Maya Sharma by her Daada—her gapi-kan. The language is many centuries old, but from what I understand was, at the time of the colonists, still spoken on Earth—though Maya Sharma herself rarely set foot on the planet. She was born on Luna, you know.

Most of this means nothing to Joy. Her head nods in time with the simple tune still running through her mind, a light ONE-two-three, ONE-two-three.

Please teach me more! she thinks, and the sparkle in her eyes dances to the rhythm. *I mean, what's next?*

A good question. How about some accompaniment? Keyboard, perhaps. And Joy's inner ear is filled suddenly with a rhythmic chiming that enriches the song, filling its empty spaces and embellishing the melody with lush, harmonious chords.

Ooo... thinks Joy. *Can Lightning sense this?*

If you wish her to.

I do!

And so, the Book adds another set of verses.

Mushkilen padhen to hum pe
Itna karam kar
Saath den to dharam ka
Chalen to dharam par

Khud par hounsla rahe
Badi se na daren
Doosroon ki jay se pehle
Khud ko jai karen
Humko mann ki Shakti dena

Mann vijay kare
Doosroon ki jay se pehle
Khud ko jai karen
Humko mann ki Shakti dena

When Lightning's spiky head begins swinging left to right and her stride alters to match the subliminal tempo, she initially takes little notice, too focused on her own worries. But that changes as Joy's delight grows, her cares for the moment cast away. Lightning peers back at her rider, never interrupting the music nor breaking stride. It isn't long before all the kezel become aware of a simple tune, light-hearted and addictively rhythmic, to which their steps seem drawn like smoke to the sky. Cliff especially finds the ONE-two-three time pleasing, but even Thunder can't help nodding his head, and his spirit is lightened.

Humko mann ki Shakti dena, they think to themselves in unison, and not a one bothers to ask from where the magic comes or what the words mean. What a sight for other kezel had they seen it: three haggard jabis, hungry and tired, marching in time, heads swinging, a bright fire in their eyes. The cheerful tempo sweeps away fear and resignation, the meaningless lyrics stirring in their hearts something like hope—or perhaps defiance. It is a sublime feeling that, in light of their circumstance, some might have thought unwarranted.

But Lightning doesn't question it. She marches on, ONE-two-three, ONE-two-three, and the weight on her back feels like a privilege.

+ + +

In time, however, they come down out of the Spine, and their path meets the River Tongue, talkative as always. The tale it tells now is one of violence and death, and no song can wish it away. Not long after, still on the western bank, the party comes to the place their noses have been warning them of. A great trampling appears, the snow stained red and blue and the ground scored by deep claw marks, clods of soil cast all about as if the planet itself had been the enemy. As they continue on, they see the long, gory trails where bodies have been dragged away to the northeast, following the river.

They quicken their pace, keeping the Tongue to their right and moving as stealthily as possible; some element of surprise might play in their favor if combat should be their fate. They circle to the west of the Skull, remaining downwind while Shimmer's pluripotents go ahead to scout. When they return, the news they bear is ambiguous and difficult to interpret.

Many sharksha stand near the caves, thinks Shimmer's prime. *But only two with tails of white.*

Lightning curls her lip, her mind racing.

Hop off, she thinks to Joy. *Wait with the others.* And she moves toward the Skull, creeping into the shadows and out of sight.

The sharksha is a fool, thinks Shimmer. *But she cannot deny its bravery.*

The falling snow begins traveling diagonally, and the kezel lay their ears flat against the wind. Joy hugs her sling and dims her eyes, her nerves taut. Thunder rises to two legs and stands with his nose to the wind, his eyes half-closed against its sharpening bite. Cliff turns north, wary of downwind trouble, and his tail twitches.

The howl that comes their way moments later startles them all badly, Cliff most of all, whose surprised yelp inspires from Thunder a stream of florid profanity. A second howl reaches them soon after, and sensing its tone, Thunder shakes his head as if trying to dislodge a clinging, unwanted thought.

Before you start wetting yourself, he thinks to Cliff, *make sure you understand the message. Lightning's OK. We're being summoned.*

+ + +

Cliff has never been to the Skull before. It doesn't take him long to recognize the source of the cave's name. The wide mouth from which the River Tongue unspools is topped by two other entrances, much smaller, which give the impression of hollow eye sockets set in a leering face. All that is required is a bit of imagination to make a nose out of the uneven cavity set between the two.

Cliff scowls at the sight.

I thought you said a rogue kezel lived here.

Lightning's snout wrinkles.

I might have made that up.

Beneath the Skull itself are a warren of recesses and alcoves, not proper caves, but sheltered spaces, overhung by the Skull's jutting jaw and the falling river. In one of these, the Redteeth are imprisoned, guarded by a pair of bristly-spiked bibijas. But in another, the grief-stricken Measure slumps over the body of her fancy, Crunch. And there also are Bridger and Pounce, mourning the loss of Blue, their beloved woti. They look up at the sight of the newcomers, and they exchange emotion-laden thoughts. But the jabis aren't allowed to sense the details, for Brook appears above them, waving them up. Shimmer and her pluripotents will have nothing to do with it, and they fly to a sheltering ridge far from the kezel, the soldiers huddled below.

The mouth of the cave can only be reached by climbing rock or rope. Lightning and Thunder choose the former, Cliff and Joy the latter, and they are soon inside, the river's voice echoing throughout.

Welcome, thinks Brook. *I'm glad to see you.*

Thank you, Lightning replies, but she sniffs and worries. *Where is our api-kan, please?*

This way. It's not far.

Brook leads them into darkness, by a rocky way bordering the chattering river for a hundred strides until they reach a crystal-lit chamber, horizontally striped in humble shades of brown and gray. Inside are representatives of three kezel clans: Fang, the Brigadier Bone, the bow-legged Vale, and two Whitetail strangers. They gather around a lone figure, larger than the rest but prone, wrapped in bloodstained bandages and lying on a bed of talihew hides.

Api-kan, thinks Lightning, and she hurries forward. The gathered kezel part to make room. Vale and the Whitetails step back uneasily at the sight of Joy, but Submission's eyes blink open.

Little Spark, he thinks softly, and he sighs as she

steps close and buries her nose in his spikes.

I'm so sorry, she thinks. Submission makes no reply, but he breathes deeply, taking in her scent and that of Thunder, who has also drawn near.

Don't you worry, thinks Brook. *He'll be OK; tough bones in this one. But no pestering with questions. Rest is what's needed.* She looks to the largest of the two Whitetails, a portly bibija whose muzzle matches the color of his tail. *Piedmont here was just telling us a story. How about I send for some food, and he can start over?*

The Whitetail she refers to bows, as does his companion. Except for his tail—and his grizzled snout—Piedmont's spikes are auburn, his vest nearly as snug on his hefty frame as Lightning's is on hers. His considerably smaller bibija companion is tri-colored, her vest dirty yellow and untrimmed. No one bothers to introduce her. Neither they nor Vale can take their eyes off Joy, but she is accustomed to being the focus of attention, and she sits calmly on the hassock near Submission, buzzing a low tune while she waits. Eventually, one of the Bristles returns with a modest but much appreciated offering of dried cremlin and tubers. Joy's share is some of the awl stashed in the pack that Cliff carries, and she gnaws on this as Piedmont re-starts his tale.

Well-ee, he thinks, *like I was a-sayin' afore, everbody knows we's a noble clan, us Whitetails, always lookin' to follow the Way and all that. We got morals, see? Yeah, so when we's a come sniffin' over to the Bristly hills, it aint cuz we's the greedy type, or tryin' to start up no kinda trouble, no sir and ma'am. We's just roamers by nature, don'tcha know. Sure-ee! Everbody's knowin' that! Can't keep us set in a place no matter what our chief says—that's the Big Fork, that is, but ya probbly knowed that—Whitetails is always lookin' for somethin' new. Always curious 'bout what's over that next rise, or 'round that bend in the river. You know how it is, yeah?*

The Sugarfeet and Bristles politely nod that they do indeed, but the latter do so as clearly read skeptics. Sharing a border with such "curious" neighbors is not as innocent a thing as their guest makes it seem. Still, they do not interrupt.

Anahoo, Piedmont thinks, *this is all for sayin' we's goodly friends, us Whitetails and Bristlys—and Sugarfeet too, sure-ee!* He pauses to look at Cliff. *You a Render?*

No sir.

Ain't no Sugarfoot.

No sir.

Some kind o' furriner?

Cliff holds up one hand.

Clawpaw, he thinks.

Oh, sure-ee! thinks Piedmont. *Ain't you though. Didn't know there was a one o' you left in the accrete.*

More than one, thinks Cliff.

You don't say! Well-ee! Anahoo, like I was a tellin', we's goodly friends, us Whitetails, with all o' the clans on this side o' the wedge. Even them ol' Clawpaws we didn't know was still a thing. Only ones we got issues with is them danged ol' dirty Redteeth. Won't wear a decent vest no sir, always thinkin' bad about Moondwellers, thinkin' they know so much—you know how they do. So, a while back, I get called by our chief, the Big Fork, right? And he ain't gettin' any smaller, for all you who ain't seen 'im in a while. No sir! Anahoo, he calls me, and I come runnin'.

"You heard the news?" he asks me.

"Sure-ee, boss," I say. "I heard. Sugarfeet are back. Or some of 'em anyway. What a thing!"

"Not that news," he says, cuz he's always ahead o' the game, see? Can't slip one by 'ol Forkie. "Redteeth are comin' for the Skull," he says. "Probably afore the Red."

"Golly, Boss," I say. "What are we gonna do?"

"You," he says. "Not we. You're gonna spread the word: stay off Bristly toes until this here trouble blows over. No sniffin' over the border, no secret-like hunting parties, no cache robbing"—not that old Piedmont ever done such, you know, that ain't what the Big Fork was sayin' nor Fluvial here, my one an' only, and here he points at the Whitetail to his side. *But ol' Forkie was clear 'bout it, no mistake. "We all's gonna keep it real peaceable-like," he*

says, "so's our goodly neighbors the Bristlys can focus on keeping them rotten ol' Redteeth on their stinky side o' the wedge." And he chop-chopped with his teeth, just to make the point, not that old Piedmont needed the help.

"Sure-ee, Boss," I says. "You can count on ol' Piedmont to spread the word. Who better? But folks aint gonna like it. Just gettin' used to havin' a grip on some new turf, yeah? Likin' to have a little more space, see?"

So then Big Fork says, "You'd rather be the cause for Redteeth startin' a new clan in our back yard?"

"No-ee, Boss," I said. "No-ee for sure! But what say we take the chance and see if a few of them Bristly ah-lahs wanna maybe try life with a Whitetail or two, you know? The ones who ain't busy fightin'?"

But you know the Big Fork. He wasn't takin' no for an answer. Tell you what, when he gets riled, don't matter how big and slow he is, he's a terror, see?

Piedmont's audience assures him they do.

Well-ee, I did like he said, spreadin' the word far an' wide—and Fluvial here, she helped, can't forget that, not the talky kind, but she can make 'er point when she wants to—and we all backed way off, all us Whitetails, like you probbly noticed. And it wasn't no trick, neither.

Never said it was, thinks Brook.

Sure-ee, but you was thinkin' it. Big Fork knowed you'd be thinkin' it. That's why he sent the Offering.

What offering? asks the Brigadier.

Piedmont nods to the one called Fluvial, and she exits the cave, gone for long moments before returning on two legs, carrying something Lightning at first can't identify. She places it on the floor near Submission's hassock, where the others can get a good look and smell. It has the gray, grimy look of something burned and battered, but only when Fluvial turns it over (quickly, as if reluctant to touch it) do Lightning and the others recognize its form. Growling exclamations and curses are followed by poking, sniffing, and puzzled expressions.

That's a head! thinks Fang. *Tell me it's not.*

Sure-ee, thinks Piedmont. *And a couple o' arms, or*

so reckons the Big Fork. Plus, a middely part—watcha call it? Torso? But ain't no thing like this livin' in the accrete. Not that ol' Piedmont never seen. Don'tcha think it oughter have some legs or somethin? Don't it look like it's bottomy half's a missin'? But then ya smell it, and it ain't no livin' thing anahoo, so what good would legs do it, see? It's just a... Well golly, who can say what it is?

The Sugarfoot kezel, all of whom have recently encountered the trio of bipeds they named Moondwellers, recognize this thing is indeed the remains of a body like theirs, but hairless and skinless, dull gray for the most part, aside from its eyes, which are a bright silver. The lower half of its body, wherever it may be, must have been torn asunder by some tremendous violence, for its outer shell, which is hard as stone, is punctured and ripped, its edges bent jagged and sharp like a cutter. Inside what remains of the torso is stuffed an intricate array of dangling filaments, bent rods, and the stain of dark, leaking fluid, its scent evocative but unpleasant.

What in Weaver's name is it? Vale wants to know. He, out of them all, is most willing to touch the thing, and this he does, slowly and reflectively.

None of the Sugarfoot kezel raise the topic of the bipeds, but all arrive by smell at the same conclusion: this thing, despite its form, is a different beast altogether. The one called Captain had smelled deliciously edible. His companions had not, but they had none of the acrid, toxic scent of this thing. It stares up at them with its metallic eyes wide and dead.

So...this is your offering? thinks Brook. *This is the thing that's supposed to convince Bristles to step away from their border and trust you?*

Sure-ee, thinks Piedmont. *It's a Moondweller thing for clear, see? Lotsa pride in finding it, yes ma'am, but we aint a keepin' it for ourselves, nope nohow. Big Fork's willin' to give it up as a goodly will sign, see? Just so yous can take care o' your business with them danged Redteeth. And that ain't all! Cuz Big Fork's said it clear: Iffin' Whitetails don't keep their bargain, you can keep us as hostage*

—me and Fluvial here—and the thingamajig, too.

Vale and Brook exchange glances, their thoughts difficult to read. Submission has long ago fallen into an uneasy slumber, his breathing shallow.

Afore you gimme your answer, thinks Piedmont. *Check out this here.* Reaching down, he moves his hand around to the back of the battered, gray head, feeling for something, his eyes half closed. Both Lightning and Joy peer close to see what transpires.

Click!

Piedmont steps away and watches as if expecting something to happen. And a moment later, something does. The bright, silver eyes come to life, glancing up and around, seeming to look for something they can't find. The other kezel scramble away as the thing's mouth opens and closes like a beached awl. A sound comes from it, tinny, distorted, and completely meaningless.

"Fairzas nokstun uppa palitch," it says, then repeats the words, once, twice, a third time, until every kezel but the two Whitetails, who have presumably heard it before, are so disconcerted their spikes stand on end.

Make it stop, orders Brook, and with a click! Piedmont quickly reaches behind the thing and silences its exclamations, its eyes freezing in its sockets.

I've heard that before, thinks Joy, to her own surprise. *Or sounds like it.*

But before she can explain further, Gapi-kan the Red announces his arrival with a shocking burst of thunder and a wicked, howling wind.

+ + + + + +

Stone limps westward, doing her best to ignore her two droning but invisible traveling companions. Once, she feigns having passed out due to her injuries, hoping to lure them close enough to catch, but they are clever and wary. They simply alight in the fanning reaches of a nearby accrete, watching her. Hurling rocks is equally futile. Even had she been in prime shape, she isn't sure she could hit these targets, for they are elusive and quick. But she is far from prime. She quits this and focuses instead on finding the fastest route to the northern wedge crossing. Damn the scion and damn Submission for allowing them into the accrete. If they follow her to Redtooth turf, so be it. They'll get theirs...

She stops to press handfuls of snow against the worst of her injuries, baring her teeth at the wind.

Never getting there before the storm, she thinks.

But she underestimates her will. Although she must curl far to the north to avoid detection by any scouting Sugarfeet, she makes steady progress, clenching her jaws in pain and wasting no more energy on curses or rocks. She skirts the southern edge of the sulfur fields and is nearing the northern crossing when Gapi-kan comes to call. The scion are able to weather the driving snow while sheltered by the accrete, but when Stone steps out into the broad clearing that marks the crossing, they are at last forced to end their pursuit. They hunker in the relative safety of gnarled, twisting forks, and there they remain, droning miserably.

You have to be kidding, thinks the Redtooth sentry when Stone reaches the crossing. He peers out at her from his modest shelter, a small recess dug into the western bank, a space large enough for two, though he does not invite her inside. He squints his eyes against the icy burn of the wind, taking in Stone's battered form and the message she shares.

Well? she thinks. *Are you going to tell the others or stand here staring at me?*

The Redtooth steps most reluctantly out into the elements, his spikes bending and rippling.

Look. Just because you're not wearing a filthy vest doesn't make you one of us, he thinks. *If my chief hadn't ordered against it, I'd finish what someone else started.*

You'd try, thinks Stone. *But it doesn't matter, does it? Your chief did order against, and unless your goal is to make him mad, you'd better be on your way.*

The Redtooth pins his ears and snarls, but whatever he might be thinking, he turns away from Stone and heads into the wind, soon disappearing into what has quickly become an all-out blizzard.

Stone slouches into the shadowy recess, settling to a sitting position and licking gingerly at punctures and scratches as she listens to the storm. Madly swirling snowflakes, children of the Red, adopt a scarlet hue as if sparks from a fire, fueled by their brother the wind. An enemy could have approached to within a stride or two, so bad is the visibility. But Stone is beyond caring about such things. Her bleeding is staunched, but she is exhausted in body and spirit. She closes her eyes and leaves her nose to sentry duty. A surprising thought, unpleasant but insistent, bubbles up from the depths of memory: Ancian and her tale of exile and being caught aboveground in a similar tempest.

Silly old rotter, she thinks wearily and only half in earnest. In fact, thinking of Gami-kan reminds her of what she has done, its finality, brutal and irreversible. *No forgiveness,* she thinks.

But she is in no mood to grant forgiveness, and so seeks none for herself. She had known the moment Submission invited scion to fight on their behalf that she would never return to the caves where her fancy and wabis had perished. Her only regret is that she hadn't long ago disobeyed orders and simply killed as many of the blue slime as possible when she had the chance, out on the plains, perhaps, honor be damned.

No road back, she thinks, and she curls herself into a large, spiky ball, her bitterness for the moment like everything else a slave to the passing of the Red.

Chapter Ten
Sister

VIKTOR WAITS IMPATIENTLY for the storm to move on, but like most associated with the Red, it is in no rush to do so, battering the coastline and threaten Cyclonia's lone tower with vicious, briny wind and hellish lightning but—as is always true south of the landfall—precious little rain. The sheltered cove is whipped to a froth, and even Twenty-Seven chitters nervously as the tower sways. But scion engineering has been tried and proven over millennia. The tower, like its mates in Albion and elsewhere on the coast of the Great Saline, is meant to yield before the wind, bending rather than breaking, and this it does.

Will he tolerate a question? asks Twenty-Seven.

He will, thinks Viktor. They are alone in the room, a chamber removed from the main of the living quarters, and he fears no eavesdroppers.

Earlier, thinks Twenty-Seven, *he was able to sense Cyclonia's queen referring to the place where the vumierre flying device fell from the sky into the bay.*

It is so.

Were divers sent?

They were. He wonders what they discovered?

He cannot help being curious.

He is unable to satisfy that curiosity. The divers could not explain what they saw, and so, neither could Queen. Something as big as an alp, she said, hard as rock and with a shape unfit for this world. Vumierre mischief through and through, and the divers were afraid of it, though it did not move or make any sound.

And yet, thinks Twenty-Seven, *it is the device that*

carried the vumierre across the sky, and when it did so, it moved faster than a derka and was louder than an alp.

So he has been told.

Is it not possible such a mighty thing could rise from its watery prison? Perhaps it is simply biding its time.

He has considered this. But recall what you know of the wretched slavers. Their contraptions did nothing without their command—indeed, from what legend tells, not usually without their direct presence.

So, he believes they may return for it?

It is possible, but he will not wait to see. If they do not return, valuable time will have been wasted.

So, he will follow?

He will. He is rested and ready. Viktor's lone antenna bends slightly, and he tilts his head, listening for a change in the storm. *Queen believes the vumierre will lead him to answers.*

What answers does he believe they will have? In what way could he hope to communicate with them?

That shall be revealed. Enough! Ready the others and prepare the alp. The storm is passing.

+ + +   + + +

Captain Monroe wakes from an epic dream which lingers in the form of nostalgia but no precise memories. There may have been a dark-haired woman with pretty lips, and perhaps a feast, but that could be wishful reconstruction, the effect on his waking mind of the room made bright by sunlight through an open hatch.

"Morning, Cap'n," says Lieutenant K, and he looks up from the documents spread out on the table before him. "Or whatever time it is. Storm has passed. A real knockout, too. Eclipse, sleet, the works. I wanted to wake you, but you know the ensign.

"I sure do."

"Orders, sir?"

The captain stretches and rises to his feet.

"None at the moment, unless you know a place to

get huevos rancheros and maybe some black tea."

"No sir, no such luck."

The captain climbs the stairs and peers out the hatch to a world made blinding and white. The snow is not deep, but it is wet and heavy, bending every yellow blade of grass. It has already begun melting and promises a sloppy day of travel.

"Finding anything good, Nikki?"

"I'll let you be the judge, Cap'n." The lieutenant indicates the oversized sketchpad, filled with simple but well-composed images, carefully colored. "Little B was an artist, and a pretty good one at that. We got all sorts of critters drawn and described, copied from that guidebook. Then there's the oldest one, the one they call Marquita. She liked math." He rifles through a stack of notebooks, each filled with meticulous characters arrayed in formulas, expressions, and equations, complete with graphs, diagrams, and charts. The captain squints at these, and he rubs a hand over his head.

"I just woke up, Lieutenant. I appreciate the pretty pictures, but this is too much."

"Aye sir, not my specialty either. I was hoping Carmela might have some thoughts."

"And she is...?"

"Still trying to get the ATV running."

"Still? That's not like her."

"No sir, but I'll let her explain it."

"And what about our new friend?"

"No change. Don't really expect there to be."

And so, after a cursory wash and groom for the captain, aided by one of the manual water pumps and towels located in the living quarters, he and the lieutenant move to the service bay. He gnaws a small brick of ration as they walk, scowling at the taste. When they arrive, they find the ensign beneath the ATV, tools at her side. Charging cables snake across the floor, one to each of the ports near the vehicle's four pairs of oversized tires, but the ATV stands silent like a beast in slumber. Sensing their arrival, the ensign lets her wrench fall with a *clang!*

and she curses softly.

"That doesn't sound promising, Carmela." The captain peers beneath the vehicle, forehead wrinkled.

"I'm sorry, sir." She slides out from under the vehicle, wiping her hands on a nearby rag. "I've done what I can, but until we get a power source more stable than the work light batteries, we're not going anywhere in this."

"And our mysterious generator?"

"Still a mystery. I think I understand the principle. It appears to be a type of cascade system, where the first phase is liquid metal spun into a vortex. The second stage is where confined plasma is released, bombarding the sphere I showed you. That leads to the third stage, which is excitation and fusion. The final stage—"

"Carmela, you're making my head hurt."

"Sorry sir. Well, in theory, I should be able to get it running, but everything I've tried is a dead end."

"It's OK, Ensign, you did your best."

"No sir, it's not OK. Unless we plan to harness one of those giant quadrupeds, we'll never extract *Valiant* without this ATV. I'm sorry..."

"Don't be. I have an idea."

"Sir, if you're thinking of trying to revive the android, I hope you understand it could very well turn out to be hostile—it could literally blow up in our faces."

"Do you think that's likely?"

The ensign rises to her feet.

"Nothing we've been able to read indicates as much, but we weren't able to penetrate all her coding. She—it—is a very complex machine for how old it is. As far as I can tell, it was made to pass as human. But that type of design was highly illegal at the time."

"Meaning," adds the lieutenant, "it's a synthetic who knows its very existence was criminal."

"Exactly," the ensign agrees. "Who knows what that's done to its programming? For all we know, she—it—is why there are no colonists alive."

"That we know of," the captain clarifies.

"Yes sir, but why was she disabled?"

"You said it yourself, Ensign. She's a couple centuries old. I might topple over too, if I was her age."

"It's possible, sir, but the diary..."

"Look," the captain waves. "I know you have worries, OK? I have 'em too. I know history; I know what happened on Mars. But she—can we just call her she, please?—she's the only person we have who might know how to make that power station, you know, power."

"Unless Carmela can maybe find something in those notebooks," says the lieutenant.

"Fair enough," the captain nods. "Dig through 'em, Ensign, but not long—is an hour enough? Less? Good. If you can't find anything, I want you to wake up Sleeping Beauty. Take all the precautions you think are necessary—but wake her up."

+ + +

Ensign Morales needs much less than an hour to arrive at her conclusion about the notebooks.

"Homework, sir."

"Excuse me?"

"Yes sir, if I had to hazard a guess, I'd say she—this Marquita person—was doing exercises, like schoolwork. Lots of repetition and steps shown in detail that wouldn't normally be necessary unless someone was trying to show their work for a grade."

"And they don't mean anything?"

"Not that I can see. Nothing more than our Marquita was a good mathematician."

"No patterns, no hidden codes?"

"Not unless they're hidden really well. As far as patterns... It's more about recurring themes. There are a lot of formulas of the type used in superluminal physics—faster than light travel—and quite a few expressions in temporal theory—moving through time—but they're free-standing, detached from one another, so it seems unlikely they represent a unified project."

"So, homework then."

"Yes sir, that's what it looks like. Pretty high-level, sophisticated homework, but nothing useful."

All three look from the table where they sit to the rumpled figure lying on the floor.

The captain purses his lips.

"You OK with this, Nikki?"

The lieutenant gets to his feet, setting aside Abbott's diary and stepping close to the white-haired figure. Its eyes stare sightlessly, frozen in surprise.

"OK's probably too strong a word for it, Cap'n. Nothing in that diary expressly says, 'don't wake her up,' but..." He leaves this thought unfinished.

"But?"

"Every time he—our friend Abbott—mentions Sister Janet, he sings her praises—until the end. Then he cuts himself off like he's afraid of saying too much, you know? Writing something that someone might find and not take kindly to."

"Someone like the good Sister here?"

"Could be. Aw, shoot, Cap'n, there's no way to know. And the clock is ticking. We need power!"

The captain nods and gets to his feet.

"Then do what you need to do. I'm not crazy about this either, but like you said: tick-tock."

+ + + + + +

Queen Allura, her magister, and a company of bristly-legged soldiers await in tight formation as Viktor limps to where the Albion contingent has wakened and loaded their giant alp. The bone-plated beast spent the storm like all its kind, hunkered low to the ground and sheltered beneath its armor. Storms, regardless their severity, cause no dismay to a full-grown alp. Of greater concern are its stomachs, most empty, and it waves its tentacles, impatient for the upper land and the yellow grass it hopes to consume by the bushel.

If the vumierre return for their device, thinks Allura, *what does he wish her to do with them?*

Interrogate! thinks her magister. *Is it not reported in legend that some among them could use the old scion language? Interrogate and torture if necessary.*

Allura's eyes flash so brightly her magister's antennae wilt, and he bows low.

Apologies, Queen, he was out of turn.

Allura turns away from him, waiting instead for Viktor's response. He considers carefully.

If he may be so bold, Queen, he desires they be held captive, and in separate cells, so they might not conspire. Fed and watered as necessary, yes, but neither questioned nor harmed until his return. The submerged device? That they should leave where it lies, for who can say what evil might befall any who dare move it? How does this seem to her?

She deems it wise. But again: is he sure he can follow these vumierre? Will he not lose their trail?

Albion's Queen Benica marked the black-suited one before her untimely passing—both its body and the black gear it wears. No Albion alp could miss that sign, even if covered in snow.

Then she advises depart at once. He has all she can give—indeed! Even some of his color has returned.

This is a generous overstatement, but something in the giving of obeyed commands and the close company of a supportive queen has brightened his eyes and restored a spring to his step. And his skin? Still gray as ever, but now with a sheen as if newly washed.

She is generous and wise, he thinks. *If his need were not so urgent, he would beg leave to remain. But it is not to be. He must not delay his departure with lengthy farewells. If possible, he will return, but until then, he hopes she will accept his gratitude.*

She will, thinks Allura. *And if his tale hadn't made her doubt the good it would do, she would pray for Ozag's grace on his mission. As it is, she will say only this: do not underestimate the vumierre. Nothing we have been taught about the slavers bodes well for the unprepared.*

Viktor bows, and his eyes are dim. Then, with no

further comment, he climbs aboard the alp, joining its handlers, who struggle to control the restive beast. How noticeable is his effort? How awkward and slow? It matters not; pride is an indulgence he can't afford. Once settled on one of the mighty creature's armored plates, he waits as Twenty-Seven and the Cyclonian soldiers climb aboard, then whistles, long and shrill. At this sign, the alp lumbers to the west, where the upper and lower land come finally to a passable way.

+ + + + + +

In the infirmary, the lieutenant finds a pair of restraining straps, adjustable and strong. These he uses to bind the android's wrists and ankles. They move her to a sitting position, resting her back against the wall. Though it seems pointless, the ensign adjusts her tunic and tucks the white-streaked hair back into place, hiding it beneath her coif. Her glasses are beyond repair, but the ensign removes the broken lens, straightening the frame and placing them carefully on the android's lap.

"What do you think, Cap'n?" asks the lieutenant. "Should we shackle her to the wall? The door maybe?"

The captain looks to Ensign Morales, but she frowns and shakes her head.

"We want her help. Restraints are one thing..."

"Understood," says the lieutenant, and he takes his sidearm from its holster. "But one wrong move and I'm shutting her down."

The ensign nods and steps forward. She runs her hand up and down Sister Janet's back, feeling carefully.

"You realize, of course, there's at least a fifty percent chance this won't work."

"Some people consider those great odds," the captain replies. "In our current situation, I'm one of them. And hey, for now, I'm Captain Julius, OK?" He peels the name patch from his suit and tucks it in his pocket. "Save the Monroe until we know what we're dealing with."

"Yes sir," says the ensign. "Here goes."

A muted *click.*

The results are immediate. The android blinks once, and her eyes snap into focus. Her posture straightens, and her lolling head and slack limbs compose themselves. Her torso moves in a perfect simulation of taking a deep breath and exhaling.

"Good morning," says the captain, watching her closely. "Can you understand me?"

The android looks at him with her plain, brown eyes, but she does not answer. She glances at his companions, then away, quickly taking in the scene. Nothing escapes her sharp gaze, not their gear, the papers and books—or her restraints. She rises to her feet, returning the single-lensed frames to their home on the bridge of her nose, and she smoothes her wrinkled cassock as well as the restraints allow, taking extra care to adjust her close-fitting headdress.

"Can you hear me?" asks the captain. "Are you OK? We found you here lying on the floor."

The android's attentive gaze settles on each of them in turn, sweeping from head to foot, seemingly unaware—or unconcerned—that she is being addressed. If she is able to speak, she shows no sign.

Ensign? thinks the lieutenant.

Clearly no telepathic abilities, sir, the ensign replies. *And no damage that I can detect. I guess she's not in a talkative mood. Or maybe she's testing us.*

Shoot. We have exactly no time for this. The lieutenant turns to the captain.

"Mind if I try, sir?"

"Be my guest; begin the trying."

"Listen, friend," says the lieutenant, and his tone is firm. "Do you know what we are?" Here, he points to himself and the ensign. "Do you recognize family? We're not going to hurt you, but we sure could use your help. It's why we woke you up."

He could just as well have been talking to the wall. The android ignores him completely, turning instead to the sealed transporter. Her glance moves quickly from its control panel to the dormant workstations nearby, from the open hatch to the sun outside. To their surprise she begins shuffling awkwardly toward the stairs, moving past them as if they were invisible.

"Whoa, easy," says the captain, and he steps away, giving her a clear berth. "Did you hear what he said? We're not your enemies. Don't go running off."

But the android is less running than waddling, forced by her restraints to shuffle like a penguin. This she does, silent and resolute, until she reaches the base of the stairs. Once there, she stands in a rectangle of sunlight, seemingly entranced by the dripping of the slowly melting snow. The lieutenant and ensign are close on her heels, attentive to any false move, but she makes none, simply staring up at the sky. Then, remarkably, she closes her eyes, and a single tear escapes, running down her cheek and falling to the ground. Ensign Morales glances at the lieutenant, then the captain.

"Sir," she says. "May I?"

The captain throws up his hands.

"Sure. Why not?"

The ensign takes a step toward the android.

"Please," she says. "I think you can hear us, and I think you know what we are. I also think you know we could disable you if we wanted. But that's not why we're here. Honestly, we were just looking for your help. But maybe...there's something we could do for you?"

The android's eyes open, and for the first time, she looks at the ensign as if really seeing her, her gaze thoughtful as she considers the words she hears. She wipes the tear from her face and turns to the captain, pointing at the insignia on the front of his ebony suit, a glittering spiral of stars.

"I don't know this sign," she says.

"This?" says the captain. "Galactic Guild, Enforcement Division. Captain Julius at your service. This is Lieutenant K—please don't ask me to pronounce his name—and this is Ensign Morales. Are we correct in assuming you're Janet MacLean? Chaplain of *Destiny?*"

The android wrinkles her brow.

"I've never heard of the Galactic Guild." She looks at both the lieutenant and the ensign, her expression pinched. "You're wearing stolen gear."

"Borrowed," says the lieutenant. "Just temporary. We didn't think anyone would mind."

"I mind. Are you common thieves, rummaging through the belongings of dead people?"

"I don't like to think of us as common *or* thieves," says the captain. "And we weren't trying to dishonor anybody. But we were in a tough situation, and my people needed clothes. I figured you'd be sympathetic."

"Did you? Why?"

"Well, you know...you're both..."

"Both what?"

"I think what the captain means to say," says Ensign Morales, "is that we're synthetics. Like you."

"I don't know what you mean."

"C'mon, Sister, no offense," says the lieutenant, "but we really don't have time for games. We scanned you, we took a trip through your software and your hardware. We know what you're capable of. You knew we were synthetic the second you laid eyes on us, glasses or not. There's no point in pretending."

Sister Janet turns up her nose.

"I see. Well. What do you want? Are you with the System? If this is a rescue, why am I tied up?"

"Things have changed, Sister," says the captain. "May I call you Sister? There is no more System. It's been the Galactic Guild for about fifty years. And no, actually, rescue wasn't our mission, although we're open to it. Frankly, we didn't expect to find anyone alive."

"Then what is your mission?"

"Confidential, at the moment. But like I said, we're not here to hurt anyone. You're tied up because we weren't sure what to expect when we, you know, woke you up. Maybe you could answer some questions. If you gave us some help, we'd be inclined to untie you."

Sister Janet slowly pushes the broken glasses up

the bridge of her nose and turns away from the sun, shuffling toward the service lift, pausing to inspect the documents spread out on the table.

"You have no right to be ransacking private quarters," she says, her tone fit for chastising a disobedient child. "Whatever your mission is, does it include breaking and entering? Molesting clergy?"

"Now hold on," says the captain. "There was only a bit of breaking and absolutely no molesting."

"C'mon, Cap'n," says the lieutenant. "We don't have time for this."

Sister Janet fixes him with a stern look.

"You have less time than you think."

+ + + + + +

Lightning' ears pin. She had disliked the strange, metallic object long before it had begun making its eerie sounds, for it has a scent like burned scales that settles in the back of her throat. And the storm that has left Viktor and the captain behind still rages outside, adding to the sinister effect. Whatever the sounds mean, they make her like the object even less. But Joy and Thunder agree; they are similar to sounds they have heard before, in the drought-stricken land of Albion, spoken by the presumed Moondwellers.

What does it mean? asks the Brigadier.

Ain't no clue here, Sugarfoot, thinks Piedmont. *Not a single one, not even a pretend-I'm-a-smarty kinda guess. Fluvial here's a pretty bright crystal, but she aint got no clue neither, nor Big Fork, and he's the big brain what got it talkin' in the first place, see? Though he aint the one what found it—way up in the mountains 'twas, north o' the sulphur pits, and he ain't been up that high sincin' he was just a little fork—'twas his oliwot Pluton what gets credit for findin' it half buried in the snow. But Pluton don't know what it's a sayin' any more than the restuvus—iffin it means anathing a' tall.*

It does, thinks Joy. *Don't know what, though.*

But that is a lie, although only Lightning recognizes it as one. The others accept Joy's claim at its face. Some return to examining the object, smelling it from a distance and on occasion daring to touch it, scuffed, hard, and in many places dented as if the loser in a rock fight. Neither Thunder nor Cliff want anything to do with it. Cliff especially shies away.

Should have left it where it was, he thinks.

But Joy's gaze turns more than once to the object, hairless skull, skinless torso, battered arms stretched to the side. Her eyes are dim, as if having an internal conversation, and she whistles softly.

Lightning motions to the stone water bowl Vale uses to clean Submission's injuries.

We'll fill it up, she thinks, and Joy takes the hint, following her down to the river's edge. *Well,* thinks Lightning. *What is it? What's on your mind?*

With one hand, Joy twists locks of her hair into springy spirals; the other has slipped absently inside her sling where it moves in unhurried circles.

I don't know exactly, she thinks. *But it's not happy.* Lightning doesn't have to ask what *it* is. That the artifact should be able to express unhappiness—or any thoughts at all—remains vaguely disquieting.

It's not the only one, she thinks. *What is that thing, and what were those sounds? It knows, yes?*

Yes. It seems to.

What does that mean?

It's hard to explain, thinks Joy. *It uses...strange words.* She clicks quietly. *I don't always understand.*

Then we'll work on it together. Tell me what it's saying and we'll see what we can come up with.

What does synthetic mean?

Um...

The thing is synthetic.

OK.

A synthetic human. Android.

Oh, piss biscuits, thinks Lightning. *Is that the best it can do? What language is that?*

Joy's whistle is mournful.

Like I told you, she thinks. *It is very frustrating. And what were those sounds?*

"Ghost on the bridge," thinks Joy. *Over and over again.* She sighs. *"Ghost on the bridge."*

+ + +

While the storm continues to rage, the Whitetails, Piedmont and his escort Fluvial, put themselves to work, aware their sincerity remains in question. Under Brook's supervision, they help fortify the Skull, blocking some entrances and gathering throwing stones near others. Their offering of the Moondweller object, whatever use it may have, is appreciated less than the calories they burn in this effort, and for the moment, the disfigured thing lies where it was presented, watched at a nervous distance by a Bristle jabi named Berm.

The scion, huddled miserably around their queen, are invited into the lower alcoves on the condition they help watch over the bound Redteeth. The invitation is accepted warily, and only Lightning and Joy are allowed anywhere near the queen's company. The poisoned Redteeth have begun to stir, recovering from multiple scion bites. Some sit passive and stupefied, but others are determined to escape, and they claw and nibble at their bindings. These are given one warning only; if unheeded, they are promptly bitten again. Among these is their leader, Spike. At first waking, he froths and convulses, his eyes rolling as he strains to free himself. No amount of warning leads him to see reason, and soon enough, buzz-buzz, he is slumping to the floor, unconscious.

Idiot, thinks Lightning.

The smell of food—simple, dried battle rations—drifts from one of the innermost caves, as Lightning and Joy return to where Thunder and Cliff stand near Submission. Vale, scarred and bent, diligently changes his bandages, and Lightning feels a sympathetic shudder at the sight of the gaping wounds.

Vale looks up as they approach.

Hand me that dow grease, he thinks, pointing to a stone bowl. Submission drifts on the edge of awareness, but he blinks in recognition as Lightning retrieves the antiseptic and approaches to stand nearby.

Happy birthday, he thinks, his thought faint.

It will be when you're healed, she replies, but in truth, she had forgotten all about the anniversary.

Submission nods. But when Vale begins to apply the dow grease, he bares his teeth and closes his eyes, and he offers no more thoughts.

What can we do? Lightning asks, her tone worried and her ears drooping. Vale finishes with the grease and wraps new bandages around the injuries. Once done, he takes a deep breath and drops to four legs.

Wait here and keep him company until I get back. And you two, he looks at Thunder and Cliff, *come with me and put on your smelling noses. We need spotted fungus. Kills the pain and raises the spirits, but it's hard to find. Won't grow in a lit cave.* He drops slowly to four legs and limps away. Thunder briefly touches noses with his apikan and then follows, but Cliff hesitates.

Will they attack, do you think? he asks Lightning. *The rest of the Redteeth? Once the storm has passed?*

Why are you asking me?

I don't know...I thought... He glances at Joy. *I thought maybe you knew something the rest of us didn't. 'Cuz of that...that thing she's carrying.*

What thing?

C'mon, Lightning. Who are you thinking to?

Apparently someone who spends too much time snooping in other kezels' private thoughts, replies Lightning, and she leans in close, sharing a tightly focused idea: *And don't ask me again.*

Cliff scowls, clearly unsatisfied, but when Vale sends a scolding thought from out of the dark, he drops the subject and hurries away.

+ + +

OK, thinks Lightning. *Tell me what's happening.*

She and Joy sit next to Submission, listening to his shallow breath. The report of occasional thunder does not wake him, and when Lightning tucks the talihew hide close, he stirs, but his eyes do not open. Outside, the wind sings an anthem to itself, or perhaps to Gapi the Red, and its tone is rousing and prideful. But the recuperating kezel is beyond its reach.

Joy hugs the sling to her chest, her eyes dim.

I'll try, she thinks. *Where should I start?*

Lightning considers. There are so many things she desires answers to. Her world had been so simple two Reds ago—challenging in its own way, to be sure, but straightforward, with guidelines, expectations, and consequences that were predictable and made sense. Since locating the Thing on the plains, clouds have been blown away from her vision, exposing a world full of mystery and menace. Not only have countless scion been living a parallel existence totally hidden from kezel, but legendary Moondwellers have apparently been carrying on clandestine business of their own, their motivation unclear, their dwellings and devices impacting her life in a way Gamikan would have thought impossible. Where to begin in such a mess?

How about ask it if we're in any immediate danger from that syn...synthetic thing. Or anything else—like those Whitetails, for example. Never did trust that clan.

No, they're being honest, thinks Joy, and she clicks a certain cadence. *They don't like Redteeth.*

But they'd love to have these caves, I bet.

Yes. But not now.

OK. So how about that awful looking...what's it?

An android.

Sure. Ask about that. Like what in the world does 'ghost on the bridge' mean?

It doesn't know. Sorry.

Well, what does it know?

Joy asks it as much, choosing her words carefully.

Beyond it being the remains of a standard System

labor android, the Book replies, *I can't say anything. How it got into this condition is anyone's guess.*

Is it a threat?

Perhaps not directly, as far as I can see, but I am seeing with your eyes, hearing with your ears. There is much lacking in my knowledge.

Not directly? Indirectly then?

It is possible.

Can we learn more?

Perhaps if we can find my other Reader.

And he is where?

As I believe I have already said, I don't know. I worry that something terrible happened while I was dormant. I do not know what or why.

Can't you sense him?

If he was in range—and alive—I could. But in my current condition, no.

Joy does her best to relay this information to Lightning, who has been sitting, idly caressing her api-kan's spikes and listening to the fading storm.

Who is this other Reader? she wants to know. *Is it like you? Scion? Or a Moondweller?*

In response to Joy's question, the artifact is quite clear, its tone almost pedantic.

Moondweller is an imprecise term. Some of the original human colonists were indeed from a moon, but not one of Aranae's. The kezel—who were still called keel at the time—simply explained their descent from the heavens in the only way that made sense to them: the newcomers must have come from one of the moons. My first Reader was a woman named Grace, born to one of those original colonists, the youngest surviving member of whom was my last Reader. Together, First and Last, they worked to create you. The effort cost Grace's life, a loss from which the planet may not recover.

Well, that sounds depressing, thinks Lightning upon sensing Joy's painstaking translation. *I don't suppose it cares to elaborate on that last part?*

But their conversation is cut short when they hear

Thunder and Cliff returning from their search.

Vale's heating the fungus, thinks Thunder. *He'll be here in a bit and wants to show us how to apply it.*

Then food! thinks Cliff. *The storm's almost over.*

+ + +   + + +

Cyclonia has faded in the distance, and Viktor's body aches from the jarring stride of the alp. Long disuse has not prepared him for such rough travel, and one torpor in the comfort of Allura's quarters is hardly enough to recover from the wretched depletion suffered in the moons of Albion's drought. His eyes are sure to bounce straight out of his head, and no amount of the queen's lova can soothe the feeling.

Upon reaching the plains, he allows the alp to move at a grazing pace, its dangling tentacles tearing neat sheaves of yellow grass from the ground and shoveling them into its gaping mouths. Though it is invisible, the alp can sense the Albion queen's marker as clearly as if it had been painted in front of them. It travels unerringly north, out onto the plains, until all horizons appear the same, yellow and infinite.

Twenty-Seven buzzes as he addresses Viktor.

Is he pleased? he thinks. *Have they done well?*

Well enough, thinks Viktor. *But he will reserve judgment until the vumierre are safely in captivity—a thing Queen Allura believes may be less easy than the experience of the black-suited one indicates.*

They will be no match! thinks Twenty-Seven. *New Magister—now dead magister—had mastery over the one, and his was a brief tenure, not well tested. What hope would any vumierre have against a company of fit soldiers and the leadership of our magister, whose experience and Command are famous?*

Only time will tell, thinks Viktor, but self-doubt haunts his private thoughts, and he whistles for the handlers to prod their steed. The great beast, its hunger soothed for the moment, increases its pace, and its hammering gait overwhelms clicks and chitters. But for all its speed, neither the horizon before nor the one behind seem to move a single stride.

+ + + + + +

"What's that supposed to mean?" Lieutenant K wants to know as he closes the hatch. "'Less time than we think?' Is that some kind of threat?"

Sister Janet turns and shuffles toward the stairwell leading to the lower levels.

"I don't make threats, Lieutenant, if that's really what you are. I am a mendicant of the Vierges Noires, no more in need of threats than a moon needs a map."

She reaches the door to the stairs, but before she can open it, Lieutenant K steps in front, blocking her way. The captain and ensign watch but do not intervene.

"Fair enough," the lieutenant says. "So, it's not a threat. Then what is it? Friendly advice? We didn't wake you to play guessing games."

"Then why did you wake me?" But Sister Janet directs this question to Captain Monroe as if oblivious to the lieutenant. Her eyes lock with his.

"Honestly?" he asks.

"No. I want you to lie to me."

"Sorry. That's a bad habit. We woke you because we need your help. Bottom line: we intend to fire up that ATV, and we need power. We thought you might know how to get the generator operational."

"For what purpose?"

"Well, like I said, that's a need-to-know question. But we'll bring it back when we're done—undamaged."

Sister Janet furrows her brow.

"I wake to find myself tied up and surrounded by strangers. They don't bother to explain themselves and they answer none of my questions, but they expect me to help them use our power and borrow our equipment. Why in the world would I? For what possible reason?"

"Maybe we can trade," says the captain. "I'm guessing you weren't just taking a nap. Either you had a system failure or someone disabled you. Am I wrong?"

"My system did not fail."

"Then someone did this to you."

"No one would do this to me. And if they arrive and see the way you're treating me, you'll be sorry."

"Are you sure? Because we've been doing some reading, and it seems like not everyone was so happy about you. Did you scram the power station?"

"No."

"Shut down the transporter?"

"No."

"Then someone disabled you, left you here, and didn't want you following them. That's my take on it."

Sister Janet pauses for a moment, and her eyes lose focus; her fingers make small pinching motions.

"If what you're saying is true," she replies, "what help do you offer in trade for my assistance?"

"Well, I suppose," says the captain, "the first payment's already been made. We could have just left you gathering dust, you know."

"Bound and captive is hardly better."

"Prove you can be trusted, and we'll untie you."

"And then?"

"One thing at a time. Power first."

"I can't work without my hands."

"Ensign Morales will help you. Tell her what you need, and she'll make it happen. She's good like that."

"Assuming you know what you're doing," adds the lieutenant, "and you can really get it running."

When she turns to look at him, Sister Janet's tone is soft but perfectly disdainful.

"You lack faith, Lieutenant. Or are incapable of it. Of course, I can get it running. I designed it."

The lieutenant scowls but waits for his orders.

"OK," says the captain. "You three make it happen. I'm going to round up supplies and load the ATV. Regular contact and report anything unusual."

The sister's bound feet render the stairs impractical, and no one bothers suggesting she be carried. As such, Lieutenant K slides opens the service lift and steps inside, waiting for Sister Janet to do the same, her shuffling feet echoing in the passage. Before Ensign Morales can join them, the captain grasps her by the arm and leans in close.

"One false move, Carmela..." he whispers.

She nods.

"Don't worry, sir, we're on it."

+ + +

Lieutenant K turns the hand crank that slowly lowers the service lift to sub-level two. The chaplain remains silent, and Ensign Morales, though she has many questions, keeps them to herself. When they reach their destination and the door is opened, the three proceed without incident down a dimly lit corridor to a pair of heavy double doors, the lock damaged.

"Sorry," says the ensign. "Only way I could get in."

She swings the door wide and leads the way into the room housing the power station. The dynamo's main body is joined by metal casing to three sub-units, all of which are paired to a bank of controls with lights now dormant. Connected to the central core by a traffic jam of cables, as if by afterthought, a device of clearly different origin and design stands to one side, taller than the bipeds but not much larger around, coiled in wires and dominated by a clear cylinder inside of which rests a single sphere, small enough to fit in one of their hands, identical to the one the ensign had earlier shown the captain but clear as ice.

Sister Janet's assessment is quick and decisive.

"This pilar is nearly spent," she thinks, indicating the sphere. She moves to the control panel.

"Easy, Sister," says the lieutenant. "Before you go pushing buttons, tell us what you're doing."

"Would you understand even if I did?"

"I probably wouldn't," admits the lieutenant. "But

she would." He points to the ensign. "And until she gives the green light, hands off the controls, capisce?"

"As you wish," the sister replies. "But the different stages of this system can only be accessed via biometrics. Booting the primary computer will require my hand on that sensor—as will starting the reactor *and* the generator. So...green light?"

"Of course," says the ensign. "But how are you able to pass a biometry screen?"

"Skip it, Ensign," says the lieutenant. "No one cares about the finer points of whatever modifications our friend made so that one machine accepts another as alive. Just make it go, please."

"Yes sir." The ensign briefly examines the controls and the security panel, a small rectangle with the image of a hand. She shrugs her shoulders. "It seems pretty straightforward, sir. But there's no way to know for sure until she actually does it."

"No booby traps?"

"Not that I can see, but again..."

"Sure, sure. No way to tell until she does the thing. OK. Do it. But I'm not in a great mood, Sister, so do yourself a favor and don't play games. Gain access to the system, but save the other buttons for Morales."

Sister Janet peers out from under her coif, regarding the lieutenant with a look that is difficult to read. But she makes no comment, and as well as her bindings allow, she places her right hand against the security panel. The image illuminates briefly. This appears to suffice, for soon enough, a series of small lights springs to life across the control panel, followed in sequence by backlit gauges with wavering needles and several large screens across which scroll characters and words in code.

"Normal so far," thinks the ensign, her eyes scanning the data displays. "As far as I can tell." She points to a monitor flashing red. "What's this?"

"This is bad news," says the chaplain. "Whoever shut down the system didn't follow the proper steps, perhaps by mistake—perhaps on purpose."

"And?"

"And we're going to have to re-initialize the entire system. I hope you're as smart as your friend thinks."

"Um, we're not friends, Sister."

"Of course. He's your commanding officer, and you're both part of something called the Galactic Guild."

"Is that so hard to believe?"

"Yes, actually. When I left the System, people like us were illegal—and sometimes killed. Our creators were criminalized. Or perhaps you aren't really from the System and don't recall what happened on Mars."

"We are and we do," snaps the lieutenant. "And we don't have time to discuss history. Get it done!"

"Yes sir," says the ensign, frowning. She points at the controls, looking at Sister Janet. "OK. What do I do?"

+ + +

What she does, as it turns out, is a combination of keyboard entry, data analysis, and sequential adjustments, performed using various combinations of the dials and levers profuse across the control panels. The process threatens Lieutenant K's patience, but the ensign finds it fascinating in spite of herself, and she often has to quell the urge to compliment Sister Janet on her clever design. When Captain Monroe arrives much later, wiping grime from his gloved hands, the reactor has begun to glow, and the generator hums softly to itself.

He smiles, sensing good progress.

"Well done, Ensign. You too, Lieutenant."

"All I did is stand here, sir, and not lose my cool."

"I'll take it. What's the word, Morales?"

"Well, sir, good news, bad news, good news, bad news, I guess. We can charge the ATV to get us...to get us there. But if we do, no transporter."

"And the other good news?"

"Sister Janet knows how to get more of these." She points at the sphere, encased in its clear housing, now pulsing in gentle cycles of rainbow. "They're called pilars."

"But let me guess: she won't tell us where."

"No sir."

"I'm disappointed, Sister. Not surprised, but disappointed. So. What do we have to do to get more of those pretty little marbles of yours?"

"Untie me and tell me who you really are."

"Hmm... Any other options?"

The sister's cool glance is answer enough.

"Well, then," says the captain. "I guess we deal with one thing at a time." He motions to the lieutenant. "Let's get that buggy running."

"Aye Cap'n. Please tell me I can drive."

"Wouldn't have it any other way, Lieutenant."

"Shotgun!" blurts the ensign.

The captain laughs. "Nice try. But I need you in the back keeping an eye on the good Sister here."

\+ + +

With Lieutenant K at the wheel, the captain to his right, and Ensign Morales overseeing Sister Janet in the crew compartment, the party sets out, at first slowly, in a rough, lurching fashion.

"Sorry, Cap'n." The lieutenant struggles with the controls. "Gonna take me a minute." The giant ATV stutters and nearly dies, rocking the passengers in their seats. "OK. Maybe two minutes."

In the back, Ensign Morales and Sister Janet sit appraising one another. The sister is first to break the silence, pushing her glasses up the bridge of her nose.

"You know an awful lot about the details of the *Destiny* mission," she says. "How? Why?"

The ensign shrugs.

"I'm surprised you have to ask. Every synthetic I know has at least a passing knowledge of the ship and what was going on at the time of its disappearance."

"And why is that?"

"Well, Watt MacLean, of course. Your brother—or maybe you prefer that I call him your designer." She glances up at the captain to see if this course of discussion meets his approval, but he makes no sign. The chaplain's reaction is subtle but impossible to miss. She tilts her head back, peering at the ensign through one broken lens, her eyes distorted.

"What about him?"

"The life and the legend, naturally. The life is easy; you know that part better than I do. Correct me if I'm wrong. Radical designer of synthetic life, creator of the MacLean Process. His ideas were rejected by the System in favor of the much faster and less expensive—but ultimately disastrous—Computational Process, and he was made an outcast among his peers. On the brink of homelessness, he got a job on the *Destiny* project and eventually worked his way to Chief Programmer. His last act before launch was to give away all the details of the MacLean Process for free. Its core principles are now the common form underlying creation of synthetic life throughout the galaxy. His sister was *Destiny's* chaplain. I never suspected you were synthetic, but I guess I should have. It makes sense in retrospect."

"Does it?"

"Please," says the ensign, and her tone is hungry, almost pleading. "Can you tell me about him?"

Sister Janet's fingers pinch together as if against her will, and she folds her hands in her lap.

"As much as I would like to engage in friendly conversation with you, dear Ensign, I'm struggling to see you as a friend. At the moment, I see you as a tool, a machine being put to use by some purported," she emphasizes this word, turning forward to the captain, "*purported* member of an unknown enforcement agency related in some unclear way to a System that was once dedicated to melting people like me to slag and imprisoning their makers. You will forgive me if I don't feel much like sharing."

Deflated, the ensign sits back.

"I understand, really, I do. I wish there was some way to prove our motivations were benign."

"Tell me about my brother's so-called legend."

The ensign smiles.

"It's popular among many synthetics to attribute *Destiny's* disappearance to being commandeered by Watt so he could escape System control and start a new civilization where synthetics and Sentiri could be free."

"Excuse me? Sentiri?"

"Sorry. I guess they hadn't been named yet, but yes, human telepaths. Technically, they're not a separate species, of course, thinkers and talkers can fall in love and reproduce—and often do." Here she once again glances at the captain, but he and Lieutenant K are having their own conversation and pay them no attention. "Anyway, after the System collapsed and the Thought Protection Act was abolished, biologists started using the term to distinguish what they considered to be a major evolutionary division: homo sapiens and homo sentiri. Sentiri hold many—who am I kidding?—*most* of the major positions within the Galactic Guild."

"And synthetics?"

"That's complicated."

"You mean you can't tell me."

"I want to, I really do."

Sister Janet considers this information in silence, looking through the window at the grass-covered terrain passing beneath the vehicle's knobby tires. They cross the river bridge and crunch their way through the thorny vines, the passengers bouncing and swaying in time with every bump and hollow of the pathless way.

"I want to believe you," she says finally. "Nothing would make me happier than to know the TPA was relegated to the trash bin of history where it belongs. And that my brother is viewed as a hero...that there are enough synthetics to hold that view..."

Her thoughts trail away.

"But your legend is wrong on at least one point. Watt never commandeered a sandwich let alone a spaceship. He was on board, but that was practicality, not heroism. He had a partner, Maya Sharma, and they were pregnant with their first child. The TPA had just been ratified, and they were both telepaths. You can imagine when the opportunity came, Maya joined Watt on board *Destiny* and left the System. But the mission's goal was no more noble than basic colonial commerce. The only reason *Destiny* never returned was—"

But Sister Janet is given no chance to finish.

"Head's up, people," says the captain. "Incoming!" He indicates a tiny blip on one of the vehicle's monitors. "Five K and moving straight at us. Lieutenant?"

"Can't say for sure, Cap'n. It's biologic—and big. Bigger than the ATV and moving about as fast."

The captain turns in his seat.

"Sister?"

Sister Janet's expression has hardened; her eyes grow narrow, and her jaw clenches. When she speaks, her voice contains intense but mixed emotions.

"You're about to meet the source of our power, Captain. I hope you are prepared to fight."

+++ +++

Allura, thinks Viktor. *Queen Allura. What a wise leader, what a scion!*

As the alp lumbers its way across the plains, tracking their quarry like only an alp can, Viktor drifts in and out of torpor, the Cyclonian queen the focus of his mind's wandering. He had been a fool, so long ago, to reject her offer of Cyclonian magistery. The pride and strength engendered by his ascent to power in Albion, greatest of the scion hives, had clearly gone to his head, and to what end? Now he has aged before his time and beyond even Allura's use or interest, has been stripped of title, prestige, influence, and color.

Still, his sleepy mind thinks hopefully. *She did restore some vigor, no? That was unsolicited. And she gave Command over a company, which she needn't have done. Perhaps her current magister fails to satisfy. He is clearly a buffoon. Maybe there is still a chance...*

Sharp whistles bring the alp to a sudden, jarring

stop, and Viktor's daydreams are dashed away by the alarmed thoughts of Twenty-Seven and the chittering of handlers and soldiers, clinging to their perches.

He will please wake, thinks Twenty-Seven. *Something has appeared on the horizon.*

He is awake! thinks Viktor, his irritation untempered. *He was not sleeping.*

As his eyes brighten and his lone antenna grows straight, he scans the northern horizon. There, an object travels toward them, not quickly, but steadily, smaller than the alp, but not by much. He recognizes it as one of the vumierre devices used once upon a time by the two-legged slavers to transport things from one locale to another. Twenty-Seven's anxious whistle tells him he has recognized it as well. Similar devices had been modified by Albion wit to be pulled by babelracks and had proven most useful. This particular version appears to move under its own power.

It is just as Allura suspected, thinks Viktor. *The vumierre are coming back for their sunken treasure. Fools. They will regret that decision.* He whistles a commanding staccato, and his company falls silent. *Prepare to ram them!* he thinks. *Victory for Queen! Glory for Hive!* And the handlers prod their alp to a full run, its ululating battle cry terrible and thrilling.

CHAPTER ELEVEN
Vow

LIGHTNING AND THUNDER'S sixth birthday feast isn't what either of them had hoped. Most of the kezel are too busy to attend the proceedings, and Submission sleeps through the entire affair. Of the meager rations, the twins are allowed more than usual, but full is not the word to describe their stomachs when the last crumb finds its home. Had Brook not offered a brief invocation in their honor, Lightning would have thought the anniversary forgotten by everyone.

Don't feel bad, thinks Cliff. *I don't even know for sure when my birthday is. Here.* He offers part of the withered cremlin tentacle that was the largest part of his share at the feast. Lightning politely nibbles a few of the suction cups but declines the rest, which Cliff gobbles whole. Thunder scratches morosely at his ear, looking out of the cave at the clearing sky and the titanic mounds of snow banking either side of the Tongue. Joy, having downed a bowl of awl broth, stands nearby, her gaze distant and her thoughts sheltered.

Where do you s'pose this Ozag is? thinks Thunder.

Far Colossus, thinks Joy, though the question was not directed to her. *It's north and east.*

What's a colossus? And how far north and east?

A really big mountain, Joy buzzes. *Far. Thousands of strides.* She offers no other details, but this news is discouraging enough; Thunder wants no more. In any case, here comes the Brigadier Bone, joined by Pounce, Lightning and Thunder's black-spotted amoti and himself a respected member of the brigade. Their mood is difficult to read. When they approach, the jabis lower their tails and avert their eyes. Bone unfastens the belt around his thigh, freeing the cutter and its sheath.

Six whole Reds, he thinks. *One more and you'll qualify as ibiwas. Think you can stay alive that long?* This doesn't seem to be a question intended for answering, so the twins hold their thoughts.

A lot of trouble in such a short time, thinks Pounce, *and you at the heart of most of it,* he looks at Lightning. *Chasing you across the sulphur fields! Almost getting scrapped by a bunch of Redteeth at the northern crossing! And now my poor woti Blue dead and gone. But I'm starting to see there are bigger forces at work here, so for what it's worth, I don't blame you.*

Lightning bows her head and relaxes her ears.

It's worth a lot, she thinks. *Thank you amoti-kan.*

Pounce sits on his haunches.

I remember your ami better than either of you, he thinks, *and how your api-kan used to be, you know, before... Well, she was amazing, and Submission got his energy from her. Crystal had enough to spare! You should have seen the two of us when we were jabis. She was more than my oli-mu, she was one of my best mates.*

All the while, Bone idly flips the cutter end over end, catching its handle with the ease of long practice. When Pounce is finished, he flips the blade one last time, then points it at Lightning.

Brigade members are blood, he thinks. *Even if they're not family. So whatever makes Pounce happy makes me happy. And he loved your ami-kan, so I want you to know when I do this, I'm doing it for him in her memory more than any particular honor owed to you.*

Um, thinks Lightning, *do what, please?*

Give you this cutter. It's a Brigadier's privilege.

Cliff's surprised inhalation fills the silence.

Hold out your hand, thinks Pounce. It takes Lightning a moment to grasp what is happening, but she does as instructed, daring to peer up.

Now, thinks Bone. *There's a ceremony that's sup-*

posed to go with this sort of thing, but we don't have time. The part that's important is this: carrying a Moondweller weapon—one that's granted, not stolen—is a tremendous honor, but it brings with it a responsibility. From this point forward, you are sworn to use this weapon in service of the clan. The pain and the scar will remind you of that oath.

The pain...?

And the scar.

Pounce grips Lightning's wrist like an awl jaw. With a swift, clean motion, Bone draws the edge of the cutter across her forelimb, resulting in a shallow but immediate line of crimson. Lightning's eyes bulge, more from surprise than pain, though there is plenty of that.

Swear the oath, thinks Bone.

I swear, thinks Lightning, gritting her teeth.

Virble turds. Don't just copy the thought. Mean it!

Lightning closes her eyes, and she strives to concentrate. Beyond Joy's anxious clicking and the conflicted thoughts of Cliff and her oti-mu, in a place deep inside her, something small but powerful opens its eyes. It seeks to rise to the surface and express itself, an affirmation of belonging only waiting for its proper time.

I swear, she thinks. *It's what I've always wanted.* And the tingling sensation that accompanies the words confirms their truth. When Lightning opens her eyes, she knows the others have sensed it as well. They fix her with unblinking gazes, ears and antennae high and alert.

Good, thinks Pounce, and he releases Lightning's arm. *Get some clean water on that—and a wrap, if you can find one. Then find that queen of yours. Her two bronze friends are back.*

+ + +

Queen Shimmer is impatient with guard duty and displeased at being underground. When Lightning and Joy deliver their message, she and her small company gladly follow them outside. Once there, they are reunited with the weary pluripotents returned after having trailed

Stone to the wedge.

The traitor crossed the ravine, thinks the one.

When it was long out of sight, thinks the other, *they came back to share the news.*

It appeared, thinks the first, *to have no intention of returning to its home. But they cannot be certain.*

They could have stayed longer, thinks the second, *or followed farther, but the Red had passed and they were beholden to rejoin Queen. Have they disappointed?*

They have not, thinks Shimmer. *Hers are pluripotents beyond reproach. But these sharksha!* She clicks like a hailstorm as Bridger, Bone, Vale, and Brook climb down from the cave. *They pile delay upon delay. The storm is long past! Even Ozag the Undying will have grown old by the time she is given a chance at revenge.*

It can't be helped, Queen, thinks Bridger. *There's more going on here than just your precious revenge.*

And how long will this "more" take?

That depends on our uninvited Redteeth guests.

They are no longer Queen's concern, Shimmer whistles harshly. *She will need her soldiers on the quest for Ozag, not depleting their poison serving sharksha!*

Then we kill 'em, thinks Vale. *End the lot of 'em or they'll just go back and join another raiding party.*

At this, Joy buzzes low notes.

Killing won't end killing, she thinks, her tone quiet but certain. *Blood doesn't end bloodfeuds.*

This unsolicited comment brings the group to a pause, and they regard her soberly.

Easy to say, thinks Brook. *They didn't murder your api-kan—or your fancy,* and here she looks to the alcove where Measure remains with Crunch, huddling over his motionless body and caressing his ears. She has shielded him from the worst of the snow, for she hasn't moved since before the storm. Brook sighs heavily, but she eases her tone. *Don't worry. We haven't sunk to their level yet. But I agree we can't just send them all back and hope they've learned their lesson.*

Then just send one, thinks Bone. *Get Spike to vow*

peace and send him back alone. He can share the news of their defeat—and our clemency.

A peace vow won't mean nothing to that one-eyed villain, thinks Vale. *Better to put an end to 'em all.*

Maybe so, thinks Bone. *But we'll have thirteen of their best fighters tucked away like fungus in a virble cache. Their chief will have to know any stupid play on his part will put their lives in jeopardy.*

Hmm... Vale looks at Brook. *What say, Boss?*

She sits on her haunches, coiling her tail around her and gazing off into the accrete.

What do you think my api-kan would have done?

Aw, says Vale. *Squall was a softy, all heart. And I loved him for it. But this is different.*

He wouldn't have killed them.

Naw, I don't suppose he would have.

Fetch their leader then. She looks at Joy. *If you and your queen don't mind helping, I have an idea. And Lightning; that cutter please, just for a while...*

+ + +

Spike is defeated, truculent, and hopelessly dizzy when he is led from his cavernous prison. He blinks at the light and scowls at his captors. Every Bristle, Whitetail, and Sugarfoot fit enough to strike a menacing pose has gathered to surround him.

Dirty rotters, he thinks, and he curls his lip.

But Brook steps forward, the cutter held before her like a threat, and Spike shies away, eyes downcast, his tail brushing the snow.

The less I sense from you, thinks Brook, *the longer you'll stay alive.* Spike scowls but keeps a tight wrap on his thoughts. Moondweller weapons are bad enough, but the presence of Whitetails is even more discouraging. A clan he had hoped would play in Redtooth favor has apparently joined the enemy.

The worst is yet to come, for the Brigadier Bone now approaches, and he stands on two legs, holding aloft the battered remains of the Moondweller creation, metallic head, torso, and dangling upper limbs. The thing has been activated, and its mouth opens and closes as if it is gasping for air.

"Fairzas nokstun uppa palitch," it says, its voice chilling and unnatural. "Fairzas nokstun uppa palitch." Over and over it repeats, eyes sightless but glowing.

Around Bone march in tight formation the last of the scion soldiers, and in the air, buzzing fiercely, Queen Shimmer and her pluripotents trace glittering circles. Poor Spike has never seen nor heard the like. He forgets his hatred and bravado, unable to take his eyes off the bizarre object and the inexplicable escort of scion attending the bibija Sugarfoot. What evil fate awaits him he can only guess, and he hunkers to the ground, sure a terrible end is only moments away.

Bone presses the switch that silences the object.

You have broken the Way, thinks Brook in her most chiefly tone. *You have trespassed, you have stolen, you have murdered. For this, the penalty is death.*

Do your worst! thinks Spike, pinning his ears. But his words are empty, and his tail is tucked.

No, thinks Brook, pointing the cutter. *Instead, we will do our best. You sensed me; I said we will repay your Waybreaking with mercy, your crimes with forgiveness.*

Spike peers up, his one good eye half closed. Is he being played with?

You will go back to your side of the wedge, commands Brook, *and you will never return unless you are invited—or death will be the price for you and those we hold captive. Spread the news to your chief: there will be no second forgiveness.*

Spike glares, but he thinks nothing.

Around you, Brook waves, *you see gathered an alliance like nothing you can create yourselves—or even understand. So don't try. Go home and tell your clan: east of the wedge is a land of Moondweller power that will destroy the first hostile Redtooth foolish enough to break the vow—maybe destroy invisibly, with poison, or from a great distance with fire and noise, or maybe even face-to-face, led by the awful power of the Talking Head!*

And if I don't make this vow? thinks Spike.

Then you'll die sooner! And Brook slashes the cutter a whisker's length from the Redtooth. He yelps and ducks away as his enemies close ranks, baring their teeth. Wobbly-legged and sick to his stomach, the poor bibija can see only one way out. With unmistakable sincerity, he bows to the snow, vowing never to return. As Queen Shimmer and her pluripotents buzz and dart overhead, the groggy combatant shuffles away, humbled and overwhelmed. The scion ride his tail until he has tottered into the western accrete and out of sight.

Well, that's that, thinks Bone.

Let's hope so, thinks Brook.

But Vale only scowls and wrinkles his snout.

+ + + + + +

Lieutenant K doesn't need Sister Janet's warning to tell him what he can clearly see with his own eyes.

"They're coming straight at us, Cap'n," he says. "Doesn't look like they plan to stop."

"Dirty kamikaze bugs." The captain clenches and unclenches his fists.

"You're wrong," Sister Janet is quick to disagree. "They're not suicidal. Before impact, their soldiers will jump from the alp. When the vehicle is disabled—and it will be, if you let them hit us—they'll overrun us and try to poison or ensnare."

"Not if I have anything to say about it," growls the lieutenant, and he turns the wheel, attempting to angle away from the oncoming collision. But the vehicle is not designed for speed or evasive maneuvers.

"You can't outrun them," says the chaplain. "If you have weapons, now would be a good time."

Captain Monroe has already determined that. He has fished the last grenade from the lieutenant's pack and powered down his window. With the press of a button, the grenade becomes live. A moment later, its target acquired, it flies from the captain's hand, whizzing away, eager to keep its appointment with the alp. The monstrous beast, plated and tentacled, hammers toward them, oblivious to the trouble headed its way. When the grenade explodes, scorched scion fall from their perches to lie motionless in the snow, but the alp, its armor smoking and some of its tentacles shriveled, cries out in a terrible voice—and continues toward them at full speed.

"Aw, geez..." The captain turns to Ensign Morales, buckling the chaplain into her seat. "Suggestions?"

"Charge the body," Sster Janet says, looking with worried eyes at the alp, now so close they can feel its beating stride. "It's a one-time defense, and it drains the batteries, but it's the best this vehicle can do."

"Carmela?" the captain asks.

"It's worth a try," the ensign replies, strapping into her seat. She points to an array of backlit buttons near the lieutenant's right knee. He presses these in quick sequence, at the last moment flipping the largest switch.

"Hold on people!"

The collision lifts the vehicle from the ground with the deafening sound of tortured metal and a crackling, electric discharge that envelops the alp in arcing, jagged light. For a split-second beast and machine seem glued together, haloed in electricity. Then the vehicle flips on its side, rolling over twice as it hurls chunks of dirt skyward and finally lands, bouncing and battered, upright, two tires ruptured, its cargo compartment torn open, and its windows shattered.

The alp lies crumpled and silent, breathing heavily, though its armor is singed and its remaining tentacles hang slack. A dozen scion sparkle blue against the backdrop of windswept grass, having leapt from their steed before impact just as Sister Janet had said they would. But one scion remains aboard the alp's broad back, nestled within the protection of its bony plates, gray and bent, its lone antenna twitching.

+ + +

Ensign Morales' eyes blink open, her blonde hair disheveled and her backpack thrown open, its contents strewn about the compartment. The first thing she sees is Sister Janet unclasping her harness. She appears undamaged, but her coif has come loose, freeing her white-streaked hair, and her glasses are nowhere to be seen.

The ensign follows her example.

"Stay where you are, Chaplain," she says once her own harness has been unbuckled. Sister Janet acquiesces without comment, calmly adjusting her headdress and peering out the cracked window.

In the front compartment, the ensign finds Lieutenant K slumped over the wheel, his blue eyes open but unresponsive. The captain is likewise motionless, a neat red line running from his forehead to drip onto the collar of his sleek, black uniform. Casting a quick glance back at the chaplain, who has found her glasses and is occupied straightening their now lensless frames, she reaches forward and pulls Lieutenant K upright in his seat. Turning his head to face her, she looks intently into his eyes as if about to ask him an important question. Instead, two beams of light emit, one from each blue eye, pencil-thin and intermittent. They meet those of the lieutenant, and for several moments the beams of light pulse, brightening, fading, then brightening again.

"Ensign," the lieutenant says suddenly, sitting up under his own power. "Good to see you."

"Yes sir," she says. "But the game's not over. Are you damaged?" The lieutenant pauses, considering the question and peering down at himself, wiggling his fingers and turning his head side to side.

"Fully operational. Thanks for the wake-up." He tries to make sense of what he sees through the vehicle's damaged windshield, crazed from top to bottom with spidering cracks. "What's our status?"

"It's hard to say. The captain's injured. Whatever bugs are left are circling us, trying to decide if it's safe to get any closer, I guess. It looks like we knocked out their ride, and that's got them worried."

"Not for long," the chaplain assures. "If they have a leader among them, he'll order someone forward as a test. They're obedient to the death if someone strong is giving the commands. When they realize the charge was a one-time defense..."

Lieutenant K quickly unbuckles himself from his restraints and retrieves his pack from where it has lodged beneath the center console.

"Switch places with me," he says. "I'll take care of the bugs. You tend the captain."

This she does, once she has stowed the loose items in her pack, examining the captain's injury and checking his pulse. All the while, having taken her place in the passenger compartment, lieutenant casts worried glances through the fractured windows and back at Sister Janet, who watches him, placid but attentive.

"Any advice?" he asks.

Her cheeks dimple as she considers his question.

"Their bites won't have any effect—on us, I mean, excluding your so-called captain. And there aren't enough of them to overwhelm us with force. But their webbing could be a problem. And if they decide to burn us out..."

"Excuse me? Burn us out?"

The blue circle draws closer to the vehicle, and one of the scion dares to step near. Its antennae bend backward as if reluctant to follow where its body leads, and it reaches out a bristly forelimb to touch one of the doors, clicking a nervous tempo. When nothing happens, it becomes more assertive, its forelimbs running from the door to the tires to the shredded canvas that once topped the cargo bed. Its companions, recognizing their quarry is safe to approach, do so boldly, half clambering atop the vehicle, the other half turning their nether regions, aiming them at the ATV.

"Ultrasonic!" suggests the lieutenant, but the ensign is quick to reject this plan.

"It might drive them off," she says, "but it will also

damage the captain—and I can't wake him."

"Well, heck," says the lieutenant, unstrapping his sidearm. "Guess we do this the old-fashioned way."

"Free me," Sister Janet holds out her hands. "You'll need the help."

"Negative." The lieutenant points his weapon. "You move one inch and you'll be my next target."

"Have it your way. But whatever you're going to do, you'd better hurry. We're on fire."

And even as she speaks, bitter fumes and toxic, black fingers of smoke work their insidious way through the broken windows and into the vehicle. The ensign is quick to reach under the center console, wrapping her hand around a short lever and pulling upward. A cloud of white foam billows from the engine compartment, suppressing the blue flames that have begun licking their way toward the engine batteries. But more spring up to either side of the vehicle.

"Watch the webbing," thinks Sister Janet, pointing as Lieutenant K gives up trying to open the jammed door. Instead, he clears away the last of the glass shards from the nearest window.

"I see it," he thinks, though the strands that have been strung across the opening are nearly invisible. He wastes no time trying to clear them away, but instead extends his hand, the fingernails growing in a blink from practical and short to sharp-edged blades several inches long. These slice through the web intended to trap him, and he crawls easily through the window, leaping through the smoke to the ground below. At once, he is beset on all sides by biting scion. But their poison has no effect, and with brutal efficiency, he dispatches any who linger within reach. He is dreadfully quick, his strength far greater than anticipated. Worse still, their camouflage is useless, and when those who remain turn to flee, he picks them off, one by one, with careful, precise bursts of energy from his sidearm. He never misses.

"Wait!" Sister Janet yells when she sees him aiming at the last and largest of the soldiers, scuttling to take shelter behind the unconscious alp. "We need him!" She has blithely disobeyed his order to remain seated and is helping Ensign Morales lower the captain through the window. Blue flames engulf all but the engine compartment, and they are just able to get themselves, the captain and his helmet—and both packs—out of the vehicle and to a safe distance before the remainder of the ATV disappears in ugly, black smoke.

Sister Janet's exit from the vehicle has left her muddied and unkempt, but she is typically demure as she adjusts her coif, wiping dirt from her tunic and returning a runaway shoe to its place. The ensign carefully lays Captain Monroe on a dry patch of ground, his head resting on a pillow of grass, while Sister Janet shuffles up to where Lieutenant K stands near the fallen alp. Two scion hunker before him, trembling and pointlessly camouflaged, backed against the bony plates of the beast. The blue one is larger and more robust than the gray, its eyes bright and its antennae quivering. But it is its lesser companion, limping and missing one antenna, who steps forward at the sight of her. Its clicking is rapid and sharp.

"Tell me quick why it is we need these two bugs," says the lieutenant, pointing his weapon at them.

But Sister Janet doesn't respond to his question. Instead, to his surprise, she makes a series of her own clicking sounds, directed at the gray scion.

"Hold up, Sister. What are you saying to them?"

"That we will spare their lives if they help us."

"That remains to be seen. What kind of help?"

"Transportation. When this alp wakes—and it will, they're remarkably resilient—scion are the only creatures it will obey. Bigger and faster than an ATV and just as suited for the job you have in mind."

"How do you know?"

"I'm guessing. Am I wrong?"

The lieutenant glares at the massive creature, its bony plates heaving gently as it sleeps.

"OK," he thinks. "The bugs control this thing, but who controls the bugs?"

"I will."

"And what's to keep you from telling them to run it off a cliff or roll over and crush us?"

"I will say only what you tell me to say."

"And how will we know that's what you're doing?"

The alp shudders and exhales. Eyes at the end of its many topside tentacles blink open.

"I'll give you proof. What do you wish of them?"

Lieutenant K glances over his shoulder to where the captain lies still, overseen by Ensign Morales. He looks back, waving his sidearm for emphasis.

"Tell them to keep this critter calm, or else."

Sister Janet's clicking is clear and decisive. When the alp rises to its feet, both scion stand nearby, chittering and buzzing to it. The creature bellows once, strident but docile. The noise wakes the captain, who sits up, looking about groggily. Lieutenant K keeps his weapon moving between Sister Janet and the scion, but he calls over his shoulder.

"Got us a new ride, Cap'n!"

+ + +

Not all the scion handlers were killed by the grenade. Those fortunate few, wakened and dazed, have been put to work controlling the grumpy alp, on orders from their magister, inexplicably in converse with a vumierre of all things. Lieutenant K stands careful watch while Ensign Morales loads what gear had been saved from the ATV on to the broad, plated back of the alp. The creature shifts impatiently, trying to forget its recent trouble by plucking grass and stuffing it into as many of its mouths as it can. Captain Monroe, his head bandaged and the blood cleaned from his face, stands near the lieutenant and Sister Janet, who has, when necessary, continued her communication with the scion.

"What're they saying?" the captain wants to know. He scowls and rubs the back of his neck as if remembering the feel of poison fangs.

"They wish to know your plans for them."

"Nothing fancy," says the captain. "Let them live if they cooperate, kill them if they don't."

"Seems pretty clear," says the lieutenant.

Sister Janet adjusts her glasses.

"I think they already understand that," she says. "I believe they're worried about what will happen to them after they've taken you to wherever you're going. As in, what guarantee do they have that you aren't just going to kill them anyway?"

"Fair question. Lieutenant?"

"I don't know, sir, how about Ozag?"

Sister Janet arches an eyebrow.

"What do you mean?" she wonders, and there is a sharp tone in her voice.

"I mean the only other bug I met made a big deal about someone named Ozag. Maybe there's a play."

"Yeah," thinks the captain. "She was all juiced up about revenge against Ozag, or whoever crashed that rocket into the middle of their little show."

Sister Janet starts, and she looks at the captain as if he has begun to speak a foreign language.

"Crashed a rocket?"

"Like an arrow to a bullseye. Not that I'm crying about it, mind you, but they might be more keen on helping us if they thought we plan to find the culprit and bring him, her—whatever—to justice, you know?"

"A lie?" says the chaplain. "Not my first choice." But she pauses, considering. "I'll make the attempt."

The message she shares, in rapid bursts of clicking and low, chittering phrases, makes no sense to the captain or his companions, but it creates an immediate response from the scion. In spite of the weapon pointed their direction, they begin pacing slow circles around one another as soon as the last buzzing note has left the chaplain's mouth, the gray, limping scion the center of the others' orbits. They do this for long moments, silent all the while, their antennae bending toward one another.

"What, are we having a dance?" asks the captain.

"I can't say for certain, sir," says the ensign, "but I'm reading brain activity very much like what we would expect from creatures practicing a form of telepathy."

"Are you surprised?" asks Sister Janet.

But the ensign doesn't answer her, instead sharing a thought with Lieutenant K.

Just like the silver one, she thinks. *Same frequency, same amplitude.*

Yeah, thinks the lieutenant. *But I could read that, and I can't read this.*

No sir, neither can I.

Are we sure the good sister can't read them?

One hundred percent. She wasn't designed for it.

At that moment the scion stop their posing and pacing, and their leader, small and gray, turns to Sister Janet, clicking a brief, sharp cadence. She replies in kind, her response followed by a brief bow.

"They have agreed to help us," she says, turning to the captain. "On the condition that they, and no one else, will be allowed to serve vengeance to the destroyer of their city's population."

"No problem," says the captain. "Tell them when we find the dirty rascal they can have all the vengeance they want—we won't interfere."

"Great," the lieutenant waves his sidearm. "If we're done playing 'Let's Make a Deal,' Cap'n, can we get this show on the road?"

+ + +

No creature on Aranae can cross the open plains or the arid coast like an alp, but plenty would offer a smoother ride. Captain Monroe's head, already sore, is soon aching like the early morning after a wedding party, and Sister Janet must order the scion to slow the alp's pace, though it grates on the lieutenant that it must be so. He straddles a bony ridge between the chaplain and the six-legged creatures she commands, clenching his weapon and cursing on occasion for reasons known only to himself. Ensign Morales sits next to the captain, observing him with a concerned expression and often inquiring about his condition.

"I'm fine, Ensign," he says every time. "Just keep your eyes on the road."

The road, which is no more than the beaten path created by the alp on its northern trek, goes on toward the elusive horizon as if it plans to do so forever. The snow is soon left behind, replaced by endless fronds of yellow grass, bowing in rippling waves before the wind. The alp keeps a time they could have set a chronometer to, the scion communicate telepathically, if they bother to communicate at all, and Sister Janet sits, stoic and serene, her thoughts a mystery.

To take his mind off his aching head, Captain Monroe broaches a pressing subject.

"You said, 'You are about to meet the source of our power,'" he says to the chaplain.

"Yes."

"Well? What did you mean by that? This stinky critter? Or what?"

The bumpy ride seems to have no effect on Sister Janet's bearing; she remains cool, tranquil even.

"You continue to make demands of me, Captain. Asking for information, requesting my help. And yet, what have you done for me, aside from waking me because—once again—you needed me for something?"

"You would have preferred gathering dust?"

"I would prefer being allowed to go my way."

"And what way is that, exactly? Looking to find whoever shut you down and scrammed your generator? Or back to doing whatever it was that inspired them to do it? I don't suppose I could blame you. But listen; you help us get what we want, and we'll help you, yeah?"

"Like you plan to help the scion get revenge?"

"Just keep these bugs in line a while longer," replies the captain, evading the question. "And maybe tell me what you meant about the 'source of our power.'"

"And if I don't? Will you simply disable me? Or will

you allow your lieutenant that pleasure?"

"We don't work like that."

"So you say. Either way, Captain, this is my home, and you are trespassing. Until I know your motives and trust your designs, I think I'll keep my answers."

And yet, thinks the ensign to Lieutenant K, *she helped us when we were attacked, and again getting these creatures to cooperate. There's something in it for her.*

Selectively helpful, the lieutenant agrees. *Doesn't make me trust her any more.*

Yes sir. I'm keeping my eyes open.

+ + +

Under Sister Janet's direction, the scion steer the alp south and west to where the landfall begins, a rocky slope allowing the beast to pick its way from the grassy plains to the pale, arid land below. From there, they move east, the wall to their left growing as they descend into a region of heat and briny wind. Soon, the looming wall is many meters above them, frowning with rough holes like dark eyes in and out of which flocks of gargantuan yits fly, screeching at their passage.

"There is a hive southeast of here," Sister Janet says to the captain. "Our current course will bring us well north of there, but it is possible we may run into patrols or hunting parties."

"Can't be helped," he says, but as the alp makes its way eastward, Lieutenant K rubs his weapon as if relieving an itch, and the captain, who had been resting his achy head, keeps his eyes wide, glancing left and right. But Ensign Morales rarely allows her gaze to leave the chaplain. Though she suspects it will do little good, she continues seeking answers.

"Who disabled you, do you think?"

"I can't say."

"What was their motivation?"

"I'm not a mind reader, Ensign. And whose mind would I read if I was?"

"I was hoping you would tell me."

The chaplain's smile is enigmatic; Mona Lisa herself couldn't have done better.

"Continue hoping," she says.

The marshy edge of the bay creeps into view, and not long after, the smell of saltwater rides the wind to greet them. They guide the alp along the northern shore, looking to reach the place where, hidden beneath the reed-choked water, *Valiant* lies waiting. Long before they arrive, however, Lieutenant K issues a warning.

"Life signs, Cap'n. Looks like a bug party."

Ensign Morales confirms this.

"I count a couple dozen, sir. Looks like they're standing watch where we went under."

"OK," says the captain. "Have 'em hold up, Sister." Sharp, clicking commands bring the alp to a lurching stop, its undamaged tentacles waving.

"I doubt your promise to avenge will carry much weight with these," says the chaplain, calm as ever. "Different hive, different motivation."

"Don't you worry about that," says the captain. "I may've taken a good crack to the coconut, but I still have a trick or two up my sleeve. Tune in and make sure the bugs behave if they want to live. Here's the plan..."

+ + +

The company of Cyclonian soldiers bides their time patiently. They take their turn at watching over the northeastern tip of the bay as previous companies before them have done ever since the departure of the one called Viktor. Never have any seen such an unlikely claimant to the title of Magister, and yet Queen Allura was decisive in her orders. And so, they wait and watch.

Never coming back, one of them thinks.

No, thinks another. *Never coming back.*

Lost on the plains, thinks a third.

Yes, thinks yet another. *Lost forever.*

Or trampled by the alp, thinks the first.

Yes, trampled, the second agrees. *Sad way to lose a company, following old, gray Magister.*

Yes, thinks the third. *Old and gray and weak.*

No Command, the fourth is sure.

No, the others agree. *No Power, no Command.*

And so, imagine their surprise when, shimmering like a mirage, the massive form of an approaching alp grows in the distance like a plant fed and watered by their doubt. For several long moments they stare, antennae bent to the west, their eyes sparkling, neither click nor whistle disturbing the silence. At last, the alp draws close enough for its passengers to become visible. The Cyclonian scion break into astounded chittering.

The gray magister, Viktor, and his adjutant, the one numbered Twenty-Seven, ride atop the alp, which is controlled, just barely, by a fraction of the original team of handlers. Of the soldier company that had set out with them, not a single one remains. And yet, beyond all odds, they must have been successful, for there, lying across the alp, their extremities bound, are the vumierre they had sought to capture, the brown one, its two pale companions, and a fourth, smaller and wrapped in odd, vumierre fashion. As the alp comes to an impatient stop, the leader of the Cyclonian soldiers steps forward.

Beyond belief, he thinks to Viktor, *he has captured the vumierre! He has Command,* and he bows low.

Yes, thinks one of his companions. *They were just thinking: the Albion magister has Power.*

Yes, agree the others. *All thought it; great Power.*

But when he replies, Viktor does not use his mind. Instead, adding to their surprise, he issues his orders, simple and short, in rapid, clicking bursts.

But...but... The Cyclonian leader struggles to understand. *Does he not wish to inform Queen?*

Again they receive a terse, clicking command, this time accentuated by Twenty-Seven's loud buzzing, his anger at their delay evident. The Cyclonians bow, none of them willing to challenge such an unlikely Power in spite of the order's unusual nature. They turn to the north and begin marching in a long, zig-zag file, on their way to the storage hole on a quest for the yellow grass that will, they are told, help bring a great plan to fruition, though none of them can guess what that plan might be.

They will do as ordered, thinks their leader, and his company echoes the sentiment, bowing low.

But Viktor offers nothing in reply.

+ + +

The "great plan" is quite simple. When the Cyclonian scion return with grass for the insatiable alp, they see the vumierre untied and laboring under what appears to be the command of Viktor and Twenty-Seven, though they can scarcely believe it.

They are brought under control, thinks their leader. *Does the Albion magister not fear they will rebel?*

Fear is for the weak! thinks Viktor, but then he returns to using clicks and whistles to communicate. "Back to the storage hole! More grass!" is what the sounds mean, though only Sister Janet among the bipeds can understand them. Chittering to themselves, the Cyclonian scion hasten to obey.

In the meantime, Ensign Morales has dived into the bay, swimming confidently beneath the surface, returning from the submerged ship with a thick rope which she and the lieutenant tie around the alp's bone-plated legs. The captain all the while sits nearby as if resting, but the lieutenant's sidearm is hidden in the pack he has on his lap. The alp, inspired by insistent clicking and the lure of yellow grass held before it, pulls with all its might. No word has ever come of an alp having truly full bellies, and the smell of grass being dangled just beyond its remaining tentacles inspires a tremendous effort in spite of its injuries. Each strenuous, heroic stride is rewarded with a sheaf of grass, and the scion thus divested must scurry off to retrieve more. A full fifty of its giant strides pass, laborious and slow, then a hundred, before *Valiant,* draped in weeds, muddy water dripping from its V-shaped chassis, is at last hauled to shore.

"What now, sir?" asks Ensign Morales.

"Time to cut ballast," the captain replies. And with that, he orders Sister Janet to send the Cyclonian company east to Albion. "Tell them to start digging holes, or go fishing, or count the sand, I don't know. Keep 'em busy and tell them to stay there until called."

The Cyclonians, amazed by what has transpired and sure that some great Power is at work, don't protest Viktor's orders. They stare in awe at the waterlogged ship, a thing unlike any they've ever seen, but then they turn dutifully and march east, their blue bodies soon twinkling into the distance.

The captain sighs and takes a container of dehydrated food from one of the packs. He chews thoughtfully as Ensign Morales examines *Valiant*, cleaning away weeds and removing service panels.

"How's she looking, Carmela?"

"Wet, sir. I recommend you don't turn our ride loose just yet—or our drivers."

"Wasn't planning on it. But once you work your miracles and we're airborne, what then?"

"No offense, Cap'n," says the lieutenant, "but once we're airborne, they're not much use any more."

"I don't think we can just kill them," the ensign says, though she looks at Sister Janet as she does so.

"I don't see why not," says the lieutenant. "That was pretty much their plan for us, I'm guessing."

"You underestimate them," says Sister Janet.

"So what do *you* suggest?" asks the captain.

"You made a deal with them, Captain. As you did with me. If you break theirs, I must assume you'll have no problem doing the same with mine. I recommend you keep your word; they will respect that."

Lieutenant K scowls as if remembering a bad smell, but the captain nods.

"Fine," he says, rubbing his temples. "Tell them to stay put or else. We'll get to them in due time." He closes his eyes and takes a deep breath.

"Captain?" says the ensign. "Are you alright?"

"I'll be fine. Just tired." He opens his eyes. "Well? What's our status? Will she fly?"

"Terrestrial flight, yes sir, I think so, once it's had a chance to dry—but that will likely take hours, even with this wind. And there's no astral drive, at least for now. Everything will be manual until I can get the electronics repaired and the computer rebooted. And I mean everything, including ignition."

The lieutenant frowns.

"That means we'll need—Cap'n!"

His cry is sudden and grievous, as Captain Monroe, his eyes rolling back and his knees buckling, collapses without a word onto the hard, dry ground, still clutching his food.

Chapter Twelve
Parting

THE SUGARFOOT JABIS prepare for the journey ahead as Joy sits nearby, her eyes dim and her sling close. They, with Cliff's help, load supplies into Gami-kan's pack and another like it, though it is larger, newer, and a great deal cleaner. This latter was a gift from Brook, who returns from the inner caves walking bipedally with something else borne carefully in her arms.

Cliff steps aside as she approaches.

For you, she thinks to the twins as she sets down two worn but sound vests, simple garments made from brown talihew, their buttons unpolished stone. *Sorry,* she adds to Cliff. *Maybe when it's your birthday…*

Wow, thinks Lightning. She picks up the smaller of the two vests. *I don't know what to say.*

Say thank you to Berm and Bite. It was their idea. But don't worry; I think they know it means they'll be getting replacements soon enough. Anyway, you can't go on a quest in something that doesn't fit—and you can't go naked. Here, try them on.

She gives Thunder the larger vest and steps back to observe Lightning trade her old gear for new. She had grown accustomed to walking around uncomfortable and constricted, half her buttons left unfastened. The feeling of a properly fitting vest—perhaps a bit large, but Gami-kan would have called that room to grow—satisfies like a deep breath after being submerged. Likewise, Thunder's vest will suit him better when he's recovered from too many moons of too little food, but being clothed transforms him from something bestial to a proper kezel.

Not bad, thinks Brook. *I know brown's not your color,* she adds to Lightning, *but it can be dyed. Here. I'll keep the old one 'til you get back—because you are coming back, yes? In one piece?*

Lightning tucks items into her new pockets.

That's the plan, she thinks. Then she notices poor, naked Cliff. *You know,* she thinks, *there's talk of making you an honorary Sugarfoot. Boots, gloves, and all.*

You're just making that up.

Am not. Just wait; you'll see. Help us keep this promise, and you'll be the best-dressed Clawpaw anywhere. Her own boots and gloves are tucked into one of her old vest's pockets; they have grown too small to wear.

Thunder fastens his last button and bows.

Thank you, he thinks.

Well sure, replies Brook. *You're like family, you know. Your api-kan and I... Well, you know. We go way back. He's a pain in the tail, but he's important to me, and you're important to him. Gotta take care of family, yes?* She scratches at her ear as if considering something else to say. In the end, she thinks better of it and concludes simply. *Finish loading up. And sharpen your claws. When you're done, you should say goodbye to Bruiser.*

+ + +

As she waits for the jabi kezel to finish their preparations, Joy sits in the sun outside the cave, listening to the River Tongue and peering into the shadows of the accrete. Kezel come and go, and they exchange many different thoughts, but she doesn't focus on these. Instead, as the sun paints shifting hues of sapphire across her skin, she places her hand inside her sling, running fingers along the artifact's edges.

What will happen next? she asks.

I'm not a fortune teller, the Book replies. *Traveling to the future is possible, but I've never been there.*

I made this happen, Joy laments, thinking of the promise that had led them to the journey ahead. *How can*

I help? she wonders. *What can I do?*

Start by staying positive, the Book advises. *Assume there is a solution for every problem.*

What is that solution?

That depends on the problem you're referring to.

Joy's whistle is low, but her impatience is clear.

What do you think?

I think you are worried about your ami-kan. I think that you want to satisfy this promise as simply and quickly possible so that she can return in peace to her clan.

Good answer! What else?

I think beneath your desire to fulfill this promise with a minimum of trouble you continue to worry about the fate of the bombas you left behind. You wonder what you can do to help them in their time of need.

Yes! All the time, thinks Joy. *What do I do?*

What the Way tells you.

Nothing useful! Nothing understandable!

The Book, of course, has no reply to this. Seeing herself being tested, Joy steps back from the anxiety, seeking a clear mind. What *did* the Way tell her? Self-control, for one. That idea has been in her thoughts a great deal since being revealed as one of the principles. But what is it? How is it useful?

What does self-control mean? she asks.

Self-control, the Book replies, *is mastery over a person's feelings and—especially—actions in the face of temptations and desires, no matter how challenging the situation. It is a short-term sacrifice for a long-term gain. You demonstrated it just now when you recognized the uselessness of being afraid or angry.*

Hmm...OK. Anything else?

Indeed. Self-control is related to compassion and generosity, of being concerned about the well-being of others ahead of yourself.

Something in the tone of this thought pre-empts the question Joy had been about to ask, and she pauses for a time, considering the meaning hidden behind the message. Was she not generous? Was she not thinking about others—Lightning and the bombas most of all? Was the Book raising an indirect accusation against her? Calling her selfish? For a fleeting moment, she feels the need to defend herself, but then a spark lights her eyes as intuition leaps to a different truth.

I'm sorry, she thinks. *I've never asked you...* She takes a deep breath. *What do* you *want?*

Tucked inside her sling, the artifact radiates a soft warmth, brief but unmistakable, and it glows.

Congratulations, it thinks to her, in a tone unlike any it has used before. *You have unlocked a new level of content. It took you a while, but you got there.*

What does that mean?

It means you recognize me as someone worthy of your concern, a being with its own hopes and interests, not a tool, but a partner, an equal. It means our relationship has reached a level where I am able to reveal more and do it in a way that is easier to access.

Joy buzzes, grateful at the news.

Sorry I was selfish, she thinks. *You're not a tool.* She traces the shape of the artifact, caressing its faces, and she imagines it as a friend or a member of the family. *So, what's your answer?*

Short term, it thinks, *I desire to learn the fate of my other Reader, the one I last saw before being disabled—before I met you. I believe his fate may be tied to Ozag and the quest you are about to undertake.*

So, you will help?

With every particle of my being.

What about long term?

To work with you and that Reader—if he is still alive—to save Aranae from the doom it faces, a doom that grows closer with each passing moon.

This is not the news Joy had been hoping to learn, but she is not given the chance to pursue further, for Shimmer approaches, surrounded by the last of her attendants. The queen clicks impatiently, her foul mood easy to read, and Joy sighs, not looking forward to the conversation ahead.

+ + +

Why do the beasts take forever? Queen Shimmer demands to know. She is now entirely gold, her skin saturated in various shades of warm yellow, while her wings and antennae are a brilliant, metallic blonde. But her mood is as prickly as ever.

I'm not in charge, thinks Joy. *Try to be patient.*

Patience! Has she not demonstrated that in abundance? Greater perhaps than any queen before her? She flutters her wings. *The Oddity speaks of patience! It should consider itself fortunate that it has never seen her be anything* but *patient.*

Yes. I'll remember that.

As they wait, Shimmer's soldiers arrange woven parcels on their backs—the last bundles of precious lova and dried awl. This leaves the basket for Shimmer and her treasures: three silken bags, lumpy and bulging, their necks cinched tight.

What are they, anyway? Joy asks.

Offerings for Ozag, Shimmer replies. *If the sluggish sharksha ever get underway—and assuming the Undying Queen will accept. All signs indicate scion no longer have Her favor. In that case, they may have other purposes.*

Um, speaking of Ozag, thinks Joy, and she whistles quietly. *What's your plan, anyway?*

It need not know every thought in her mind. It need only do as it has promised. Help her find Ozag, Limitless and Vengeful, where she will either seek the Great Queen's aid in securing justice for Albion, or—if She is shown to be the traitor Herself—kill slowly and without mercy. Shimmer's buzz is low and menacing.

How will that work? Joy asks, filled with misgiving. *If she's so "limitless?"*

It doubts the abilities of the Albion Queen?

Just trying to prepare.

It needn't trouble its simple mind. When they arrive at Far Colossus, she will learn all she needs to formulate a plan. Her retinue is pathetically small, but they are brave and resilient. A way will be shown.

Ever been to Colossus?

No.

Know the best route?

Not exactly.

Ever seen this Ozag?

Of course not!

Joy's clicking is coarse and irregular. From the mouth of the cave, Lightning waves to her, indicating that she should climb up and join her. Then she moves deeper into the shadows and out of sight.

We'll be leaving soon, thinks Joy, and she moves toward the climbing rope. *Wait here.*

+ + +

By the time Joy catches up to the jabi kezel, they have already made their way to the cave in which Submission lies resting on his side, his head propped up with a thick pillow of virble fur.

How are you feeling? asks Lightning.

Weak as a wabi and just as hungry. Submission adjusts his position to see them better. He winces and curls his lip, but he does manage to sit up.

There's a hunting party out right now, thinks Thunder. *They'll bring back something good.*

Submission appraises him carefully.

You're doing my work, he thinks in a solemn tone. *Keeping my promise and taking my risk.*

Only because you can't. There's no dishonor.

No. The opposite, in fact. You make me proud. Look at you both! New vests, soon to be ibiwas, going off to secure the family honor. He closes his eyes for a moment. *Your ami-kan wouldn't have liked to see you go, but she would have been proud. Ancian too.*

Lightning senses emotion getting the better of the situation, so she makes a promise that seems fitting, though how she'll keep it remains unclear.

We'll have lots of good stories to share when we get

back, she thinks, *and some trophies. Don't know what they'll be, but this Ozag must have something good.*

Joy buzzes softly, its meaning hidden.

It'll be enough that you both return safely, thinks Submission. *You too,* he adds to Joy.

They will, thinks Cliff, puffing up his spikes.

Brook enters the cave with Vale limping beside.

I wish I could give you some advice, thinks Submission wearily, *but once you get past the Whitetail range, you'll be out of my experience.*

Which is what I came to say, thinks Brook. *Piedmont and Fluvial have volunteered to escort you through their turf, make sure you get through safely.*

You trust them? asks Submission.

As far as this promise, yes. Beyond that? Who knows? Whitetails are notorious opportunists, it's true. But they're not openly aggressive; it's not their style.

You mean they're cowards, Vale clarifies.

Maybe. But these two seem about the bravest I've met. They stuck their necks out pretty far coming here. I think they're OK.

They are, thinks Joy, and Vale leans back, glancing at her sidelong, still unused to anyone but a kezel sending him sensible thoughts.

While we're on the topic of trophies, thinks Lightning to her api-kan, *Joy supposes that offering the Whitetails brought is connected to our mission. Don't ask me how. Might provide a clue how to find this Ozag we're looking for. But I thought I should ask you.*

Is it dangerous? Submission asks the bibijas.

Vale uses a claw to pick awl from his teeth.

You know me, Bruiser. Suspicious of anything outside of normal. He tries not to look at Joy. *But lately, so many things've been...different...I'm starting to wonder if maybe normal isn't what I thought it was.*

Is that a yes or a no?

That's an I don't have a clue.

Brook wrinkles her snout.

I wish I could say for sure. At this point, anything

is possible. It makes those sounds, but it smells dead as a rock. And even if it was alive, nothing I can imagine could be so badly damaged and still function.

So, no threat then?

All I know is that the button on the back of its head wakes it up or puts it to sleep. If it starts acting suspicious, I guess one push is all it takes.

Submission closes his eyes for a time.

Take it, he says. *But don't underestimate the power of the Moondwellers. I hate to sound like Ancian, but if they did make whatever it is, it could be a whole lot of trouble.*

He looks at Joy.

What do you think?

I think you're right, she replies.

With that, Brook leans down and touches noses with Submission, exiting the cave as Vale limps behind. The others remain in silence and sheltered thoughts, though all can feel the press of time. At last, recognizing their api-kan is about to fall asleep, the twins take turns touching their noses to his.

Get better soon, thinks Lightning.

You can count on it, he thinks, his thoughts growing faint. *And you come back so we can dye that vest. Brown's good for Thunder, but your ami-kan always said: it's black for Lightning.*

Joy whistles a short tune.

We will come back, she thinks.

+ + +

Brook and Vale join the questers at the mouth of the cave, sending them on their way with farewells and advice. Piedmont and Fluvial are there, the latter carrying the dented torso on her back, its arms dangling.

Watch out for this, thinks Vale. *Look out for that.*

We will, thinks Lightning, as Joy climbs aboard.

Don't do this, thinks Brook. *Don't do that.*

We won't, thinks Thunder, adjusting his pack.

All's well, thinks Piedmont. *Nothin' bad's a gonna*

happen while we're on Whitetail turf, that's a big sure-ee.

And after that? Brook asks.

We'll do 'em proper, see? Set 'em on a good path and wish 'em well. Don't know much about the place they're thinkin' to go, but we'll do 'em proper as proper.

They are just about to depart when Pounce appears from out of the alcove housing Blue's ruined body. His fancy Bridger and their woti Digger remain inside, seated by the body, their eyes downcast.

You'll "do 'em proper," Pounce thinks, *or you'll have me to answer to, got it? 'Cuz I'm going too.*

Confused expressions greet this news.

Don't stand there with your tongues wagging, he thinks. *Trust me; it's not my first choice, but I have honor to win back. Bridger and I have been thinking it over, and we agreed. What Stone did...it's unforgiveable. Our own woli! And what did it get her? Ignominy! Exile! Her oti-su killed!* Pounce leans back and howls, rage and grief in his voice. But then he gathers himself and concludes at last: *So yes, I'm going too, wherever it is, and I'm going to earn back what Stone lost if it kills me, got it?*

This does not seem to be an offer that can be refused. Brook simply nods. Vale pats Pounce on his spiky shoulder. The three jabis stand speechless. Lightning alone musters the courage to say something, for Pounce was Crystal's oti-mu, and she had often spoken of him in the highest terms.

It means a lot to us, thinks Lightning. *Thank you.*

But Pounce has howled himself out of energy, and he merely nods, his ears drooping. Shimmer clicks impatiently, carried in her basket by attentive pluripotents, bronze wings flashing. Her twelve remaining soldiers arrange themselves nearby.

Well then, thinks Lightning. *Let's do this.*

First step is the worst step, thinks Cliff, and he tightens the pack straps over his shoulders.

And so, with nothing else to be said, they take that first step, moving to the east, following a narrow path that moves in a winding fashion toward and then into the accrete. And at their backs, fading in the distance, the River Tongue sings them a song of farewell and safe travel.

+ + + + + +

Captain Monroe wakes with an achy head and a mouth like sand. Ensign Morales kneels by his side, holding his hand, her brow furrowed.

"Wow," he says, sitting up slowly. "I feel like I lost a fight—or won a party."

"Neither," says Lieutenant K, who stands watch over Sister Janet and the scion as if he hasn't moved an inch. His attention is unwavering, though the scion lie in the shadow of their alp with eyes dim, their antennae slack in torpor. Sister Janet has taken a seat on a nearby rock, her eyes open but staring at the western horizon, seemingly unconcerned by the captain's waking.

"How is your vision?" asks the ensign. "Blurred? Seeing double? Or spots?"

"Vision's fine," says the captain, "but I feel shaky, kinda loose in the guts if you know what I mean."

"Some of that's the concussion," says the ensign. "Can you swallow? Here, take these." She hands him a canteen and two pills. "One's for pain, the other is for nausea." The captain downs the medication, nearly emptying the canteen. He sighs deeply.

"You said 'some of that,'" he notes. "What do you mean? Is a concussion not enough to keep me busy?"

"I wish," the ensign replies. "When I was scanning you for brain damage, I found something else. I can't say for sure without access to better facilities—and by that, I mean *any* facilities—but my limited tests show blood properties consistent with drug withdrawal."

"Bug bites, you mean."

"Yes sir, I guess so. From what you told us, your body spent a lot of time building up a tolerance, and now: nothing. You've basically quit with no tapering and no warning—what used to be called 'cold turkey' for some reason." She shrugs. "No idea why."

"Not that it matters." Lieutenant K scowls.

"No sir."

"So, what do we do about it?" the captain asks. He closes his eyes and rubs the back of his neck.

"Well," says the ensign, "that depends on the details. What is the exact composition of the toxin, what effect does it have on the system over time, have any organs been damaged, et cetera. If I knew that, I could synthesize a treatment to ease the symptoms and wean you off the toxin."

"Well, something has to happen," says the captain, "cuz the way I'm feeling, I'm not going to be good for anything any time soon."

"Yes sir," says the lieutenant. "We've been working on a plan for that."

"Yeah? Don't be coy, Nikki."

"No sir. Morales thinks she can get you up to full speed if she has an infirmary. Only one we know of is back at the ag facility."

"Which has no power," the captain reminds him.

"Yes sir. But Sister here claims she has a solution for that." He turns her direction. "Don't you?"

Sister Janet looks away from the horizon as if being wakened from a pleasant nap. She doesn't bother responding to the lieutenant, but directs her reply to the captain instead, speaking softly but clearly.

"You wanted to know the source of our power, Captain? Here is your chance. The infirmary is humble but should have everything your ensign needs if she is as adroit as she seems—and if your hired gun didn't totally destroy those scion he shot."

"Oh, she's plenty adroit," says the captain. "But make it simple, Sister. My head's not what it could be. What do those scion have to do with anything?"

"To begin with, they will provide the toxin samples necessary for analysis and synthesis. Also, if they are not too badly damaged, their bodies contain, in the form of a waste product, something that can be used as a fuel. It's crude in its unrefined state, but powerful, and, as you've already seen demonstrated, is easily capable of generating enough electricity to power the infirmary—if the person harvesting isn't squeamish."

"Are you telling me *bugs* are the power?"

"More than you know, Captain."

"Their waste product?"

"Like an oyster's pearl."

"Well I'll be..."

"Yes sir," says the lieutenant. "That's just what I thought. But if it's true, Carmela can take you back to the facility while I work on *Valiant.* As soon as she's flightworthy, I'll swing by and pick you both up."

"Both? What about our guest?"

"Staying with me, if you approve," the lieutenant replies, in a tone that says he intends to proceed with or without approval. "I want her where I can see her—and where we can have some leverage so she takes care of her end of the bargain. If something goes sideways with the ensign and yourself, she'll be the one to pay."

The captain tries to get to his feet but fails.

"Sorry," he thinks. "Not to rain on your parade, but how's Carmela going to handle that beast?"

"Sister claims these bugs will do the work even if she's not along for the ride."

"And how is that, exactly?"

Ensign Morales holds forth a small cube for the captain to see, its sides no larger than her thumbnail.

"With this, sir. Electronic emitter filled with synthetic pheromones. Concealed in her vocal cavity. It's how she gets their attention—and their cooperation. As long as I have it with me, they think I'm royalty."

"Not exactly," says Sister Janet. "I've told them you're a slave. But a slave to Ozag is to be obeyed."

"Assuming you can speak their language," the captain objects. "Which you can't."

The ensign smiles, and to the captain's surprise, she produces a series of soft but rapid clicking sounds.

"The sister shared a few basic commands," she says. "We tested them; they work."

The captain bows his head.

"Wow. OK," he says. "But Nikki. What if a bunch of those bugs come back and our chaplain doesn't have her fancy perfume? They can travel in big numbers."

"Not big enough to handle *Valiant's* guns, that's my bet. Which, if pushing leads to shoving, we can always fire manually."

Captain Monroe nods, a gloomy look on his face.

"You've thought it through," he says. "And I got nothing better. Hate splitting up, but..." His voice fades and he closes his eyes. "If we're going to do this," he continues at last, "sooner is better than later."

Lieutenant K motions to Sister Janet.

"OK," he says. "Work your magic."

\+ + +

From their first sight of the robed biped with the white-streaked hair, Viktor and Twenty-Seven had been unable to reconcile its vumierre form with the Queenly scent it possessed. Not only could they smell it, they could sense it with their antennae, potent and enchanting, and it would have, under other circumstances, inspired them to do anything its owner requested. But this was a vumierre, hated by scion as all their kind are. On the plains, sloppy with melting snow, Viktor and his depleted company had smelled a queen but seen a human biped, two discordant realities that froze them between attack and obedience. What had tipped the scales was hearing it speak their ancient language.

"They sense the power of Ozag, the Unbounded and Invincible," it had said to them, clicking and buzzing as naturally as one of their own hive. "Beyond their feeble imagination a vumierre is revealed to be Envoy of the Undying Queen! Do they doubt? They have seen her bring their alp to the ground and ruin their company. They have witnessed the power of her allies, the slaves of Ozag. They will make their obeisance to her and she will speak well of them upon her return to Far Colossus."

Viktor had resisted most stubbornly, and Twenty-Seven had followed his example. But the remaining handlers had soon become enthralled, their antennae making decisions independent of their glittering eyes, and they had bowed low, touching the ground.

Magister, Twenty-Seven had thought, struggling to express himself. *It...she...it...the smell...*

The mind! Viktor had replied. *Focus on the mind!*

And indeed, the mind he had sensed when he had reached out with a tentative thought was like no scion—like no other biped—he had ever met. It had not returned his thought, and he had fostered doubt that it had even been sensed. But that smell...

Don't bow! Fool! he had scolded when Twenty-Seven had at last capitulated, his eyes made dim and his antennae drooping to the puddles.

"Does the old one still doubt?" the vumierre had clicked sharply. "Has it knowledge of Albion? Has it heard of that hive's fate? It will divulge!"

"He has knowledge," Viktor had replied in grudging clicks. "He has more than heard; he has seen."

"And?"

"And Ozag has forsaken Albion. The Circle is laid waste in fire and the larvae left tenderless."

"Destruction came from the sky, did it not?"

"It did."

"And thus, he sees. Ozag knows all—though Her Envoy is privy to only a fraction of the Golden One's mind. But she does know this: Albion's suffering was not Ozag's will. The Splendid and Terrible is greatly dismayed at what has transpired. She has sent Her Envoy, only vumierre ever to be so entrusted, along with Her slaves, to secure justice for the hive—and revenge."

And so, Viktor had, after admirable reluctance, finally been swayed. The thought that such a smell, in combination with such mastery of language and demonstrations of Power, could be anything but the will of the Undying had become inconceivable. He had at last buzzed a low tune of compliance and bent his lone antenna to the ground, glad that a figure of Command had been delivered to them. Now, finally, he would get some answers—and Albion some justice.

+ + +

But answers had not been immediately forthcoming, and the route to justice was looking to be slow and convoluted. Viktor's questions had been rebuffed in an imperious fashion that would have made his own queen proud, and beyond understanding, his alp and the tattered remnants of his once-proud company had been pressed into service, sent back the way they had come and used to drag from the bay the massive vumierre device whose role in Ozag's plan was unclear.

Now, as if the creature can't make up its mind, the Envoy of Ozag orders them north again.

"They will take special care that no harm comes to the vumierre," it clicks, "for they are slaves to the Undying, and their service gives Her great pleasure."

"Might he inquire as to why?"

"No he mightn't! But Ozag's Envoy demonstrates patience learned from the Fabulous and Bewildering Herself. Here is his answer: they will return and gather the bodies of the fallen scion, and of these, Ozag's slave will select one for a special honor. It need not wonder what! The rest shall be wrapped with great respect, for in due time, they will be given traditional last rites."

This news meets widespread approval among the other scion. But even had Viktor wanted to object, it would have been futile. Twenty-Seven and the remaining handlers are now completely under the vumierre's thrall, nearly tripping over themselves in their rush to obey every order. Their certainty soothes the last of his doubt—or perhaps simply overwhelms it—and when given the order, his handlers assist the two vumierre (the black-clad and the golden-haired) into positions on the alp, followed soon after by Viktor himself and the rest of the scion company.

And with that, they are off.

+ + +

Sister Janet stands by her rock. The blustering wind snaps her cassock like a flag on a pole, but she remains as demure and serene as ever.

"Well, Lieutenant," she says, "just the two of us."

"Wrong," he replies, and he holsters his sidearm, patting it meaningfully. "The *three* of us. So you sit nice and quiet while I work, capisce?"

"Of course." Sister Janet sits on the rock, closing her eyes. "But I wonder why I've earned such enmity from you. Haven't I done everything you've asked?"

"Selectively," the lieutenant concedes, "on your own schedule and for your own agenda."

"Everyone has an agenda, Lieutenant."

"Yes, and some of those agendas are transparent."

"If you desire transparency, you might consider demonstrating it yourself."

"What I desire is for you to stop talking and let me get to work. You might've gotten the ensign in a lather with all your stories about Watt Maclean and whatnot, but I have no interest in family history."

"Of course you don't."

Lieutenant K doesn't rise to the bait. *Valiant* is his concern. He doesn't need to be looking at the chaplain to know if she leaves her seat—and he trusts she is aware of this. The ship before him is filthy, damaged by the pulse mine that had dropped it from orbit, scorched by uncontrolled atmospheric re-entry, and pummeled by its crash into the reedy bay. It is small for an interstellar craft and would be to inexperienced eyes an unremarkable vessel, but Lieutenant K loves it like a sweetheart. He runs his hands across its hull, whispering to it and at times leaning in to rest his cheek against its weed-slicked flank as if listening to its heart.

Should have seen it coming, he thinks, referring to the mine. *Should have known something was up. I'm sorry.* But of course, until her electronics are repaired, she can't understand him or reply. *That's OK,* he thinks, and he wipes away fronds of limp seagrass. *We'll get you up and running in no time. But where to start?*

He turns to Sister Janet.

"How long before the next storm?"

She looks up and shrugs.

"I wish I could say. But my internal clock was disabled along with my other systems. I don't know how long I was deactivated, so I can't say where in the lunar cycle we are. It could be several days, it could be one. Earth days, that is, if that means anything to you."

"No way to predict which?"

"I don't know about you, Lieutenant, but my sensors have a limited range. I'm more apt to know a storm is coming by sight than barometric pressure. There's a meteorology station at the ag facility, but of course it will need power, and by the time—if—your ensign figures out how to re-fuel the generator, we may be able to see a storm coming with our own eyes."

"She'll figure it out."

"You have tremendous faith in her."

"Did you tell her everything she needs to know?"

"I did."

"Then she'll figure it out. You just keep your eyes on the skies." Peering beneath the ship's belly, the lieutenant releases a half dozen spring latches. Then, opening a panel on the hull, he pulls a manual crank from its recessed position, locks it in place and begins to turn. A gasp of pressurized air spits salty water from around the edge of the hatch. Down it comes, slow and steady, hinged at one end, to form a ramp.

"Stay here," the lieutenant orders, though seemingly without need, as Sister Janet hasn't moved.

"Are you ever going to untie me?" she wonders.

"When Captain Monroe gives the word," he replies, ducking his head and climbing into *Valiant.*

When they had been awakened by their captain—the result of being allowed by New Magister to put on his flight suit—Lieutenant K and the ensign had found themselves and their ship under several meters of ocean water.

Upon escaping with all they could salvage, they had been able to manually pressurize the cabin and force most of the water from the ship's interior. Nevertheless, the lieutenant steps inside to find everything slightly damp, with a pervasive smell like salted fish.

"Let's open 'er up," he says to himself, comforted in a strange way by the sound of his own voice. "Let in some air." And so, he moves throughout the ship, inside and out, hand-cranking to the open position the canopy and every ventilation port and adjusting the louvers to maximum flow. This is just the start of his labor. Every console and control panel gets sprayed with compressed air, chasing water from the smallest spaces. He dries the interior using sterile towels from airtight containers as if *Valiant* were a sweaty champion fresh from a race, and he moves meticulously through the engine compartment and fuselage, scrubbing this and wiping that.

And all the while, he checks on Sister Janet.

Good, he thinks. *Just keep sitting there.*

By the time he moves to the charging station, where they will need to manually create a static charge for ignition, Ensign Morales' prediction of an hours-long project has long since been proven correct.

Just a bit more, he thinks, using the last of the dry rags on the charging station controls.

He pauses, looking out the window.

Sister Janet has gotten to her feet.

"Lieutenant," she says, and though he can barely hear her, he senses her alarm. He hastens from the vessel and moves to where she faces the southwest, her glasses not quite straight on her face.

"It appears we have been discovered." She raises her bound hands and points. On the far horizon, a slender column of dust is lifted on the wind, tiny at this distance, but enough to tell a clear story. A large group of scion are approaching at high speed.

"Kakawka," the lieutenant curses in Russian, and he raises the index finger on his right hand. A gleaming blade appears suddenly from its nail bed—*snap*! "I guess it's time to see if you can be trusted."

+ + +

Back inside the vessel, with Sister Janet at his side—no longer bound—the lieutenant indicates the charging station, a cramped crawl space hidden behind the service panel he has removed and cast aside.

"Here," he points. "You see?"

"Yes," she says, peering inside the unlit space.

"Just lay on your back and use the foot pedals. Pump until this indicator flips to green, got it?"

"Fast, slow, steady?" asks the chaplain. "Any particular method to this pumping?"

"Full range of motion, all the way down, all the way up, as fast as you can. Don't stop 'til it's green!"

"Then what?"

"Then you have fifteen seconds—and not a second more—to finish the sequence. First, pull these two handles to the out position *at the same time.* Once they're out, turn the left one clockwise and the right one counterclockwise as far as they'll go and *in that order.* That'll open this panel." He points. "Inside, there'll be six sliders, all in the zero position. Move the three blacks to fifty percent and the three reds to a hundred. Got it? When they're set, this big button here will turn green. Push it all the way in. Understood?"

"Completely."

"Fifteen seconds!"

"Understood."

"If you don't finish the sequence in that limit, we'll lose the charge and you'll get to do the whole thing over—with lots of buggy company."

"As I said..."

But the lieutenant has already hurried away, only peering back once to watch as Sister Janet takes her position, stooping to squeeze into the crawl space. Placing her feet against the pedals, she begins pumping as instructed, though at first they complain as if being rudely wakened from sleep, and she must bear down to make them cooperate. Moving to the rear of the ship, the lieutenant disconnects some cables and reconnects others. Some he switches from one port to another, while others are left to dangle, homeless. When done with this, he hurries back to the helm, passing by Sister Janet, pumping away in her crawl space.

"Twenty percent," she says as he passes.

"Good grief! Is that all the faster you can go?"

He moves on to the helm and takes a seat, closing and locking the canopy. The scion are getting closer, at least three companies of glittering blue, their formation tight and their target unmistakable. Cursing softly, he reaches beneath the control panel and begins flipping switches, reciting in his mind a list of actions as if recalling a memorized lesson.

Gunnery protocol overridden, he thinks. *Safety features disabled, targeting from auto to manual.*

"Fifty percent!" the chaplain calls out.

"I don't need updates! Just pump!" Moving as quickly as his fingers are able, Lieutenant K breathes a quick thank you to his designer. For Sleeo's genius is at work in *Valiant* as well, much of which can be operated absent an electrical source—including weapons. Sighting by eye, the lieutenant releases clamps locking the portside gun in place and levers it to aim at the oncoming scion, now a hundred meters away. He re-clamps the weapon and turns to yell over his shoulder:

"Firing cannon!" then lifts a switch plate and presses the button inside. The weapon coughs like a grumpy lion, and bright flashes of light streak from beneath the wing, bursts of energy that reach the marching scion in the blink of an eye, striking their midst and sending plumes of disintegrated rock skyward. The shot was well-aimed; the scion are now a fifth of their original numbers. But they are no fools. Recognizing the risk of traveling as one large target, they split into several small groups and approach from the far left and right. And as he watches this, Lieutenant K senses something else; he turns quickly. Another column of blue, coming from the east, raises its own dust cloud. Removed from Sister Janet's enthralling power, the scion that Captain Monroe had earlier sent to Albion have come to their senses and are on their way back.

Once again down the gangplank the lieutenant hurries, and he begins firing his sidearm in all directions. His accuracy is beyond human, but his opponents number in the scores and his ammunition is not endless. With only a few rounds remaining, he stops firing and climbs hastily back into the ship.

"Scrap that plan," he says, and his hands fly in a tight circle as he cranks up the gangplank and locks it, his mind filled with images of the melted ATV.

"Seventy-five percent!" calls out the chaplain.

"Not fast enough!" the lieutenant yells. "They're almost on top of us." And he lowers himself quickly down a short ladder into the belly of the ship, thinking to use the ball turret. The bugs are too close for cannon, but some fifty caliber machine gun fire might get their attention. But Sister Janet's startled cry sends him back topside before he can find out. The charging station is showered in sparks and acrid, curling smoke. Cursing, he douses small flames with a nearby extinguisher and disconnects the guilty circuit, worried they have lost their charge. But when sparks and smoke abate, Sister Janet, seemingly unshaken, continues her labor.

"Ninety percent. Ninety-five."

"Well done," says the lieutenant. "Be ready to hang on to something. We're taking off the second you finish that sequence—and it's going to be rough."

Off he goes to the helm, quickly sliding into the pilot's seat and taking his own advice as he buckles his safety harness. Just then, he hears Sister Janet exit the crawl space. She wastes no time, moving at once through the charge sequence. But already the scion have drawn close enough to touch. They have heard nothing of their brethren's misfortune with the ATV, and they clamber atop the vessel fearlessly.

"That's it!" calls out Sister Janet.

The lieutenant's fingers move over buttons and switches like a professional pianist, and a split-second later, just as the bravest of the scion has turned its rear to aim a stream of burning black, the entire ship shudders. The engines roar, at first haltingly, then, as the lieutenant makes what adjustments he can, with more confidence, a tremendous force building beneath them, lifting them slowly from the surface.

One meter. Two meters.

The scion nearby are blown away by a perfectly circular cloud of dust and the force of *Valiant's* engines.

Five meters.

Those scion still clinging to the ship's hull drop to the ground and are whisked away by its exhaust.

Ten meters.

And now Lieutenant K gently eases the vehicle not just up, but forward as well, though manual operation in these windy conditions means "easing" is a lurching, uneven affair. When Sister Janet comes stumbling onto the bridge, holding tight to whatever she can reach, the lieutenant is far too busy controlling the bucking ship to congratulate her on her success.

Ten meters of altitude becomes a hundred, and the Cyclonian bay falls steadily away behind them. The lieutenant operates like a surgeon, but he uses his feet as well, controlling pedals that adjust both the ship's attitude and its propulsion.

Sister Janet watches every adjustment.

When turbulence rocks the ship, she appears to lose her balance and stumbles forward, falling against the pilot's seat. When she regains her feet, she is holding the lieutenant's sidearm. She steps back, aiming the weapon.

"I'm sorry Lieutenant," she says, and her tone is sincere. A moment later, she pulls the trigger.

The adventure continues in

www.ingramcontent.com/pod-product-compliance
Lightning Source LLC
Chambersburg PA
CBHW032155190626
46808CB00020B/152

* 9 7 8 0 5 7 8 8 2 3 9 7 3 *